They'd had ot ⌐⌐⌐⌐⌐⌐⌐⌐ ith
the same hair ⌐⌐⌐⌐⌐⌐⌐⌐ of
the Sea' and sl ⌐⌐⌐⌐⌐⌐⌐⌐ as a
youngster," Keera told her amenable husband. Both girls had
the same complexion and hair coloring as their mother.

In their twenties, both Mauve and Moyrah had married
hardworking men and remained close to their parents who
lived two miles up the lane. Nanna Keera enjoyed spending
time with her five rambunctious grandchildren, as did Pappa
Patrick, who worked at the same job he'd done for almost
four decades—a math and science teacher at the local high
school.

"I'm concerned about Fayanna," Moyrah quietly confided
to her twin as the children played on the opposite side of the
quarter-acre garden.

"Why?"

"She prefers being by herself. She seemed fine earlier with
Wrenna but now she's sitting by herself." Both sisters noticed
a breezy ripple through the six-year-old's carroty hair as she
sat on the ground cross-legged. Leaves on the trees moved
gently.

"You know, just because we are still best friends doesn't
mean the girls will be."

"I realize that but I'd hoped our daughters would be life-
long friends. Cousins are the first friends children have.
Maybe it's because she is an only child. I'm grateful your four
are so welcoming and they all get along. The girls were like
us though when they were younger—inseparable."

"Fay's fine. You're overreacting. The girls are only six
years old, and a few months apart. See now? Wrenna is
heading back to Fay with a stack of coloring books. Don't
create problems where there aren't any. And stop worrying;
Most of what you fret about has never happened. Look,
they're holding hands like they always do. Lighten up, sister.

Anyway, I'd rather talk about meeting our new American cousin, Anne, next week," came advice from the marginally older sibling.

Their young daughters could have been twins even though they were born 2 months, 2 days, and 2 hours apart. The girls would laugh and explain this when asked if they were twins. They even wanted to dress identically, which their mothers enjoyed as they had been dressed the same by their mother also. The twins hoped their daughters would love doing their tradition forever but knew that was unlikely.

CHAPTER TWO

The cousins held hands frequently as children; when they were happy, upset, frightened, or even angry. Both girls had made that their own personal way of calming or reassuring each other. It was their unspoken language. Neither had to say a word. The grasp of the other's hand was all that the girls needed. Fay called it their superpower even though Wrenna would have preferred invisibility.

On the school playground one day, a bully was bothering meeker Fay. Wrenna, not shy about standing up for herself and others, marched over to Fay and took her hand. They strutted away peacefully after Wrenna bumped against the boy hard, causing him to take a tumble. She glared viscously calling him a "stupid boy." Fay let out a sigh of relief. "Stand up for yourself, Fay. If anyone touches you, bash 'em in the face."

In high school, Wrenna fretted about a college entrance exam. Sharing coffee one day before the test, Fay took her cousin's hand and Wrenna felt the familiar calmness envelope her. They had a cousin connection, a powerful bond, one that they were both well aware of. Together they could handle anything.

CHAPTER THREE

I n their home, located in the middle of wine country and Christmas trees in the Willamette Valley of Oregon, Peter and Anne perused the plasticized map of the island of Ireland situated in the North Atlantic Ocean. Spread out on the dining room table, he highlighted their route. His finger moved north from Dublin, stopping at Belfast, up near the top of Northern Ireland at Giant's Causeway, dropping south to Derry, into the Republic stopping in Donegal where Mauve and Moyrah live. "We will go on through Sligo toward Connemara National Park, into Galway, continuing south to the Dingle Peninsula, then around the Ring of Kerry, into Killarney, Cork and Blarney Castle, and Waterford."

"Oh boy, more souvenirs," Anne injected.

Peter touched Kilkenny circling back to Dublin. They would fly in and out of Dublin which sits across the Irish Sea, 175 miles from Liverpool, England.

"I'm excited about this trip, especially since we'll be going the opposite direction from our last time. Twenty years ago, where did that go?" Looking at her husband of several decades, his hair had gotten thinner with plenty of silver strands and she could see the bald spot growing. Just like his dad. He had few wrinkles, less than she did. She thought his rather deep-set eyes were bluer than hers. He stood just over six-foot tall and she had already lost a half inch, now five foot five inches. Always a medium blonde, her hair had turned lighter mainly because of the added gray. He hadn't gained a pound; she had, which annoyed her. She heard him talking but it was like he was miles away.

"Hello? Earth calling Anne. Where did you go?"

"Oh, just thinking about the last 20 years. This route, I will get to see the cousins sooner." She'd stopped calling them by their first names years earlier. Mauve and Moyrah was a mouthful to say. The third cousins had been shortened to "the cousins."

She crossed her fingers. "Maybe we'll find some art. Let's watch for something fabric or some textiles, not necessarily a photo or painting."

"Sounds good."

"Anything you want to get?" She looked at her husband across the table.

"Maybe a gray and black herringbone Irish flat cap or a tweed patchwork cap."

"Oh, and I have to find langoustine, they are so yummy."

"I know you love the shrimpy lobster delicacies."

"I haven't had any since Iceland and we never see them on menus at home. Oh… and Sticky Toffee Pudding!"

"Of course, your favorite British dessert. I know we've planned this Irish adventure for the past two years with Dave and Sue, and other friends, but you need to get your head around the fact we might not go."

"Yes dear," she stated, slightly miffed. She knew it was more likely they would not be going. She wouldn't leave her dad in the last months or weeks of his life, no matter what he or her mother had instructed her to do.

Surely the doctors were wrong with their diagnosis. She couldn't even say the word "cancer" and hardly could think it. Her dad was the first man she truly loved and to this day, he loved her unconditionally. He always called her his "darlin' daughter."

"Maybe the luck of the Irish will be with us and the doctors are wrong on his timeline. Plus, we have travel insurance if we need to cancel the trip which we can decide one day before our scheduled departure," she stated in her travel agent voice.

He thought it best not to be his normal realistic self, instead saying, "Yes, maybe."

CHAPTER FOUR

The next morning, Anne opened her email and saw a message from Mauve. The subject line read, "Changes."

"Oh drat, something's happened," Anne declared out loud.

"Are you talking to me?" Peter yelled from the bathroom.

"No, I'm reading an email from Mauve about some changes to their schedule. Whew, it's not awful news after all," she told Peter in a raised voice so he could hear over the running water. "Get this. Mauve's husband Brennan is being sent to Dublin for a three-day technology instructional session at the University. Remember her emailing about him being injured on the industrial construction site several years earlier and he could no longer do heavy lifting? Mauve says it turns out he has a head for technology so that's all management needed to hear about him. They are sending him to learn website design. He will be their new website designer and expert."

Mauve added a yellow smiley face emoji and a second one of an emoji head with shrugging shoulders. Anne continued reading loudly to Peter, "Mauve writes, Who knew? Since his hotel room is being paid for by his employer, I can go along. A little holiday and we can have a couple of days together while he is in classes."

Anne replied instantly, hoping to catch Mauve with it being 7 a.m. which would be late afternoon in Ireland.

You are not kidding me, are you? Seriously? Brennan is going to learn a computer program and design things for the company? I just don't see it.

Mauve sat at her computer as Anne's email popped in.

He doesn't quite see it either but I tease him about old dogs learning new tricks. I know he can do it and he seems determined since he wants to work another ten years or so. He is nowhere close to retirement. You know, I have only been to Dublin two times in my life.

Anne typed back.

What? Two times? You only live 200 miles away.

Mauve clicked away.

True, but we don't just jump in our cars and drive around like you do. We take the train most of the time. You know petrol is three times what you pay, so we think before we drive."

Anne typed then pressed send.

Fair enough. I forget how expensive fuel is for you.

Mauve answered.

We can stay anywhere we want as long as we stay within the employer's budget. Where is your tour group is staying? I want to check there first.

Anne could hardly sit in the chair.

Oh my goodness, that would be so wonderful!!!

Mauve typed quickly.

And Moyrah says she needs more than an hour or two also. So when you are in Derry she wants to come see you since you'll be there for a couple of days. And it's only an hour or so away. Since she doesn't drive, either she will take the train or bus. Or maybe we will be back by then and I can drive her to see you. Or maybe Fay but she's pretty busy juggling work and a fella.

Anne typed as fast as she could.

I'd love to see the girls, too. Girls, funny to still call them that since they're in their mid-twenties. I am so excited I can hardly stand it. But you know my dad is very ill.

Mauve hit 'send' one final time.

Yes, I know Anne dear, and my prayers are with him and your family, but somehow I think this will all work out.

CHAPTER FIVE

As a Riley, Anne was returning to her fatherland, so to speak. She hadn't grown up hearing about her Irish roots because the whole Riley connection had been disclosed later in her life.

Since the DNA test, her father had learned that his biological father's grandparents, Michael O'Reilly and Mary Margaret McGinnes, called Maggie, lived somewhere around Dublin but left by ship from County Cork. Since the Irish family revelations, Anne fantasized about Maggie. Maybe she was bareback, riding her chestnut horse carrying a pouch full of soda bread, potato scones, and cheese to share with her red-headed, blue-eyed love, Michael. All Irish seemed to be red-headed in her imagination. Did the young lovers plan a clandestine rendezvous away from prying eyes?

Had they fled because of the Great Famine hoping for a better life? They had choices of where to start anew. Undoubtedly, many of their young friends and some family were leaving if they were still alive. Should it be to America, Australia, or Canada? Had they remained, they could have been in the statistics of the one million who perished.

Undeniably into the drama of Irish history, the truth was that most of Anne's family roots were not provable. She didn't know how much her great-grandparents suffered until they departed for America.

When did they learn the devastating news that much of their crops of oats and rye were being shipped to the continent not even feeding their own people? Did they try to overtake a squad of dragoons, wearing scarlet vests and long breeches, with wagons loaded with bags of their oats and other foodstuffs, headed to a port? The laws regarding exports wouldn't be altered in time to make a difference.

They, like other tenants, needed to make money to pay their rent to their English landlords. And they could only do that by selling the food they grew. Anne's thoughts turned dark as she pictured forlorn ghosts in their dirty worn clothes, huddled along the side of a road, many clutching one bag of belongings. Proud people turned into beggars. How could their government let this happen? Anne fumed.

Anne had read dozens of historical fiction and nonfiction tearjerkers like *Trinity*, *The Princes of Ireland*, and anything by Maeve Binchy. Disturbing and heartbreaking were understatements, and then to read descriptions of how Irish properties were taken by Englishmen who were clueless about Irish traditions, turning the Irish property owners into tenants, requiring them to work and pay to live on what had been their own property, well, it was unconscionable plus dozens of other adjectives she could think of.

Most English landowners didn't even spend time at their estates and hired an agent, usually someone originally living there, to oversee the land while they continued to reside in England. Most inherited their estates through English lineage. Anne felt pretty sorry for her Irish ancestors.

She recalled her Scottish roots and her mother's family's similar situation where her great-great grandfather was the caretaker of a castle owned by an English lord. Anne had been fortunate to have visited the small village of Sanquhar, in the borderland region of bonnie Scotland.

Most Irish tenants lived in sod houses on the estate acreage that had been divided and then subdivided to accommodate the growing tenant populations. Anne saw photos of land that was split by rectangular walls constructed of brush and stone. The tenant farmers lived on these plots of land. Once, lush potato ridges, abundant with green leaves, cut across their tracts.

As more fertile potato ridges turned dark, their leaves crinkled; some called it The Plague. There were comments that the summer of 1845 had been mild and wet, excellent for growing potatoes. Some would say the curse came from the rain and wind, others blamed insects, and some feared it came from God.

More positive souls would say not to worry about such things, "luck" would provide. Anne could only imagine her family discussing these issues, realizing the crop was ruined and they'd have to start over for the spring. Without potatoes, there would be nothing to eat.

Women were taught only how to prepare food and meals made of potatoes. Did Maggie's mother ponder what to cook when potatoes were no longer available?

The Great Famine, or the Irish Potato Famine, was a horrible time of disease, mass starvation, and emigration between the years 1845 to 1849. It's estimated that about one million people died, and a million more left Ireland for a better life. The greatest areas affected were in the south and west of Ireland.

Anne's family, Michael O'Reilly and Mary McGinnes, from somewhere around Dublin, chose the United States of America. There were no accurate details of their journey. She could only speculate from the multitude of historical readings she'd perused that it wasn't a pleasant journey. Many were seasick the entire time.

The first thing that happened, coming through Ellis Island, would be the modification of the spelling to Riley. It became commonplace that immigrants reworked the spelling of their original names or altered them completely to sound less ethnic and more American. Sometimes an immigration officer shortened or wrote the name as he heard it.

Anne assumed her ancestors could only afford steerage, so they had to undergo inspection at Ellis Island. First and second class passengers received a quick inspection while on board the ship, based on the notion that "if people could afford to purchase a first or second class ticket, they were less likely to become a public charge in America due to medical or legal reasons," according to the written brochure from the Statue of Liberty; Ellis Island Foundation.

The hundreds of employees at the station had to work quickly during those first waves of immigration, processing each immigrant in a matter of four to seven hours. The inspectors interviewed 400 people in a day, processing a million a year during the peak of the flow.

Anne learned through her research that in the mid-1800s Irish immigration was not a new event. It had been increasing since the 1820s right along with dramatic increases in the Irish population itself. Data shows that the largest number of immigrants coming into the United States as a result of the Potato Famine settled in two states—Massachusetts and New York. Most were encouraged to bring enough money to move west where land and jobs were greater, rather than stay in Boston and New York City. Most however, could not head west, as the emigration from Ireland took their entire fortune. Port cities like Boston, New York, Philadelphia, and New Orleans became overwhelmed with the new arrivals from Ireland and the disease and poverty that came with them.

Michael and Maggie are documented in the first records Anne's dad uncovered. They are listed on page 39 of the United States census in 1865 in Carroll, New York. Records show sons John and Daniel were both born in New Jersey. They knew the family moved to western New York State and lived there for a while as they are listed again in 1870 still living in the same area. They also learned that Michael and Maggie had four children all born in the United States. Their first, John, was born in 1845, the first official year of the Potato Famine, followed by Daniel, Kathryn, and James. James, born in 1852, is recorded in Trenton, New Jersey.

"James is our great-grandfather," Anne told her brothers after the discovery. "So, for sure, they arrived before the Potato Famine in 1845.

"Great-grandfather James married Lina Ingrabretson, who was born outside of Oslo, Norway. However, it was spelled "Engelbretsen" in Norway. She passed on October 4, 1946, in Chinook, Montana. James and Lina had four daughters and seven sons, one being our grandfather, W. M. Riley, born in 1901 and died in 1979. Sure sad that Dad didn't know about him earlier." Anne continued, "I did learn more of the recent Riley family history about our great-grandfather James and great-grandmother Lina. Now I want to explore Norway one day. This definitely wasn't a happily-ever-after story." Both of her brothers sat enthralled with their new Irish family history. Their older sister was enjoying the spotlight revealing family history.

"So, after James and Lina married, they moved to North Dakota where Lina's brother John lived. Then they moved to

Montana because land was given to those who would be farmers. Great-grandpa James had a large farm outside of Hingham, Montana.

"Then, tragically," she said inflecting drama in her voice, "I read that great grandpa James committed suicide, shooting himself. In their barn, no less. I'll read his obituary from the *Hingham Review*, March 7, 1913:

Last Wednesday this community was shocked and saddened to learn that James Riley, a responsible farmer living seven miles south of town, had committed suicide. He shot himself in the right temple with a rifle. Mr. Riley had been in poor health for the past year and during several weeks prior to his death had been confined to his bed most of the time. He had never said anything that would lead anyone to think he intended suicide and was kind and cheerful to his family to the last. On Wednesday afternoon he walked out in the barn with the rifle concealed under his fur overcoat and committed the terrible deed, which is thought it have been the result of a temporary derangement of the mind.

Everyone has unbounded sympathy for his family and especially for his good wife, who is considered a blessing to the community in the way of caring for sick people.

The Rileys are held in high esteem by their neighbors.

"Well, that's sure heartbreaking," Will commented.

Anne nodded, "Then I found a follow-up article on March 14, 1913:

James Riley's Funeral

Last Sunday afternoon a large concourse of people gathered at Kimpel's Opera House to pay their last respects to James Riley, deceased. Mr. Riley was 61 years of age and leaves a wife, three daughters, and seven sons to mourn his loss. One son, J.E. Riley, arrived from Mobridge, SD, to be in attendance at his father's funeral.

The deceased had suffered much during the past five years from an ailment of the stomach, from which there seemed to be no relief. He was considered a good man by those who knew him. The family have the profound sympathy of everyone in the community.

"So he had this severe illness for many years which caused much pain and he couldn't deal with it any longer. Today it's called stomach cancer."

While researching history, Anne emailed the information she had learned to her Irish cousins anytime she found out something new.

CHAPTER SIX

A nne and Peter sat on the sofa as they watched BBC News on August 15. The anchor reported the 20th anniversary remembrance in Omagh, County Tyrone, Northern Ireland. The horrific bombing occurred at 3:10 p.m. in the center of town, taking 29 innocent lives. Anne felt somber, just as she had two decades earlier when they were 50 miles away from the bombing.

She turned to her husband, "Remember when Mauve told us her story of how she maneuvered her new sapphire '94 Fiat Punto into their usual spot, about four blocks from the market? She, Moyrah, and the girls eagerly anticipated every Saturday sharing one of their favorite outings, at Omagh's Saturday market, buying fresh vegetables and fruits, baked goods, and flowers.

"Mauve said it was a lovely August afternoon, and with bags gathered and girls holding hands, together they started across the street. A blast so tremendous knocked all four backward, and everyone else around them. After checking on each other to make sure they were okay, they noticed Mauve was bleeding. Nearby, a young man who also had fallen, stood up. He introduced himself and explained he was a nurse and helped Mauve and several others who were injured.

Acquaintances who parked in the same neighborhood going to the market were stunned and bewildered, too. The nurse told them he suspected something horrific had happened. He told them they needed to leave and get Mauve to the hospital so her cheek could be cleaned and stitched. They heard emergency vehicle's blaring horns getting louder and louder, and they could hear car alarms adding to the noise level. It still gives me shivers."

CHAPTER SEVEN

Fifteen days later, waking from a short nap on their Delta flight and the new *Jumanji: Welcome to the Jungle* movie still playing, Peter leaned over to Anne. "Gosh, it feels almost like yesterday not 20 years ago when we were going on the tour with Europe Through the Back Door, with 16 of our favorite travel buddies. We arrived and began a tour in Dublin," Peter noted.

"Remember, too, how after the tour we flew home on August 23? I couldn't wait to tell Dad all about our adventures and show him pictures from where his grandparents had come from. In 15 hours, we were home and I felt like a transformed woman. What was going to be a tour exploring a new country and maybe discovering some family roots became so much more for me. It turned into a trip of realization, enlightenment, sorrow, more understanding—and tolerance. Little did I know August 23 would become a meaningful day in my life, the anniversary of Dad's passing exactly 20 years later. Just nine days ago," Anne whispered through her heartache.

Her Celtic roots were tingling, jumping, and dancing a jig just like the first time she'd traveled to Ireland. *Where had 20 years gone*, she pondered as they were about to land in the homeland of her paternal great-grandparents.

Peering out the window of the airplane in the miles-wide circle, 5,000 feet below lay a plaid quilt of various shades of green attributable to different types of crops. Anne noticed a basil-colored field, probably fescue grass. A plot of celery-colored crop, the pale green she thought would be from ryegrass. In a perfectly square lot, she saw a sort of gray-green crop and had no clue what it was. The pine hue was probably a type of bluegrass.

Anne knew her grasses from growing up in the fertile Willamette Valley, where growing grass was lucrative and easy to grow due to the climate. She had even driven a combine during harvest season several summers during her youth.

Her thoughts returned to home, thousands of miles away, as she recalled what her father had made clear to her one month earlier. "Darlin' daughter, you have to go to Ireland; you can't miss this opportunity." Her reply after the third or fourth conversation on this topic became, "I will wait and see, darlin' dad."

Her father had been diagnosed with stage two (then as it turned out, stage four) lymphoma located in his spleen and in his lower abdomen. They were told by the doctor it was uncommon and the cancer would be aggressive. Her family heard the numbers "four to six months" without treatment. Treatment meant aggressive chemotherapy, which was not an option for her father due to a chronic World War II injury that he dealt with daily from age 19. He enlisted and became an Army 10th Mountain Division ski trooper, ascending Mt.

Belvedere in the Po Valley of the Italian Alps, fighting back the German army when another soldier stepped on a land mine and Anne's dad had been seriously wounded, causing a 70-year painful bone infection called osteomyelitis.

No way would Anne waste two weeks in Ireland when she could spend that precious time with her darlin' dad. He chose to do things his own way, however, and passed away before the planned trip to her motherland, or in this case, fatherland. Anne's mother reminded her that Dad wanted her to go. Her brothers and other family suggested they go also. He passed on August 23 and nine days later she sat on a plane to Ireland for a second time.

A highlight of this trip would be seeing her cousins, Mauve and Moyrah again, maybe even their daughters, Wrenna and Fayanna. Photos that had been emailed from her cousins reeled through her mind like fast-forwarding through commercials between television programs.

Peter and Anne had eight friends with them on this trip: Greg and Linda from Oregon, Bruce and Nancy from California, Chris and Jeanine, and Anne and Peter's dear friends Dave and Sue from Washington. Sue and Jeanine are sisters. Anne's secret hope, with the help of their friends, would be to return home renewed, refreshed, and healed.

Anne's long-time "sisterchick," Sue, had Irish roots, too. What is a "sisterchick?" A friend who shares the deepest wonders of your heart, loves you like a sister, and loves you even when you're being a brat. Even though they'd done a variety of vacations together, they had high expectations for this one for many years. Finally, they were together in Ireland.

CHAPTER EIGHT

Their Ireland tour would begin and end in Dublin with Collette, a land-based tour company that Anne and Peter had traveled with around the globe. Arriving in the afternoon, after about 16 hours of travel, they dropped off their luggage in their spacious room at the Clayton Hotel Ballsbridge, a neighborhood of Dublin. As was their practice, they'd arrived a few days before the actual tour began to get over any travel issues and prowl around a new (or not) city on their own at a relaxed pace, and in this case, Dublin.

They sat on the top level of the Dublin Hop On/Hop Off bus touring the city. The fresh air helped them stay awake. "No napping" had been their mantra. Greg and Linda sat near the front of the top deck and as they drove under a tree with branches a bit too low, smacking Greg in the face, fortunately not too hard. They all learned to duck after that thanks to Greg's leaf encounter.

With earphones adjusted, the first sighting of St. Patrick's Cathedral bathed in sunlight took Anne's breath away as the recorded message explained it as the oldest site in Dublin. St. Patrick is reported to have baptized converts to the Christian faith in a well that once existed north of the tower in the present park. At one time a river flowed around the cathedral. She thought at first it was a cool moat, but no, just a culvert. Because of its sacred association with St. Patrick, a church had stood here since the fifth century. In 1191 the Normans built another church in stone on this site. Rebuilt in the thirteenth century, it is the same building today.

"Come on, let's hop off and see the cathedral." Anne headed toward the magnificent building.

As they stepped over the threshold into the cathedral, the grand tall arches seemed purposely designed to raise one's eyes upward. There are memorials of old Irish regiments and a Roll of Honor containing names of 50,000 Irishmen who fell in the Great War of 1914 to 1915. An intricately carved spiral staircase leads to the organ.

The Great Organ, the largest and most powerful in Ireland, sits in an interior gallery and upper part of a choir loft. The Cathedral Choir took part in the first performance of Handel's *Messiah* in 1742. Anne recalled the many times she had sung the *Hallelujah Chorus* in choir while in high school, and many Christmas cantatas in her younger years. That first audience must have been wowed.

The cathedral is full of statues, tombs, windows, and memorial tablets, each with its own story. To Anne, St. Patrick's felt more special than any other church they'd seen anywhere. The cathedral represents the history and heritage of the Irish people from the earliest times to the present day but what she appreciated most was how it's open to anyone who wants to worship their God.

The weary wanderers returned to the hotel restaurant for a dinner of whitefish, broad plank potatoes called "chips," mushy peas, and dense white bread. Anne skipped peas, because whether mushy or not, they were absolutely not a favorite vegetable of hers.

"Would you care for anything to drink?" A waiter turned to Anne after taking the other orders.

"What's she drinking?" she asked, pointing to the eye-catching emerald cocktail.

"That's a 'Luck of the Irish.' Light and fruity, with a shot of whiskey, of course."

"Well, that cocktail seems appropriate for our first night. One of those please, but half the amount of whiskey."

"Really? You want half? Most ask for double." The waiter had a hearty laugh.

With Anne's first sip, she tasted the combination of whiskey, peach schnapps, pineapple juice, and lime. "I'll be having this again, for sure." She let Peter have a tiny sip.

The conversation bounced around regarding expectations, music, and food. Bruce shared he'd read that the island of Ireland is slightly larger than South Carolina, but if Northern Ireland is excluded, then the Republic is smaller than South Carolina. Jeanine's eyelids were already drooping as Chris led her to their room, and others followed suit with best wishes for a good night's sleep.

Turning on the faucet in one of the largest bathtubs Anne had ever seen, and after about ten minutes of filling it up complete with bubbles, she slipped in to soak away close to 24 hours of travel dust and aches. She wondered how her mother was coping, then thought of her brothers, and how they were doing with their first parent gone. Mesmerized, she stared down as her tears created little circles in the bathwater. She set the alarm on her phone, careful not to fall asleep in the tub as her knight in shining armor would be no help. Peter fell asleep in three seconds flat.

CHAPTER NINE

On their second day on the Emerald Isle, Peter awoke to a rapping on their hotel door. "Anne, someone's at the door," he muttered, trying to wake up.

"Room Service," a voice stated in an Irish brogue.

Anne ran her hands through her blonde chin-length wavy hair that had more silver now than not, slipped on a robe courtesy of the hotel, and opened the door, expecting the breakfast they had ordered the night before. There stood Mauve, her arms full of goodies crammed into a welcome basket.

She blurted out, "Brennan is already off to his first day of classes. I am all yours! You'll see him tonight." Before Anne could even say hello, Mauve wrapped her in a huge hug.

Sunny skies seemed a perfect way to begin their day of exploring historic Dublin. Strolling down O'Connell Street and standing at the base of a well-preserved statue of the man himself, Peter read snippets from Rick Steve's *Ireland* guidebook. "Daniel O'Connell was a liberator and elected Member of Parliament for County Clare in 1828 and best known for campaigning for Catholic emancipation and for arguing for the repeal of the Act of Union 1800, which tied Great Britain and Ireland into one United Kingdom."

Flanking the base of the monument are four-winged angels that represent virtues attributed to O'Connell: courage, fidelity, patriotism, and eloquence. It is large and impressive.

Peter continued, "Throughout his life, he never supported the use of violence but believed the Irish should instead assert themselves politically. Being Catholic, this prevented him from reaching the uppermost circles of his profession."

"Our first castle!" Sue jumped up and down, about as excited as a child at Christmas. Dublin Castle, made of nutbrown stone on the bottom half with reddish on the upper portion, has a six-sided clock with a pistachio-colored cap with the hands directed at 11. "I expected to see rows of gargoyles." She pointed to one that had lost its head while others grinned down, looking more charming than vicious.

Peter handed Anne the Rick Steves *Ireland* guidebook, "I want to hear her read." Anne then handed it off to Mauve. "This castle is one of the most important buildings in Irish history. From 1204 until 1922 it was the seat of English, then later British, rule. During that time, it served principally as a residence for the British monarch's Irish representative, the Viceroy of Ireland, and as a ceremonial and administrative center.

"The castle was originally developed as a medieval fortress under the orders of King John of England. Constructed on elevated ground once occupied by an early Viking settlement, the old castle stood on the site of the present Upper Castle Yard. It remained largely intact until April, 1684, when a major fire caused severe damage to much of the building. Despite the extent of the fire, parts of the medieval and Viking structures survived."

Viking history is splattered throughout Ireland, much like

Scotland, Anne had read. She had Norwegian and Swedish DNA coursing through her, too, so it made perfect sense to feel such a kinship and empathy for these people and countries.

Mauve continued, "Following the fire, a campaign of rebuilding in the late seventeenth and eighteenth centuries saw the castle transformed from the medieval bastion into a Georgian palace. The new building includes a suite of grand reception rooms known as the State Apartments. These palatial spaces accommodated the Viceroy for state occasions. In the early nineteenth century, the castle was enhanced by the addition of the Chapel Royal in the Lower Castle Yard. It remains one of the architectural highlights of Georgian Dublin today.

"On January 16, 1922, the last Viceroy of Ireland handed Dublin Castle over to Michael Collins and the government of the newly independent Irish state. The end of the British presence had come about in the wake of the Easter Rising of 1916 and the Irish War of Independence. These momentous events paved the way for the creation of the Republic of Ireland and were closely associated with the history of Dublin Castle. Irish governments have continued to use it for important national events, such as state dinners and commemorations.

"Over the centuries, those entertained at Dublin Castle have included Benjamin Franklin in 1771, the Duke of Wellington in 1807, Daniel O'Connell in 1841, Queen Victoria four times between 1849 to 1900, Charles Dickens in 1864, Princess Grace of Monaco in 1961, John F. Kennedy in 1963, Nelson Mandela in 1990 and Queen Elizabeth in 2011. My, that's a lot of reading and history." Mauve concluded her dissertation.

"She's reading all day as far as I'm concerned," Sue told Anne. "I love her accent."

Anne mentioned to Mauve, "I'm somewhat fascinated by the British royal family. I must admit I got up in the wee hours to watch the wedding of Diana and Charles, then Andrew and Fergie, Diana's heartbreaking funeral, and then of course I had to watch Diana's son William marry Kate 16 years later. Remind me to tell you the story about how we serendipitously encountered Queen Elizabeth and Prince Phillip in Victoria, B.C. Did you know she is the same age as my mother almost to the month?"

Mauve had no idea of the captivating history surrounding this castle. Inside, the guided tour started with the medieval undercroft and the mini Dublin history lesson. The guide told them that the medieval undercroft is the ruins of the original castle that is under the administration building. He led them along a stairway and walkway so they could see close up the city walls and the River Poddle that flows under the city.

Next, they visited the Chapel Royal, which opened in 1814, replacing an earlier church on this site. "The ornate and elaborate woodwork is remarkable." Dave admired fine craftsmanship.

They were led into the palatial State Apartments appearing exactly as one would expect the inside of some magnificent castle to look. The walls in each room were painted a different color with plenty of golden opulent chandeliers dripping with hundreds of glistening crystals in the shape of raindrops. The tapestries adorning the walls, the carpets on the floors, plus a splendid staircase, communicated importance and magnificence. This was no ordinary majestic staircase; it was, in fact, a Grand Staircase, and the first of its type in Dublin. Its architectural form created a regal first impression of the State Apartments. During the social season, debutantes and members of the aristocracy ascended this staircase in grand attire on their way to attend balls, dinners, and presentation ceremonies given by the Viceroy, the guide explained.

"Can you just imagine one of our ancestors dressed in finery gliding down this staircase?"

"Actually no, Anne. Ours were trying to grow crops or milk cows."

"Probably. Okay then, how about the legendary American Princess Grace of Monaco gracefully descending, almost floating, just like in the movies?"

"Now that I can picture." Mauve smiled, totally in awe.

The Wedgwood Room used the arctic and white color scheme that mimics the colors of the famous pottery. Completed in 1777 in the neoclassical design, it later became the castle's billiard room. Lit only from above by a small glass-domed roof, it had been a favorite place in the nineteenth century for the creation of temporary indoor gardens filled with exotic birds, trees, and water fountains.

Mauve touched the glass pane of a tall cabinet full of cups and saucers. "I have one Wedgwood tea cup and saucer, that's all I could afford. It's on a rack on the kitchen wall with instructions for no one to touch it."

The Portrait Gallery has two walls filling almost every inch with images of important people and a dining room where state dinners were held in the early eighteenth century. This room continues to be used for state receptions by the Irish government. The elegant dining table is laid with Waterford crystal and the Irish State dinner service, which features the national emblem—the gold harp.

Room after room appeared impeccable and elegant. The Throne Room, created in 1788, has an audience chamber in which the Viceroy received guests on behalf of the British monarch. The throne was made for the visits to Ireland by King George IV in 1821. Later, Queen Victoria and King Edward VII used it during their visits to the castle.

The State Drawing Room is chock-full of marble-carved busts, gold-framed portraits, and full-size sculptures all against imperial red walls. There is an ornate tapestry carpet with a pinkish sofa across from a grouping of uncomfortable-looking chairs, surrounded by vases, clocks, candlestick holders, and three grandiose crystal chandeliers overhead. Their knowledgeable guide had lots of interesting information to share.

They entered the Connelly Room named after James Connelly who led the Easter Rising in 1916. "We all know about him and studied this extensively in school," Mauve told them. She added, "Not only one of the signers of the Proclamation of the Irish Republic but he was also held here as a wounded prisoner. The Easter Rising being unsuccessful, Connelly was executed. This did not sit well with the Irish people and therefore increased their quest for Irish independence."

She read the round plaque on the wall. "In this room, James Connolly signatory to the proclamation of the Irish Republic lay a wounded prisoner before his execution by the British Military forces at Kilmainham Jail and his interment at Arbour Hill 12th May, 1916."

Their tour ended in St. Patrick's Hall, the largest room in the State Apartments. Mauve told them that Parliament had met in this room but now it is used for inaugurations and other stately functions. Square tapestry flags flanked each side of many mirrors. The mirrors tossed back reflections of casually clothed tourists, perhaps not dressed appropriately for the grandeur of the room.

"Can't you just feel the importance of this room by the magnificent landscapes and portraits, the royal blue carpet with columns of gold, and mammoth sparkling chandeliers?" Mauve gushed, obviously proud of her heritage.

The invasion at Costa Coffee commenced after Anne mentioned they'd stopped at many in England and Scotland. While others read the menu, Anne ordered one of her favorites, an iced chai latte. "I can vouch for their iced beverages but not any others. I'm not a hot beverage person." Peter asked for an iced cortado.

"Cortado, seriously?" Anne's blue eyes opened wider than usual.

"Yeah, I need a pick-me-up. Double espresso with milk over ice will help. Likely jet lag." His drink arrived with three chocolate-covered coffee beans floating on top.

Mauve grinned. "I'm having what he's having. I'm not used to all this activity. Thanks for the caffeine hit." She hugged her American cousin about the fifth time already that morning. "I needed this."

They met up with a local guide, Ian, whom Anne had contacted for a private tour by email months before leaving home. He had lived in Dublin most of his adult life, a retired barrister who now led tours. Walking through the Temple Bar district located in an area on the south bank of the River Liffey in central Dublin, the area contains everything from busy restaurants and bars to theaters and art galleries, situated on charming cobblestone alleyways with street performers galore. Kelly green, dazzling white and blaze orange pennants waved in the gentle breezes on many buildings and across alleys.

Ian mentioned there were over 600 pubs in Dublin. "Temple Bar is crammed not only with taverns but shops, restaurants, attorneys' and doctors' offices."

"Which one is your favorite?"

He motioned toward a pub with an emerald door and suggested, "Let's go in for a pint."

They all stood at what seemed like a quarter-mile-long wooden bar. Anne couldn't decide. "Sorry, I'm not an ale or beer drinker. Can you recommend something else?"

"How about trying a Black Velvet? It's a real Irish classic."

"What's in it? "

"Guinness and champagne."

"Still beer but okay, I'll give it a try." Anne took a cautious sip. "Gosh, that's a powerful smoky taste, although the champagne lightens it with the bubbles. This would be fun for New Year's Eve, Irish style. We need to try this at home, Peter."

"Noted." Peter was about to order Guinness to be sociable, but it wasn't his favorite. He mentioned it to the server.

"Let me get you a Snakebite. Some beer, some cider, one glass." The bartender's spirited hazel eyes barely peeked above the row of round-handled taps, handing him a tall glass of caramel-golden fluid filled almost to the top rim.

Sitting beside her cousin, Anne asked, "Didn't Moyrah mention Fayanna has some interesting things happening in her life? She alluded to some Irish mystical foolishness. But is it?"

"Well, Fay supposedly sometimes sees things. Generations back on my mother's side, women read tarot cards and tea leaves. It's claimed that mother's family has always had a talent: a special sight. Mom never did, or so she repeatedly says. Grandma either but who knows."

Back outside they meandered up a street lined with colorful Georgian doors. The doors seemed out of place, newer than the rest of the area. An emerald door and a ruby door surrounded by ivy adorned the side-by-side homes.

"Sometimes called the Doors of Dublin, Merrion Square is one of the most intact Georgian Squares and where Oscar Wilde lived," Ian pointed out.

On Lower Baggot Street, near Merrion Square, they saw many beautiful doors along both sides. Fitzwilliam Square they learned is the smallest of Dublin's great Georgian squares and one of the last Georgian squares built in Dublin. Many of the buildings were blanketed in dark green ivy.

Anne was dying to peek inside one of the colorful doors. She had become obsessed with colorful doors on a trip to Scotland years earlier. "Sometimes things happened to her because of colorful doors," Peter told Mauve. "Anne created her own special word, 'graviosity,' a combination she made up."

"True. Sometimes it happens, gravity and curiosity blend to cause a pleasant surprise around or behind or through a colorful door. Maybe it will happen on this adventure, maybe not. I do know, though, I'm feeling a powerful tug to that opulent emerald door. See? It's slightly ajar. It seems just the invitation I need." She motioned toward the door. "Ian, maybe you know the owners?" Anne sort of joked with him.

"Sorry, no I don't. But after all these years, as a barrister and tour guide, I do know countless folks. Some questionable, most fine," Ian grinned. "Don't hesitate to ask. Honestly, most living in these Georgian homes are blow-ins—new blood, newcomers over the years, not original families. The repairs and upgrades to these historic homes are very costly."

In a row, the doors they saw were painted crimson, cherry red, sunshine yellow, and slate blue with a white H in the ornate scrollwork in the fanlight. Two ebony doors stood side-by-side with one surrounded by beige and the other in white woodwork and fanlights. A fuchsia door right next to a periwinkle door, both without as much fanlight flare as the others. Two doors were almost identical shades of neon yellow except for their mail slots and door knockers.

Ian told them that these doors can be traced back to the 1700s when the old medieval city began growing and becoming quite prosperous. Fast expansion led to remodeling of the city's streets and squares and a need to develop outside the city center, especially to create residential areas. Strict codes were enforced for structural designs which created restrictions for buildings. The resulting style and period had come to be known as Georgian Dublin, named for four kings who ruled during that period. To show some individuality and set themselves apart, the former residents of Georgian Dublin painted their front doors whatever color they desired. Breaking from the strict architectural uniformity, residents started adding their own touches to set their houses apart from others. These flairs of personality or maybe independence included fancy knockers, intricate designs or fanlights above the door, and most striking, front doors in a variety of colors. Today, most of the houses have their original fanlights, some still with box-shaped glass recesses in which a lamp would have been placed.

Peter noticed Dave waving his arms, motioning him over. He gestured up. "Check out that bird, maybe a hawk? It's really fast."

"Hmm. It could be, or maybe a falcon." Peter took the caps off his binoculars and followed the bird flying in an upward spiral. He could see its blue-gray back as it dipped down towards land, then its barred white underparts to its throat to its beak and the bird was about two feet long. He pulled out his *Ireland Birds* handy tri-fold pocket guide, checking his suspicions. He always bought a nifty laminated bird and animal guide before any global trotting. This time he had gotten one for each couple on the trip.

Ian joined them. "What are you looking at, gents?"

"Maybe a falcon." Both tourists motioned up.

Looking skyward, Ian agreed. "You are correct. It's a peregrine. There are several in this area. Effortless meals for them." He nodded at the river. "There is at least one pair roosting on iconic Poolbeg chimneys that overlook Dublin Bay. Fantastic location for them at 680 feet high.

"Here in the city, they have nests on top of cathedrals and sometimes bridges. They don't build nests but make a scrape or shallow depression in existing gravel or other debris like sticks. Very uninspiring for the magnificent birds they are. Occasionally they will also use a nest vacated by eagles or ravens."

"Are you a birder, Ian?"

"Not officially even though my wife and I admire birds and all wildlife in general. I read more about birds than she does."

"So not as serious as *The Big Year* movie a few years ago?" Dave chuckled.

Ian laughed and shook his head. "Oh my, no. The film probably depicted fowl enthusiasts more accurately than some would like to admit, my avian-obsessed friends, anyway. I will disclose that Talula, that's my wife, and I, do keep track and have identified over 1,050 different species over the past decade. She enjoys watercolors and paints scenery and wildlife, and always makes sure birds are included."

Peter said, "Anne and I try to do some bird watching on all of our explorations. We have peregrines at home, too. I read an article on them in *National Geographic* and they are the fastest member of the animal kingdom. They clocked one at 242 miles per hour during its high-speed dive for food."

"We've seen a few along the cliffs and canyons of the Columbia River, too." Dave reminded Peter they'd seen the falcons while exploring Ginkgo Petrified Forest State Park outside of Vantage, the last time they had visited.

"Normally they are bird-eating raptors dining on ducks and pigeons but will hunt small mammals and reptiles. Our pigeon population is kept in check by the peregrines. Don't be surprised if you see a few on your upcoming travels."

Christ Church stands guard above the River Liffey. On the borders of the lawn surrounding the church were dayglo-orange geraniums with bushes of delicate yellow flowers filling the corners. Light and darker gray blocks of stone, lengthy and tall stained glass windows, and lots of arches were their first sights. Approaching the church gave Anne the impression that it was protecting its neighborhood from evil. And it is ancient, built in 1172 to 1220.

Ian explained that over the centuries, Christ Church accommodated many significant events including the crowning of Edward VI in 1487. Today, it houses the important Treasures of Christ Church which features manuscripts and ancient artifacts as well as a spectacular exhibition of original sixteenth century costumes.

Constructed in the early twelfth century, and still the oldest structure still in use in Dublin, the crypt is home to a mummified cat and rat. According to cathedral lore, the cat chased the rat into the pipe of the organ, and both became stuck. There they stayed, permanently. There are hundreds of relics in the collection.

Skyward, stained glass windows are plentiful along with the medieval floor tiles in every shade of amber, fading into cantaloupe with different designs on each tile. There are thousands of them. In one section there is a perfect square of four rust-colored tiles; next were black and white in a triangle pattern with sienna and caramel flower patterns in the middle. Each section around the cathedral had different tile patterns and colors. There are many magnificent stained glass windows, some narrow and long, some in a flower pattern, some typical with arched top, one even in the shape of an eye with an eyeball. The wording alongside the eyeball reads, "The church bells range in weight from a quarter of a ton to two and a quarter tons." Under a crimson crest, two large gold keys cross over each other and beside them, a plaque reads *Christ Church Cathedral was founded in 1028.*

"I've learned more today about Dublin than in any history books," Mauve said, soaking in every word Ian shared.

"Perfect timing, I'm famished." Mauve put her hand on her stomach as Ian dropped them at the front door at The Shack Restaurant, in the heart of the Temple Bar. Going in felt like a step back in time with wide plank hardwood floors, walls adorned with pictures and photographs of scenery, and still life fruit and vegetables. Doing a complete 360 of this charming dining establishment, the wooden walls blended with gray stone block walls and more artwork. Light poured in from the only window, and a section of the wall displayed colorful patterned Irish plates on wooden wall racks. Mauve's husband, Brennan, sat inside holding a table for them.

"Appetizers are called 'Starters' here, you know. How about we begin with oak-smoked Irish salmon with home-made brown bread, and garlic mussels tossed in a pan with garlic butter and white wine?"

"A good start, Mauve, but I'm really hungry," Brennan

said. "I'm the one who has been working all day while you played."

"Anne, do you see what else is on the menu?" Peter indicated the salad section.

"Marvelous! Do you want to split the Langoustine salad, please, please?"

"Absolutely."

"Very good choice," the server agreed and explained that the Dublin Bay prawns are the key ingredient along with other fresh vegetables. "You don't mind just a little kick as the prawns are first cooked in olive oil with a sweet chili sauce. We use a light citrus dressing and comes with a slice of soda bread."

"So Dublin Bay prawns are the same as langoustine?" Anne asked.

"Yes, sometimes called Norway lobster or scampi. But langoustine, although the sweeter lobster taste and texture, is not a crustacean but in the hermit and porcelain crab family."

A woman sitting close by had a stunning turquoise drink. "What's that woman drinking?" Anne signaled across the table.

"Irish Eyes" came the answer, "made with whiskey, crème de menthe, Irish cream, and cream. I think you will enjoy it. If not, I will gladly find something else for you to try. Would you like to try one?" Anne nodded with a mouth full of soda bread that had been placed in front of her. Mauve raised her hand, "Make that two, please."

"How's the Irish Manhattan?" Peter decided to try something different than his usual, an Old Fashioned.

"A very popular one, sir."

Anne cleared her throat.

"Oh, with extra cherries, please. For my wife." Peter watched the bartender make his favorite drink but with an

Irish twist, Jameson Whiskey with sweet vermouth, bitters, and adding four dark cherries.

Five minutes later, Anne lifted her drink, "Cheers, Cousins," and touched her glass to Mauve's. Peter did the same with Brennan.

Mauve said, "Oh my, they need to know the correct words for 'Cheers,' don't they, love?" Brennan had just taken a drink so could only nod. "Cheers is acceptable but you will be highly regarded if you say it as we do. It's as important as Hello, Please, and Thank you but we say, 'Cheers,' most of the time."

"Hey everybody!" A quiet fell down the long table as Anne got everyone's attention. "Mauve is going to teach us how to say, 'Cheers' properly."

Mauve had already ingratiated herself with their friends and even though a long day, seemed eager to learn the lingo from their Irish tutor who some now had put on a pedestal.

"The word is spelled Sláinte, and we say 'slawwn-chee' or you may hear 'Slaw-in-tche' which means 'to your good health.'"

All Brennan heard was the Americans trying, but butchering, one of his favorite words. Mauve just laughed.

"How is Wrenna doing?" Anne asked between sips of the creamy mint Irish Eyes.

"She hasn't discovered her niche just yet. She graduated college, as you know, a couple of years ago and has had a few jobs. The last one lasted a year or so. She's working at a popular pub in Malin Head, north of Derry for the summer. I just don't know about her future but she certainly doesn't seem concerned. She is an excellent listener and I think she'd make a wonderful therapist, as she has such an empathetic heart and is compassionate with all ages."

"You know," Anne patted her cousin on her right knee, "it's a new day and age where we stayed at home or had more long-term jobs. This generation seems to flit around from job to job. They say they are getting more experience, maybe that's so."

"She has many friends and several close female friendships but nothing like with Fay. She texted me last night and mentioned a man she is seeing. That's not unusual, she plays the field but no one seriously, I'll fill you in on the boys later. They are a topic of their own. Maybe I will get a grandchild one of these years." Mauve rolled her girlish azure blue eyes and crossed her fingers.

For the main entrée, Anne selected the traditional fare of Bacon and Cabbage. The loin of bacon is commonly cooked and served with buttered cabbage, parsley sauce and potatoes. It tasted flavorful and hearty. Peter had Irish stew made with lamb, carrots, and potatoes. Mauve ordered one of her favorite meals, lamb shank on Irish cabbage with red wine gravy.

"This is just the beginning of eating potatoes prepared in dozens of different ways," Brennan chuckled.

"We take our potatoes very seriously." Mauve scootched up, sitting straight as if morphed into a teacher. "You might as well learn some etiquette sooner than later. Murphies, poppies, praities, purdies, shpuds, spuds, tatties or totties. Boiled potato, pretty much explains itself. Boxty is a potato cake on a griddle using a mixture of raw and mashed potatoes and eggs. You can add garlic to pep it up. Champ is an Irish dish of mashed potatoes and green onions. Chips are your French fries. Crisps are potato chips. Mash are mashed potato. New potatoes are usually cooked and served in their jackets."

"Okay, that's enough about potatoes for now. I can only retain so much info."

"I'm absolutely knackered." Mauve's droopy eyes indicated to Anne it meant her cousin was exhausted. "All this walking and touring is hard business."

"I like their word 'knackered' better than 'exhausted.' You might hear it in the future, Peter."

Anne couldn't get to sleep. She went into the bathroom not to disturb Peter and typed out a quick email on her phone, checking in with her mother. She immediately replied that she was okay with diversions from family and friends, and lots of casseroles and desserts. She'd eaten an entire banana cream pie in two days, one of her favorites. Tomorrow she would start the chocolate cream. Anne burst out laughing. Her mom loved any type of cream pie. However, her mom also wrote that the task of writing her husband's obituary felt overwhelming. Anne cried for her mother who had lost the love of her life of 68 years.

One hundred forty miles northwest of Dublin in the town of Donegal, Seamus Kennedy heard his phone ping. Recognizing the name on the screen, his deep-set frosty eyes narrowed as he swore a blue streak.

> U owe me $15,000. U have 10 days or u r dead.

Seamus ran his right hand through his tousled thick chestnut hair thinking he should get a haircut before his next date. *No need, I'm great the way I am*, he thought, always impressed with himself. He didn't reply to the text. He knew full well what he owed even though it had started with the $10,000 loan. With his delays and high interest, it had become $15,000.

An hour later, sitting on a stool at his favorite neighborhood bar after downing his third beer, Seamus stammered, *"What am I going to do?"*

"Do about what?" The bartender asked, just being friendly.

"Mind your own business and just bring another." *I can't go to my sister again.* He typed a message to a woman he dated off and on for several months.

The bartender set another glass of Guinness in front of him remembering two weeks earlier when Seamus was so wasted that his blood alcohol level could strip paint off a wall and he'd insisted on more. He touched the soreness on his jaw from the last donnybrook and wouldn't be tangling with this mess of a man again.

Wrenna heard her phone, read the message then responded.

> Looking forward to our time together on Friday.

> I need to postpone.

> Ok another time.

He was ticked.
Wrenna didn't answer.

Trying another one of his lady friends, Fayanna hoped it was from her boyfriend.

> Looking forward to our time together on Friday.

> Me 2. My roommate will be away if u want to start here with appetizers...

He couldn't miss the teasing winking emoji. Seamus sat there sweating, grumbling to himself. He picked at a blemish on his scruffy chin. *I need to figure this out. Where in the world am I going to get 15 grand?*

In his stupor, he recalled the first time he saw Wrenna, or was that Fayanna? The cousins were still hard to tell apart. A stunning woman garbed in a knock-out scarlet dress with a plunging neckline highlighting her alabaster skin, lipstick to match her dress, and knee-high jet-black boots, promenaded in the bar, her shoulder-length ginger hair piled in a messy bun. She sparkled. So much sparkle. Her particularly merry greenish-blue eyes gleamed right along with her necklace. She was a curvy woman with plenty of sass, not like he recalled from their school days. Thinking back, he now couldn't recall who he'd actually met up with that night.

But Fay knew. She'd been repeatedly told by a few of her gal-pals that she acted and dressed like a nun and needed to enjoy life more. Her experiment went badly. Very badly. She wasn't anything like the woman she pretended to be that night.

CHAPTER TEN

They awoke bright-eyed and ready for another full day in Dublin. Today the visitors would start in the center of the city after a half-hour hike from the hotel through a lovely neighborhood of homes, small businesses, and a few restaurants and pubs, scouting out where they would have dinner.

At the Dublin Church, a plaque caught Anne's eye as the last name sounded familiar. It read *Erected by the citizens of Dublin to the memory of John McNeill Boyd*. They had special friends at home, Tim and Heather, with the last name of Boyd so she hoped it could be some long-lost relative of Tim's.

Peter started to read a lengthy inscription and Anne interrupted him, "Let's have Mauve read it. I want to hear her as long as we get her."

"John McNeill Boyd, R.N. captain H.M.S. Ajax born at Londonderry 1812 and lost off the rocks at Kingstown Feb. 9th, 1861, in attempting to save the crew of the brig, Neptune. Safe from the rocks, whence swept thy manly form the tides white rush. The stepping of the storm, borne with a public pomp, by just decree heroic sailor! From that fatal sea, a city vows this marble unto thee, and here in this calm place, where never din of earths great waterfloods shall enter in: when to our human hearts two thoughts are given, one Christ's self-sacrifice, the other heaven: here is it meet for grief and love to crave the Christ-taught bravery that died to save, the life not lost, but found beneath the wave. All thy billows and thy waves passed over me: yet I will look again toward thy holy temple."

On a corner, Anne scanned Reilly's pub decked out in black proudly displaying the gold Guinness sign and shamrock promoting the 'National Lottery Sold Here' signage along the top. Peter took a picture of Anne and Mauve flanking the wooden post trimmed in shamrock green.

The cherry red-painted Queen of Tarts storefront had shelves lined with homemade delicacies, most topped with some type of berry. It was unusual not to see a building festooned with flowers, flags, and banners. Most buildings were white, gray, or cinnamon stone. Multiple hues of gray stones made up many churches and Celtic crosses. At Bulmer's Fish and Chips, they paid 12 pounds for an authentic lunch wrapped in yesterday's newspaper.

Sitting across from each other at a picnic table, Anne rolled her eyes, "This is the best white fish ever. Chips—not so much—pretty soggy. By the way, how are your parents doing?"

"Oh Anne, they are so upset about not seeing you this time. Honestly, they didn't think you'd be coming because of your dad. They are in Iceland and using the tour guide company you have raved about several times…"

"Friend In Iceland," Anne interjected.

"Right, well off they flew because your friends…"

"Gunnar and Saga Jen," Anne butted in again.

"Right, they had a cancellation so Mam and Dad flew off.

It's only a two-and-a-half-hour flight from here. They are gone for two weeks and are going for several days in Greenland, too."

"I'm sure they're having a fantastic time; it's such a diverse country with incredible scenery, delightful, hardworking people, and delicious food."

"I'll show you an email later with photos of them by a dozen different waterfalls, hiking a rim of an extinct volcano, soaking in hot springs by a geyser, and Mam horseback on a trail ride while Dad was doing some glacier hike. But Mam thinks they should be thinking about downsizing. They're on a good-size plot of land, too much now for Dad to take care of himself. Moyrah and I, plus our brothers, keep trying to have the 'time to move' conversation and unfortunately, our youngest brother doesn't agree with the rest of us, so it's caused some discontent. Instead, they bought an apartment in Malaga, Spain. Did I tell you that they'll be going for six months or so in the winter?"

"Malaga? That's perfect for them. Fresh seafood on the beach, paella, avocados the size of footballs, fresh fruits, and luscious Sangria. And lots of British fair-skinned tourists burning their pasty skin. Pale like us."

"You've been?"

"Yes, with friends from England who have a timeshare there." Anne shared a vivid memory after they'd checked into their apartment next to Brits Howard and Pearl. "I bounded down three flights of an outdoor staircase going to the front desk with a question when I saw two topless women, clearly senior citizens, not with perky twenty-something chests, lounging in what they assumed was the privacy of their balcony. Or they didn't care and were glad to be out of the gloom of summertime in England. When telling Pearl, she casually confirmed it and said, "Oh yes, it's topless here and most of us do."

Mauve's eyebrows about reached the bottom of her straight-cut bangs. "I *do not* see my mam going topless in Spain. But then again, I never dreamed they'd buy a place in the tropics."

Anne burst out laughing and added, "We got to visit the complex of Alhambra in Granada. Then journeyed to Gibraltar for a day, touring the fort and all the creepy aggressive monkeys begging for handouts. Oh, and one day to Tangiers, Morocco. We are not talking about that one."

"Why?"

"Another time. Trust me. It raises my blood pressure." Anne chuckled.

"We will go to visit them some winter when Brennan can get a week off work. What a perfect wintertime break from our cold, drizzly weather."

"How do they get there? Train and ferries or flying?"

"Flying. It's just three hours, whereas the train route is a couple of days, about 1,700 miles."

"It's odd. My parents used to drive three days, 1,200 miles to sunny Arizona, a couple of states away, and yours fly several countries away. Cherish your time with your parents, Mauve." Anne once again blinked away tears. "My folks are older than yours, but one never knows."

"Aye. Brennan's father passed suddenly a couple of months ago; massive heart failure. It was such a shock."

Close to Trinity College they came upon a life-size Molly Malone statue to commemorate the heroine of the famous song, "Cockles and Mussels," a tune set in Dublin. Molly lived in the seventeenth century and was known as a hawker by day (seller of fish) and a part-time prostitute by night. The statue is sometimes called "The Tart with a Cart" or "The

Trollop With the Scallops." Molly is wearing a low-cut blouse, barely covering her bustiness. On the cart sits three empty woven baskets depicting what, Anne didn't know. One American and one Irish cousin stood behind Molly as Peter took yet another photo.

They toured Trinity College's impressive Book of Kells. It hadn't changed much in 20 years except for creating a more efficient flow for tourists to view the books. Mauve knew all about the 680-page book and explained that it contains a Latin text of the four gospels copied and beautifully decorated by Irish monks around 800 AD. Since the 1660s, it has been safely stored at Trinity College Dublin and exhibited in the college library since the mid-nineteenth century. Other medieval copies of the gospels ranging from the fifth to fifteenth centuries are on display, showing that in the Middle Ages, copies of the gospels needed to be made in large quantities, all by hand.

Viewed by looking down at the open pages protected under thick glass, the printing of the letters and numbers were straight and narrow. The ink colors were vibrant and incredibly well-preserved. Display after display showed the artisans' painstaking work of this transcription. One life-size display stated that most of the text pages were written in iron gall ink made from oak galls (or oak apples), mixed with iron sulfate and wine or vinegar. Some lines of writing were in yellow, purple, or red.

Another display called "Pigments" explained that pigments were made from a variety of mineral and organic sources in early medieval Ireland. The yellow came from the mineral orpiment and yellow arsenic sulfide, known as a gold pigment. Purple was created from a dye from an orchid lichen then mixed with white to create pink. Different pigments were displayed in photographs of a dog-looking creature, a cross, a person, and script writing. Reading all of this certainly gave each an appreciation of what creative scientists they had hundreds of years ago.

Sue stood mesmerized. "I can't even imagine how long it took to find and then experiment with these plants, minerals, and other things to get these colors that withstood the sands of time."

They sauntered to the Long Room, really the main chamber of the Old Library, over 200 feet long. The dark wood columns flanking each alcove of precious materials seemed to stretch forever. It houses around 200,000 of the library's oldest books. It is kept somewhat dark to protect precious history and smelled like old books—musty. When built, it had a flat plaster ceiling with shelves for all the books on the lower level. By the 1850s the shelves were jam-packed. In 1860, the roof was raised to allow the construction of the present vaulted ceiling and gallery bookcases.

The Pantheon in the library displays busts of famous and important men such as scientists, statesmen, writers, philosophers, and thinkers from history, with not a woman in sight. Marble men line both sides of the Long Room. The farther away, the smaller the statues appeared, becoming cottony dots instead of a man's head. This collection began in 1743. Allegedly a committee drew up names of the "greats" they wanted included. Anne sized up Aristotle, who gave the impression he was very impressed with himself looking rather haughty. Also included are Isaac Newton, Plato, and then William Shakespeare wearing a collared jacket, just as they'd seen pictures of him with wavy hair, mustache, and beard. Many had curly hair and frilly collars; some were clean-shaven and some were not. There is an Irishman, writer Jonathan Swift, with a full head of wavy hair, wearing a scarf around his neck. But they all had one thing in common—they were carved out of snowy marble.

Farther they came to The Harp. "It is the oldest to survive

from Ireland and probably dates from the fifteenth century." Mauve had good reason to be proud. "It is constructed from oak and willow with brass strings." Anne always appreciated harp music and now had even higher esteem for the musicians who mastered such an instrument.

They also got a glimpse at a copy of the 1916 Proclamation of the Irish Republic. This signaled the start of the Easter Rising when read aloud outside the General Post Office on April 24, 1916.

Having worked at two universities in her career, Anne appreciated this library and the valuable resource it is for students who are privileged to study here. "I can see how one could get lost in history for days and days."

They stopped at the café for cranberry bread and a bottle of pink lemonade made in Ireland by D.P. Connelly & Sons, Merchant Family. She and Peter always tried to support local businesses when traveling and this brew did not disappoint. In the library shop, she purchased several bookmarkers and a pencil, as she did at any university she visited around the world.

Popping out of a crack in the stone wall at the cemetery grew a lone fern. Edgings of multicolored flowers sprang up beside the gravel. Dozens of stone and cement Celtic crosses towered above other lower gravestones on the walk to their next stop. Several light gray-collared doves cooed and pecked the ground. They returned 20 years later to the unchanged Kilmainham Gaol, the Dublin jail. This time the top floor displayed a historical tribute to Nelson Mandela whom Anne and Peter had seen in Oxford, England, some years earlier. "Remember when Nelson waved at me from the backseat of that black Rolls-Royce with Prince

Charles?" Anne reminded Peter who replied, "I recall he waved at me."

Entering the jail, it felt as ominous as their first visit, and Mauve became absorbed with the heartbreaking history. The jail tour guide explained it opened in 1796 as the county jail for Dublin. The doors closed in 1924. Today it is a museum symbolizing the tradition of militant and constitutional nationalism from the Rebellion of 1798 to the Irish Civil War of 1922 to 1923. On wall plaques, they read that leaders of the rebellions were detained and in some cases executed there.

The guide turned as he spoke to them standing in a circle. "Many members of the Irish Republican Movement during the Anglo-Irish War from 1919 to 1921 were also detained here, guarded by British troops. Not only were notables housed here but it held thousands of ordinary men, women, and children. Their crimes ranged from petty offenses to more serious crimes such as murder or rape. Convicts from many parts of Ireland were held here for long periods waiting to be shipped to Australia.

"The New Jail, built as a response to the poor conditions of prisons in the eighteenth century, soon had many of the same problems as the old jail, mainly as a result of over-crowding. Until the 1860s, overcrowding led to disease, poor health and hygiene, and no full separation of adult and child or male and female prisoners. The prison reform movement protested this atmosphere and encouraged a move to single cells and facilities for hygiene and health.

"Many Irish revolutionaries, including leaders of the 1916 Easter Rising, were imprisoned and executed in the prison by the British. Not only notables but many were there for stealing a slice of bread to feed their family, or for throwing a stone breaking a window." He showed them a plaque outside a prison cell that read, "John Shaw (32) Shoemaker. Breaking a window and stealing bread thereout. Sentence: One Month."

The exterior of one cell door had been painted orange at one point, then black. Patches of orange bled through the peppery faded color, like a bright personality trying to escape darkness. On the back wall of another cell hung an oval picture of Mary holding baby Jesus. There were scribbled names etched in the walls. Spiral staircases led to the second and third floors. Three stories of rooms in a circular fashion are lined up directly above the next. As Anne stepped into a cell and closed the heavy solid wooden door with only a small hole for identification, communication, or light, she felt a chill of dread and was thankful her relatives didn't end up here as she didn't find one listed.

Sue leaned into Anne. "So do you believe in ghosts, spirits, fairies, and whatever else seems to be important to this history?"

Instead of a direct answer, she replied, "Well, don't you believe in ghosts?"

"I believe some people do. To each their own, right?"

"Fair enough. I like to visualize ghosts wandering over the moors."

"Wonder what Mauve believes?"

"Good time to find out. Mauve..."

"Well, we were raised believing in all sorts of spirits, fairies, ghosts, apparitions, trolls, and other world visitors, and I think, why not? How did the stones get to Stonehenge? How did the Pyramids in Egypt and Machu Picchu get built? Certainly not by humans. There are too many unexplainable happenings."

"Do you have first-hand knowledge of something?" Anne stepped closer to her cousin.

"I do. One weekend Brennan and I slipped away to a small Bed and Breakfast along the shore. It had a reputation of a rambunctious child ghost who loved music. The story goes that the child developed a lung disease, consequently a retched passing.

"That night I woke from a sound sleep hearing the piano downstairs playing a few notes. I listened, being wide awake, and again it played four notes. I tossed back the bedding, slipped on my slippers, headed across the dark bedroom to the hallway, and slowly tiptoed down the stairs. I could hear the wind whistle through the cracks in the siding. A dim floor lamp shined in the corner behind a chair in the living room. I stepped in, glanced around, and pulled back the lacey ashen curtains to see outside as the piano lid thumped down. I probably jumped about six inches. I grabbed a poker from the fireplace. There was nothing or no one there. I told myself to calm down, my heart racing. I rushed back upstairs and couldn't fall asleep. When I told the owners that morning about the piano, the lady nodded her head and told me it had happened before. I laugh about it all now but who I am to say anything about ghosts? It felt real to me, I am a believer."

A shiver ran down Sue's back and the hair on the back of Anne's neck stood up.

"I remained convinced someone had been in the home, but the owner, probably 35 years old, located no trace of anyone outside and no footprints. The ground was soft but there wasn't a single footprint beside his own. I remember him saying something funny when I mentioned I was going outside for some fresh air. Then he said he'd join me and give a gander again around the house."

"I rudely laughed out loud and said, 'gander,' not many people use that anymore."

He cackled sort of spooky-like, "I'm bringing it back."

Now Anne and Sue were laughing, no longer quite so nervous about the ghost situation.

For dinner, they ate at their hotel's restaurant and started with vegetable soup with Irish soda bread. The soup, called Dublin Coddle, is made of Irish pork sausage pieces in a potato and herb broth. Peter and Anne shared a grilled chicken fillet with herb stuffing served with pepper sauce, and a baked fillet of salmon with Cajun sauce, sautéed leeks, and brie cheese in puffed pastry with cranberry sauce. Anne learned quickly that even though Americans don't pronounce the "h" in herb, Irish do. So, Herb could be a man's name or an herb (erb).

Most ordered a pint of something but Anne surveilled a few bottles of wine and asked if the server had a favorite. He brought over a local bottle of Lusca Irish Wines, that comes from Llewellyn's Orchard, a small-scale winery run by fruit alchemist David Llewellyn in Lusk, County Dublin. The private orchard has grown to produce balsamic apple cider vinegar, cider vinegar, apple syrup, craft cider, and apple juice as well as wine from Irish grapes. He offered Anne tastes of Cabernet Sauvignon, Merlot, Dunkelfelder, and Rondo.

"Dunkelfelder? I've not heard of that one."

"Dunkel means dark which deepens the color in the wines. It's used as a blending ingredient and rarely made into varietal wines. The few released are dry, with acidity and body and somewhat neutral flavors. It's best with steak and kidney pie or a tomato pasta dish." After the sip, Anne decided to go with the Merlot.

Dessert wasn't particularly traditional, a typical chocolate brownie but with the bonus of the Irish liqueur ice cream, it turned into something lip-smacking. A dollop of whipped cream decorated with raspberry drizzle made an appealing and delicious dessert.

The cousins sitting side-by-side visited between bites. "Anne, how's your brother Will doing? Did he retire?"

"Yes, in June after over 35 years with the county sheriff's office. He decided not to run for sheriff again because it's a four-year term and he's pushing 55. Plus with our elderly parents, he wanted to be more available to help out. He never expected he'd be dealing with our dad's passing so soon. He has a myriad of interests, so he'll be fine. He even enjoys grilling and some cooking, lucky Michelle. They enjoyed meeting you and Brennan when you visited a few years back."

"We loved meeting them, plus their three children and granddaughter Brooklyn. She's a peach. And your brother, Max, and his wife Lola, are each so interesting with their various lives and jobs. And five children and passel of grands. I appreciated seeing your state and the driving tour you took us on. I can't believe Oregon is over three times larger than Ireland. I especially loved that area in the central part with all the tall mountains named after your American presidents. But my favorite was going to the headwaters of the Metolius River where you spent much of your childhood camping. And that Peter's family camped in the area also. Then we drove along that long gorge, what is it called?"

"Columbia Gorge."

"Em, yes, with that amazing 700-foot-tall waterfall, Mult-nomah, right?" Anne nodded. "Brennan enjoyed the coastal drive; he's enjoys water. We did have a hard time with all the town and some of the river names," she laughed.

"You're not alone there," Anne assured her cousin. "Most tourists do, many names and words coming from original American Indigenous words."

"But I have to say," Mauve winked, "my absolute favorite was the wine tasting at several of the excellent wineries close by your home. The two bottles we carefully carried home didn't last long. Do you want to stay here or go to Trad night, traditional Irish music? It's where a group of locals get together and plays songs everyone knows"

"I'm good with staying here and catching up with you, Mauve. We will have plenty of opportunity for Trad nights later in the trip."

Anne was curious about Mauve's oldest child. "How's Finnegan doing? Did he get settled?"

"We traveled to see him in Wales about four months ago. He is thriving at the Llanelli fire station. The town has around 25,000 people and sits on Loughor estuary. It's quite scenic with its squatty washed-out lighthouse and rocky beach that's not really for sunbathing but more for beach-combing. We visited the fifteenth century church, St. Ellyw's, and whoever built it used rubble stone from the beach. It's lovely with a basil-green slate roof and terracotta ridge tiles. He didn't mention any particular lady but he's easy to click with so has plenty of friends. They do a tremendous amount of charity work within their community, car washes, food drives, and many other things. They seem well respected and appreciated by the locals. He's a bit of a daredevil. I heard him tell his father he wants to skydive, and I pray he's not reckless when working."

"Ohhhh, I have a fantastic fundraising idea for him. Tell him they should do a firefighter's calendar. I've seen this in other communities and those hunky firemen make lots of money that way for charity. Who doesn't love a man in uniform?" Both cousins snickered.

"And PJ?"

"Well, our PJ now prefers to be called Patrick," Mauve faked an uppity voice. "He lives for research. If he could, I think he'd be a student all of his life. He knows he needs to work but it's not his focus. He's decided to get his PhD and being a perfectionist, he'll do very well."

"PhD In what?"

"Neuroscience."

"What?"

"He's been accepted as a research associate at the University of Sheffield in northern England for the Division of Neuroscience. The research project focuses on decreasing the diagnostic delay of people with motor neuron diseases."

"How in the world did he decide that path?"

"I truly don't know. Maybe from his workaholic grandfather being a science and math teacher?"

"What's he doing for fun?"

"He loves rock wall climbing, which makes me extremely nervous. I don't think I'm a worrywart but I told him sometime back not to tell me before he does something crazy, but instead after he's done. He's very private and doesn't share much about his personal life. He's close to Wrenna and the only thing she's gotten from him is that he has a friend. I'm not expecting any grandchildren from him." Mauve shrugged her shoulders.

"Wow, he's an impressive lad and only in his early thirties."

"I'll tell you about Conor later. Brennan refers to him as our wild child. Want another glass of wine?"

"Absolutely. What happens on vacation stays on vacation."

CHAPTER ELEVEN

The next morning their official Collette tour began and their guide, April, graciously allowed Mauve to join the group for the day. Anne's cousin quickly became a hit with other American guests. "Who doesn't love an Irish accent?" one woman commented in a syrupy voice, obviously somewhere from the southern part of the US.

Anne took an immediate liking to April with her infectious smile and high cheekbones, smoky black shoulder-length thick hair, and sparkly mahogany eyes. Cherry red lipstick worked well for her. Her personality felt magnetic as she welcomed everyone warmly.

Anne's original group of ten were joined by twenty-two others from around America. April told them she was of Scottish origins; no wonder Anne felt a fondness for her. Their driver Bill lived in the area. He had the appearance of what tourists envisioned as characteristically Irish with medium height, wiry, light reddish hair, blue eyes, fair complexion, and a pleasing smile with a thick accent.

They headed to Merrion Square Park in one of Dublin's five historic Georgian squares, where a local guide joined them for the morning. Alexander gave the impression or one might guess, would be an elder Irish statesman: lanky, with a thick head of collar-length snowy hair that matched his bushy eyebrows and a pinkish glow to his face.

Sue whispered to Jeanine, "He could hide behind a telephone pole."

"Right? Mosquitos would leave him alone." Both sisters chuckled.

He wore a royal blue shirt with a snazzy cobalt and ecru tie, with a gold fleur-de-lis pattern and a gray sport coat with dark slacks.

He explained that the park memorializes the famous (and infamous) Oscar Wilde, author, playwright, and poet who was born in 1854 at #1 Merrion Square, just across the road from where they stood. The memorial consists of three pieces—the stone sculpture of a reclining Oscar, a pillar with a bronze of his pregnant wife, and a pillar with a bronze male torso.

Their knowledgeable guide stated the memorial's Irish sculpture was commissioned by the Guinness Ireland Group in 1997. The artist used polished colored stones and interesting textures to create a striking lifelike pose of Oscar relaxing, laying back on top of a 35-ton boulder of pale quartz from local mountains. The artist wanted to depict Oscar's love of beautiful objects as well as his colorful personality. Even his clothing is unique, as Oscar wears a sage smoking jacket with a pink collar, long pants, and shiny black shoes. Alexander made sure they all carefully noticed Oscar's face. One side looks joyful and the other forlorn.

They read several quotes on the front of stones around a square: "It seems to me we all look at nature too much and live with her too little." And another: "There is only one thing worse in the world than being talked about, and that is NOT being talked about." And Mauve's favorite Oscar quote, "With freedom, books, flowers, and the moon, who could not be happy?"

Before this Irish adventure, Anne thought about what she wanted to learn and glean from her second time here and decided she would pay more attention to meaningful people like Oscar, not just charming historical architecture and spectacular scenery.

St. Stephen's Green (or "park" as Americans call it) is right in the center of Dublin. There is an official national holiday on December 26 for the man who is believed to be the first Christian martyred sometime around 33 AD.

Anne felt an immediate calm overcome her even though traffic surrounded all sides of the square. The 22 acres were extraordinary with well-maintained historical monuments, trees, and oodles of different flowers in perfectly manicured beds. A small girl wearing yellow pants and a striped pink and purple blouse sailed her toy boat in a large water fountain. Ponds filled with quacking ducks were being fed chunks of white bread by local children.

It wasn't just the beauty and serenity but the history that was especially meaningful. St. Stephen's Green was one of the areas the Irish held during the 1916 Uprising that ultimately won them independence. They saw an abundance of statues of lords, poets, a knight, a king, and the famous Three Fates. Down a pathway through an arch of greenery is a stone sculpture garden and a somber reminder of the Great Famine. The tallest person is headless. A scrawny dog is barely alive. Another headless person is holding a pole in her left hand that touches the ground, with her other hand reaching out to a person sitting on the ground. All a somber reminder that it is part of history for this country. On a lighter note, it's the only place in Dublin where they eyed a stationary elephant and tiger.

Right across from the Green is the main shopping street,

Grafton Street. To the left Alexander pointed to the Gaiety Theatre, Chester Beatty Library, City Hall, and Dublin Castle. To their right stood the National Library of Ireland and the Royal Hibernian Academy. This particular academy is a result of about 30 Irish painters, sculptors, and architects who petitioned the government for a charter of incorporation in 1832.

Within a short distance down the street, through an archway, they came face to face with a life-size Pieta. Alexander told them he attended here regularly. They continued through large wooden doors entering a lovely, peaceful, small Catholic church called St. Teresa's Carmelite Church, established in 1792. Anne thought the ornate scrollwork on the altar and alcoves were magnificent. Locals came for a time of prayer. A sunbeam worked its way through awe-inspiring stained glass windows that reflected a kaleidoscope of rainbow colors onto the tile floor. They saw exquisite statues with their individual altars where one can light candles, whether Catholic or otherwise. Mauve suggested they light a candle and make a wish, an Irish tradition.

St. Teresa, born in 1515, was a prominent Spanish mystic, nun, author, and theologian who led a contemplative life through what was called "mental prayer." Anne asked Alexander about 'mental prayer' and he answered that it meant nonverbal. Being a Carmelite, she lived, prayed, and worked to serve God's people.

After all the expended energy it seemed time for a treat and they'd heard some reports about fudge, Irish fudge. Alexander escorted them into an open-air market with stalls displaying pastries, meats, sandwiches, clothing, candles, jewelry, and about anything else one could want. Sue sighted it first—the Man of Aran Fudge—with its promise of creamy, buttery fudge. The fudge creator grew up on one of the three Aran Islands off the coast of Galway. His grandmother fixed a toffee mixture like no other. When he departed for school in Galway, those sweet memories never left him, so he decided to take her recipe and make fudge for the masses. He makes the same original flavor today called Tiger Butter Fudge, with plenty more flavors to sample. Anne selected Salted Caramel Fudge, Hot Irishman Fudge, and Peppermint Chocolate Chip Fudge and requested that he cut them into small cubes to share with her friends. She bought a separate piece of the salted caramel just for her.

Hoping no one would go into a diabetic coma, they continued their walk to City Hall, where Daniel O'Connell has an immense statue in his honor. As they stood under the stone arched gate, Alexander read, "'Gates of Fortitude and Justice Erected in 1750,' the pair of massive inner arches which flank the Bedford Tower and large sculptures of Fortitude and Justice at the gates."

Then he directed their attention to Ireland's most famous writer, James Joyce, standing on a marble block located right off O'Connell Street, near the Spire of Dublin monument. The novelist is leaning on a walking stick, his bespectacled greenish eyes looking upward from under a hat as if daydreaming. He is dressed in a shirt with a tie, slacks, and shoes, with an overcoat that touches his knees.

"The Spire, also called the Monument of Light, is a large, stainless steel straight-pin-like memorial completed in 2003," Alexander said. Almost 400 feet tall and consisting of eight hollow cone sections, it didn't seem to fit into the architectural correctness of this area, but Anne knew that Ireland is a country of monuments no matter the reason or cause.

Behind the castle, they saw buildings painted in bright colors in shades of yellow, red, lime, and lapis. The yellow building had a sapphire front door. A short distance away is an oval plaque that Alexander read, "#7 Hoey's Court (now demolished) about 100 feet northwest of this spot reputed that Jonathan Swift, dean of St Patrick's Cathedral, was born on the 30th day of November 1667. He died on the 19th day of October, 1745."

"Readers recognize his name as the author of *Gulliver's Travels*. Swift was an Irish author, clergyman, and satirist. His father died two months before he was born, so Swift grew up under the care of his uncle. He received a bachelor's degree from Trinity College and then worked as a statesman's assistant. He became dean of St. Patrick's Cathedral in Dublin. For some reason, most of his books were published under pseudonyms." Anne hung on every word and detail Alexander shared with them. Using a local guide provides insight that one might miss when wandering on your own.

Down the street, they saw a third-story window to which was firmly attached what appeared to be a gigantic peeping tom—a black and white peacock made of cloth and feathers. Alexander shrugged his shoulders, clueless about this peculiarity. At Kennedy & McSharry, a well-known men's store where hats, caps, and ties are available for purchase, Anne thought of her father, a true tie man over the decades. He always dressed up for work. While an elderly salesman held a traditional tie showing it to an equally mature patron, Anne wondered if this shop would be around in another 20 years.

Across the square, Handel's Hotel is several stories high with an impressive statue of a man standing on a thin 20-foot tall pedestal using both arms as if he is conducting a choir. They would have missed it if Alexander hadn't told them to glance up.

On the corner stood a bright teal-tinted building that houses the cheerful little Chorus Café. Special "Chef's Dishes" were posted on a stand-up menu board at the door: Mexican chicken wrap and chips, Chicken burger and chips, BLT and fries, for about the same prices as at home. About mid-day, the café had become a popular lunch stop with people from all over the US, sharing where they were from and why they'd come to Ireland. Especially interested in learning why people were visiting her country, Mauve gleaned that the majority of the tour group had Irish roots.

The cousins sat together sharing an order of fish and chips across from Peter who had struck up a conversation about flyfishing with a man from Minnesota.

"So, why are you calling Conor your wild child?" Anne questioned in a lower voice.

"He was a lot. Antisocial. Inattentive. Stubborn. As a child, he acted so differently than his siblings. Strong-willed, maybe describes him better. He became a real challenge to us with his stubborn streaks and always wanting to learn things for himself rather than listening to what we had to say. Especially when it came to safety. I remember one time he started to climb a tree at Mam and Dad's that Dad knew was rotten and would fall in the next gale. He told Conor not to climb it for that reason. It's like Conor wanted to be in charge of himself and wanted to be right above everything else. He climbed it anyway, and of course, a branch broke off with him on it. Crashing to the ground Mam thought the worst but he was okay and laughed it off. This emboldened him more. Like, 'See, I disobeyed and I am fine.' That didn't go over well with his grandfather.

"When his heart got set on something, his brain had a hard time switching gears. He felt passionate about things, more for wildlife and the outdoors. We read some things about this type of child and decided we didn't need to be involved in power struggles with him. We didn't have to argue with him about everything. I learned to take a deep breath and walk away. Brennan, not so much. He let Conor push his buttons all the time."

"Did you ever have him tested for autism or one of the syndromes like Asperger's disease?"

"We thought about it but took another path and let him take charge of his own activities and decisions, as long as he remained safe. I started talking to him differently, not nagging him about everyday things. Being able to have choices made a tremendous difference."

"Like what?" Anne sat mystified by this conversation.

"Example. It's freezing outside but he doesn't want to wear a jacket. Instead of telling him to wear a jacket, I learned to say something like, 'Okay, you don't want to wear your jacket today. I think it's cold and I am wearing one. Of course, you are in charge of your own body, as long as you stay safe and healthy, so you get to decide whether to wear one or not. But I am afraid that you will be cold once we are outside and then I won't have time to come back to get it. How about I put your jacket in the backpack, and then we will have it if you change your mind.' I had to realize he wasn't going to catch pneumonia. He would ask for it once he got cold. He couldn't imagine feeling cold when he was warm in the house and a jacket seemed like such a hassle.

"I didn't want to undermine that self-confidence but just teach him that there's no shame in letting new information change his mind. And I had to learn to listen to him. Listening calmly was not easy because he just didn't make sense to me. Or Brennan. Only by listening and reflecting on his words, did I come to understand what came across as opposition. I don't know if it's because he's the youngest but he acted like he was fighting for his own place, for respect."

"That's fascinating. I am so impressed." Anne wiped a teardrop that had escaped.

"He always loved the outdoors, animals, and not so much people, probably because of all the rules and regulations. So he decided to be a park ranger. Or a wilderness guide. Or even a wildlife photographer at one point. He's done some college and got hired as an intern for the summer as a park ranger assistant in Scotland at Loch Lomond and Trossachs National Park. He's responsible for maintaining the park's natural resources, ensuring visitor safety, and providing information to visitors, so some people skills but all outdoors. He can even lead some groups on outdoor adventures such as hiking and camping. And he's learned to flyfish, too. When he calls, I can hear the excitement and fulfillment in his voice."

"So, interning means no salary?"

Mauve nodded. "Indeed, just a stipend that includes room and board, but they've promised him a full-time job soon. Two of my sons seem to think money isn't a priority. Somehow they will get by."

"Your children certainly do have interesting professions which makes them so unique."

"I don't expect that I'll have grandchildren from Conor or Patrick, maybe for different reasons. Finn and Wrenna are my only hope and I don't see that happening right away, either."

"You're too young to have grandchildren." Anne put her hand on her cousin's hand.

"Of course you are right. I will need time to go to Spain in the winters to see my parents." Mauve gave her cousin a double wink.

Alexander aimed their attention to the historic Liffey Bridge, commonly called Ha'Penny Bridge built in 1816 because a toll was charged until March 1919. Its original name was Wellington Bridge, and since 1836 has been officially called Liffey Bridge. It spans the Liffey River and is now a pedestrian-only bridge. Dozens of people were taking photos under the white-iron-scrolled archway with a lantern perched at the top, right at the crest of the bridge.

While walking, he mentioned that Ireland is a mecca for memorials, historical places, and public sculptures but few are as somber as the Famine Memorial on the bank of the River Liffey at Custom House Quay. The collection of statues designed and crafted by Dublin sculptor Rowan Gillespie was given to the city of Dublin in 1997.

This memorial is a permanent reminder of the many people who emigrated because of the Great Famine. It's built on the site of the *Perseverance*, one of the first famine ships to leave the area in 1846. The 74-year-old ship's captain quit his office job to transport the starving people from Dublin to America. All of his passengers arrived safely, and the *Perseverance* remained one of the first of thousands of ships to make that epic crossing.

Each wandered through the memorial of emaciated people trudging along the riverbank, with their various facial expressions of sadness and anguish, yet determined to save their lives. The bronze sculpture also includes a starving dog staggering behind his people. The skeletal figures, four males and two females, are shabbily dressed and wearing nothing more than rags. The first two figures are each clutching one bag tightly against their chests. The third person is a man carrying his belongings in one hand against his chest with his tattered hat in the other hand. The woman in the back isn't carrying anything; her bony arms and thin hands are at her sides. Her face is tipped heavenward with a questioning look on her face. The last male has a smaller corpse wrapped around his shoulders, maybe his child. They are not wearing shoes. Just a few steps away from the memorial is a tall ship moored in the water that is set up as a famine museum. The *Jeanie Johnston* is a replica famine boat. This stretch along the riverbank felt very oppressive and heartbreaking to Anne.

Mauve blew her nose several times and didn't hold back her tears.

Not far upriver, sparkling in the sunshine is a white bridge. The design caught Peter's attention. "Do you see a harp laid over on its side?"

"I do see that." She inquired about the unusual expanse. The guide replied, "It is called the Harp Bridge by many but it is the Samuel Beckett Bridge, which opened in 2009."

"Ah ha, something else new since we visited in 1998."

Alexander said, "Beckett was awarded the Nobel Prize in Literature in 1969. It is the second bridge designed by Calatrava, the first being the James Joyce Bridge farther upriver."

For dinner that evening they experienced Indian Tandoori, boasting authentic Indian cuisine. She didn't know how authentic, but it tasted delicious. Anne and Peter knew only one other Indian restaurant with which they had to compare it in Oxford, England.

After dinner, they wandered back to the hotel stepping over cables through a well-staged movie set with laundry carefully hung on two lines between buildings. Pants, shirts, blankets, sheets, and bloomers were precisely placed. Extras rushed around as two actors sat relaxed in chairs. Mauve stood star-struck and pointed out the famous duo to Anne and others. Mauve couldn't believe no one in their party recognized the Irish stars.

Back in their hotel room and eight hours ahead of the west coast of the US, Anne noticed an email from her brother, Will. The subject line read, "Warning and please proofread this." She opened it to see a photo of their father and the wording for a printed program that would be used at his memorial service. *This is real*, she thought to herself.

CHAPTER TWELVE

Anne and Peter got up early to have breakfast with Mauve and Brennan before their tour of the country began.

Mauve cried. "I will not say goodbye, instead, see you later."

"I'm so blessed to have found you."

"Aye, you too, Anne."

With last-minute firm hugs and a few tears, the Oregonians waved See You Later to their Irish cousins.

After boarding their tour bus, they hadn't been driving north for long before stopping at the Boyne Valley located at Newgrange, a UNSECO World Heritage Site, where perfectly round mounds sprouted wild grasses. Rocks surrounded each hill. April told them that this is the oldest Neolithic burial site in Ireland. Dirt paths led from one burial chamber to the next. The Passage Tomb, Si an Bhrú, is one of the most famous prehistoric monuments in Western Europe. Built over 5,000 years ago, the burial chamber is entered through a long stone passage, with the whole thing covered by a huge mound.

One knoll itself covers more than an acre and was constructed from over 200,000 tons of stone and earth. Standing 36 feet high, its diameter is about 260 feet. It is bordered by a curb, made of 97 uneven stones, many of which are decorated.

The passage alone is 40 feet long and is lined on both sides with standing stones. It leads directly into the burial chamber. April motioned to the magnificent corbelled roof, sort of a squared arch, which is 20 feet high. It has remained intact and waterproof for more than 5,000 years. They weren't permitted to go through the passage but could see down into the darkness.

One of Newgrange's notable phenomena is the small opening over the door. April explained that at dawn on the morning of the winter solstice, the shortest day of the year (December 21), and for several days before and after, a shaft of sunlight penetrates the passage, creeping slowly to the back of the chamber. To the Neolithic farmers, this may have been a sign of rebirth, with the New Year giving renewed life to crops and animals.

They wandered around this ancient site surrounded by a mammoth hedge, seeing the passage tombs, the medieval cemetery, Tower House, and standing stones. Anne stepped close to Sue. "I can't fathom how this had been built 5,000 years ago with no modern equipment, just determined backs and strong animals. Had to be aliens."

From Newgrange, they continued heading north through the Ring of Gullion, "an area of outstanding natural beauty," according to all the billboards. April told them that the ice age sculpted the rocks and terrain creating the deep valley forming a lough, numerous natural bays, and a flat plain along the coastline and now a UNESCO Geopark.

Peter drew Anne's attention to several carrot-red squirrels bounding around. April overheard him and explained they were Cooley Red Squirrels and an official group had been formed to protect and help maintain the population of the furry creatures. She didn't elaborate on the cute rodents nor did she point out the random red blotches on the roadway.

Just past Flurrybridge at the A1, they entered Northern Ireland and then turned west. It wasn't long until they reached the Ring of Gullion which contains the remains of 20 or so large stone tombs situated in prominent places. Stopping at one, they saw spectacular views of the surrounding area. Several anglers were flyfishing as families lollygagged along the river bank.

They saw golden acreage of stubble where barley, oats, or wheat stood. April mentioned that each crop would have been 3 to 4 feet high before harvest last month.

Just 12 miles from Belfast, they approached the village of Royal Hillsborough by a famous residence where the royal family stays when visiting Northern Ireland. The uninspiring two-story Georgian mansion made with blocks of light and tawny stones reminded Anne of any college building that could be at Oxford University. Four sets of two columns hold up a portico. Arched windows flank the entrance with other square windows painted clean white. Even President George W. Bush stayed for one night in 2003. They saw a quick glimpse of the meticulous park and lake creating a pictorial setting.

Driver Bill mentioned that Hillsborough hosts an International Oyster Festival in late August every year that attracts thousands of visitors. Events include racing, parachuting, garden fetes, oyster eating, and Guinness drinking contests. He and his wife tried to attend each year and added he hadn't won any contests but had given it his best.

Bill skirted to the east of Belfast, avoiding the vast city, and their group eagerly boarded a train for a scenic trip to Bangor, a coastal town. It sits on a pretty harbor with a clock tower and historic buildings. They stayed at the Royal Hotel on Quay Street. Their bright and airy room had a separate sleeping area with a large bed through an arched entrance with a sofa, table, television, and desk in the living area.

Several sauntered along the harbor wall seeing watercraft of all colors and sizes from yachts to fishing boats and even kayaks and canoes. They all returned to the hotel for traditional afternoon tea, coffee, and snacks in the Library Lounge.

That evening they enjoyed a delicious, hearty dinner of tasty beef, root vegetables, and potatoes as the main course at the hotel's restaurant, called The Quays. Anne noticed several bottles of wine and asked the waiter named Rian, about local choices.

"Excuse me, I'll be back." Nabbing three bottles, he returned. "David Dennison is a small-scale Irish wine-making enthusiast, based out of County Waterford. The farm is located in the southwest of Ireland, is family-run and also home of a small cider orchard. The vineyard has been known to have as many as 2,700 plants of grapes, including Rondo which is red, Solaris and Bacchus, white, and Pinot Noir."

"We will be in Waterford later in the trip. Can we get it there?"

"You should be able to find it at most restaurants."

He held up another bottle, this one from Thomas Walk Winery near Kinsale in County Cork. Rian told them, "The winery is owned and run by German wine-lover Thomas Walk, and it has been in production since the 1980s. It is one of Ireland's longer-standing operating vineyards.

"This bottle is a fruit wine from award-winning Wicklow Way Wines, winery and home to Móinéir Fine Irish Fruit Wines in County Wicklow, also known as 'the Garden of Ireland.' It's a real favorite." Rian poured about an inch of red liquid into a glass and handed it to Anne.

"What do you smell?"

"Raspberry?"

"Right, and they are available in strawberry and blackberry flavors, too. Fruity wines are bursting with taste and delicate aromas."

Anne giggled at his flourish of words. He admitted he had read it off their website.

One hundred twenty miles away, Seamus and Fayanna were both eagerly anticipating the evening. He hadn't seen her in a week because of their work schedules. This time of year there were more deliveries to restaurants and bars because of longer days, better weather, and tourists. His employer expected more hours from his drivers.

Fayanna worked at a short-staffed senior center or nursing home, he still wasn't exactly sure. He just knew she did work for very old people. He thought it a waste of her time but she disagreed. She liked helping others, totally the opposite of her boyfriend of six months or so.

Seamus acted sulky and she called him out on it. "I haven't seen you in what seems like forever. What's wrong?"

"Oh, just some stuff with work." He shoved thoughts of his debt to the back of his brain for a few pleasant hours. He noticed she smelled like the vanilla candles his grandmother used to burn at Christmas, and her vanilla pound cake with fluffy vanilla frosting, sometimes with sprinkles.

Fay made it her goal to help her grumpy boyfriend relax, which didn't take long. They started at her apartment, and with her roommate away, they had more time than usual to spend alone. She liked looking at him, but teased him about his sparse beard, even though he had a thick head of chestnut hair. His eyes, nose, and mouth were evenly proportioned and his teeth were white and straight. She disliked stained, crooked teeth. A couple of hours later, they ambled to a popular bar in the neighborhood for dinner and drinks.

"You're staring at me. Why?" he asked.

"You just look amazing tonight. I appreciate your effort."

"So do you, except you're drop-dead gorgeous." He glanced down her neck.

"You'll make me blush."

Both Mauve and Moyrah wanted to know their cousin's whereabouts, so each night Anne promised to text them updates. Trying to condense an entire day of activities onto a phone screen was proving difficult. After a full day, too much food, and two glasses of wine, her phone woke her up when it dropped onto her chest.

CHAPTER THIRTEEN

Seamus wasn't in any hurry to get out of bed since he didn't need to report to work until one o'clock that afternoon. He had the afternoon and evening shifts due to covering for a friend who had a family emergency somewhere in Slovenia. His mind drifted to the previous night with Fay, then abruptly switched to his current financial dilemma. His friends were tapped out or knew better than to give him any more money. *Why haven't you thought of them before?* He hit his flat palm on the side of his head.

Fay heard a familiar ping as her phone lit up. She read a text from her boyfriend.

> Grand time last night. Meet me Wednesday at 10:45 out back Farren's. I need to c u.

> Sure, spending a few days with my cousin, will b in that area anyway. I'll introduce u.

She added her signature pink heart emoji.

Perfect he thought to himself. *Time to get all this out in the open anyway.*

After a delicious Irish breakfast, Bill delivered them to the Europa Hotel in the center of Belfast. During The Troubles, journalists from all over the world stayed here. The hotel was given the name "Europe's most bombed hotel," and is one of the largest and most important in Belfast's history. It remained despite being bombed 33 times by the IRA between 1970 and 1994, April told them, before handing them room keys. Anne and Peter rode the elevator getting off on the 11th floor.

"Ok, I'm puzzled. These are all suites. Look at this: The Clinton Suite. The plaque reads "President William Jefferson Clinton stayed here 30th November 1995."

"Wow, this one is the Titanic Suite. There is a plaque here as well. The Titanic Suite Welcomes Hilary Clinton US Secretary of State Sunday 11th October, 2007."

"Keep going; no, we are definitely not in one of the suites, check the number of the room at the end of the corridor." Opening the curtains they saw the view down to the street and the lively Crown Bar.

A jovial local man named Thomas joined the tour group as their guide for the afternoon. He thanked them for coming to Belfast and mentioned the economy appreciated their contributions, too. He pointed out Belfast's coat of arms prominently displayed in many locations.

His description brought to life seventeenth century Belfast starting as a typical small village. Then came industries such as linen, rope-making, shipbuilding, engineering, and tobacco. The population grew rapidly to over 300,000. The citizens built the City Hall. Construction began in 1898 and completed in 1906, built in the Classical Renaissance style in Portland stone. It's rectangular enclosing a quadrangular courtyard. Sitting on top, like a crown, is the great dome, wrapped in copper but aged in patina. The dome is 173 feet high and made for an easy landmark. Ornate lamps are situated on either side of the main gate. The lamps are adorned with cherubs and seahorses, symbolizing the industrial and manufacturing heritage of the city. Six similar but less ornate lamps are evenly placed on each side of the main gate.

Inside the hall, he directed their attention to marble memorials and statues of famous Belfast-born people. The walls at the entrance are dramatic along with salt and peppery marble tiled floors.

At The Grand Staircase, Anne whispered to Peter, "'Grand' is an understatement," looking up at the magnificent dome with multiple types and colors of marble with fancy plasterwork. Sue caught Anne's attention and they moved toward sunbeams shining through stained glass windows creating rainbows around the area. Standing straight as an arrow is a bronze statue of the Earl of Belfast, and Anne took a picture with Peter on one side and Bruce on the other. On either side of the Grand Staircase are two more incredible stained glass windows illustrating historic events including the bombing of the City Hall during World War II.

They stepped into the Council Chamber with its entry having arches springing from piers 17 feet high stretching to the richly decorated dome. The galleries and oak-paneled walls are intricately carved as are the seats for members. There is an elaborately carved oak screen that forms a backdrop for the Lord Mayor's Chair, with smaller chairs for other city staff. They didn't allow visitors to sit in the chair that resembled a throne. But they did get to sit in the gallery as they listened to Thomas give them the rundown of this particular room. Various large portraits adorn the spacious walls but Anne only recognized Queen Victoria.

The Great Hall on the east side of the building is protected with a vaulted ceiling rising to 40 feet. The room brightened with sunlight streaming through the several stained glass windows, reflecting prisms around the hall. This hall was almost totally destroyed by a German air raid in May 1941. Fortunately, in 1939 the unique windows had been removed for safekeeping. When the Great Hall was rebuilt the original windows were reinstalled.

The Banqueting Hall was topped by a dome rising to 36 feet with plasterwork on the vaults and domed ceiling. The walls are paneled in carved oak to a height of nine feet and the windows are filled with stained glass showing the Royal Arms, The Coat of Arms of the City represented by mean-looking seahorses with chains and snarling mouths, and two Lords.

Anne figured if someone could only visit one place in the city, it should be here to learn all the history in one place. The outdoor gardens and grounds are equally as stunning with a marble statue of Queen Victoria and bronze figures symbolizing shipbuilding and spinning. There is a short stone column bearing the inscription *U.S.A.E.F. (United States of America Expeditionary Force) landed in this City 26th January 1942,* and many more memorials.

That night Anne and Peter ordered room service and stayed in enjoying their luxuriously spacious room. Lights from below flashed neon, and apartments and homes glowed in the darkness. The bathroom had a bathtub, so she slid in for some soaking time before a good night's sleep. She texted her cousins about the day but kept it brief, setting her phone on the floor, afraid she'd fall asleep and her phone would take a deep dive.

She had a vivid dream about her dad. He was in Ireland with her taking the place of Peter. The only thing she remembered the next morning was his words, "Everything is going to be all right, darling daughter." She would argue with him on that. It would never be all right again.

Mickey typed on his phone. He knew his boss wouldn't be happy.

> Didn't find him, boss.

> > u better and remind him of our deal. 1 week or else.

Seamus had gotten sidetracked making delivery after delivery and finally got a break around 10:30 p.m. He grabbed his phone. Wrenna had just about fallen asleep when she read a text.

> Meet me Wednesday 10:45 out back
> Farren's. I need 2 c u.

> > Working that day depends on how busy we r.

She typed very annoyed he would assume she'd be available. *I'm done with him.* She started texting him her decision, being no, but instead decided to just tell him that day. His cocky personality and vague messages were immature, and she didn't like him that much anyway. He had been more like something to fill some random time. *Just like high school nonsense which I am so over,* she told herself.

Try

He thought about adding the word 'please.' But he wouldn't beg anyone, especially a woman.

Wrenna turned her phone off and didn't reply.

CHAPTER FOURTEEN

After breakfast, a local man named Sullivan joined the group for a driving tour of Belfast. He pointed out the Parliament buildings, one of the most iconic buildings, River Lagan, St. George's Market, Victoria Square with four levels of shops, Titanic Quarter, Cathedral Quarter, St. Anne's Cathedral, and Clifton Street Poor House. Opened in 1774, it existed as a nursing home and hospital for older people.

They drove slowly down the most famous of the peace walls. Decorated with hundreds of murals, it runs for several miles that divides the Falls and Shankill Roads in the western part of Belfast. It is interrupted at several junctions by enormous metal gates across the roads. At the height of The Troubles, these were used as security checkpoints.

"That's my favorite mural." Nancy pointed to the Solidarity P.O.W.'s, showing two hands grasping together out of jail cell windows. One shirtsleeve is green, white, and orange, the Irish flag colors. The other has green underneath the white with a red rumpled cuff.

On the Shankill Roadside, navy, red, and white Union Jack flags hang from houses and poles on the streets. Ropes tied across the main street proudly display flags with British colors, and images of the queen are all around. At one point there is a slogan written across a wall that reads, "Open your arms to change but don't let go of your values."

Attached to a telephone pole is a sign that reads "Alcohol-Free Area. It is an offense to drink alcohol in public places in this area. Maximum penalty 500 Pounds."

They stopped briefly at McHughs, established in 1711. It boasts "Welcome to the oldest building in Belfast. Home of the 'Potato Boxty' & 'Steak on the Stone.'"

A public art metal sculpture which stands 66 feet tall and constructed in 2007, is called the Beacon of Hope or Thanksgiving Square Beacon and stands overlooking the pretty River Lagan. It is crafted of stainless steel and cast bronze and spirals upward, holding the Ring of Thanksgiving. The globe indicates peace and harmony. It's not a solid sculpture but is see-through and light and airy.

Their next stop was the Titanic Experience. Samson and Goliath are the gigantic cranes at the shipyard that built the Titanic. Titanic Belfast opened in 2012, marking the 100th anniversary of the launching of the legendary liner. The striking building reflects the front of a large ship.

They were not going to miss a thing in this exhibit, and their strategy was to start at the top and work their way down. They rode the elevator to the sixth floor. The self-guided tour allowed them to go at their own pace, exploring sights, sounds, even smells, and stories of the Titanic.

Located where the ship was originally built in 1912, the exhibition follows the story of the ship from her conception in Belfast, through her construction and launch to the famous maiden voyage and subsequent tragic place in history. Using state-of-the-art design, explanations, and technology, each of the nine galleries focuses on a unique part of the story.

-Boomtown Belfast, showing the city at the start of the twentieth century through stories and pictures of the works.

-The Shipyard, a mini-car ride around the rudder. Anne felt like she was right there helping to build the ship.

-The Launch, showing that process.

-The Fit Out, the fitting out of the ship on the maiden voyage, the journey from Belfast to Southampton, and from there to Cherbourg and westwards. Anne felt hopeless since she knew what occurred. Passengers' backgrounds and stories were told in this area through recorded voices. She shed a few tears.

-The Sinking, the tragic disaster of April, 1912.

-The Aftermath, the legacy of the disaster. This phase includes testimonials from those who arrived in New York.

It is meaningful, somber, and educational, all wrapped up in one well-done exhibit.

Anne's friends and tour group sat in bench seats at long tables, sharing family-style traditional Irish foods. Anne forgot to text her cousins that evening, which she didn't realized until she turned on her phone the next morning.

Both Fay and Wrenna read the same message that had been texted separately from Seamus.

Can't wait to c u in 3 days.

Me 2 pink heart emoji.

He wasn't happy to hear back from only one.

CHAPTER FIFTEEN

They woke to sunshine with the knowledge that this would be a delightful day, even though Peter and Anne would be repeating some of what they had done 20 years ago. The drive alone is spectacular with old castle ruins sitting atop cliffs jutting down into the sea, bleached beaches that stretch far and wide, and fertile mossy hills.

From Belfast driving through the scenic back roads with ditches full of scarlet poppies, through Ballymena to the Glens of Antrim, they saw O'Connor's Bar painted in bright lime with yellow trim next door to Donnelly's Family Butchers, its building coated in cherry red. The road never veered far from the indigo sea of the North Channel. They meandered through terrain of purple blooming heather, meadows of bright poppies, perfectly square lots bordered by dark pine-colored shrubs, and in one plot something bright yellow bloomed lanky and tall.

"The Causeway Coastal route has to be one of the prettiest drives in the world," Peter exclaimed. It didn't hurt that it remained a bright and sunny day, for now, anyway. At Glenballyeamon, a silvery sandy beach stretched for miles with great views of Trostan Mountain. Farmlands stretched up the mountainside.

The seaside Ballycastle, a thriving metropolis comparatively speaking to the other small villages, sits at the base of Knocklayde Mountain. The scenic bay was crammed with boats, some obviously expensive. April drew attention to Rathlin Island and even parts of Scotland on this clear day.

At Cushendun, another seaside village, free-standing buildings stretched out into the water creating an illusion that made it appear that way with the town sitting on a spit, with the backdrop of rolling hills, craggy cliffs, and a slowly meandering river. Anne glanced to her left and showed a stag to Peter.

"We need to return to the glen for a long vacation sometime," Peter noted.

Along the rugged coastline, they stopped at a famous rope bridge that was first erected by salmon fishermen in 1755. The name means "rock in the road," an obstacle for the migrating salmon as they search for the river to which they were born. At Carrick-a-rede, a few brave souls staggered across the flimsy, unsteady-looking rope bridge, some 80 feet above the sea. Not being crazy about heights, Anne didn't do it. In fact, no one in their group tempted fate, instead opting to get to the Giant's Causeway sooner.

Just a short distance beyond was their destination, The Giant's Causeway in County Antrim, where Anne couldn't wait to get off the bus and start exploring. She recalled their first visit and how being 20 years younger, they climbed higher and explored more than they would this time.

The rocks are stones of all different dimensions that made it appear they could have easily reached Scotland and

Iceland. Ancient lava flows have eroded to uncover columns of unnatural regularity.

April explained that Finn MacCool (or McCool) is supposedly the giant who built The Giant's Causeway. She told them the legend of the popular fictional character. Fionn mac Cumhaill, his real name, lived with the reputation of being the greatest leader of Fayanna, the ancient warrior band of old Ireland. "This must be how they got Fay's name," Anne surmised.

"Finn is credited with creating The Giant's Causeway as stepping stones from the North of Ireland to Scotland," April continued. "The second version tells how he threw a large piece of the land into the sea at an enemy, that piece of land becoming the Isle of Man. The hole left behind by the clump of land he threw became Lough Neagh. Another one of the stories claims Finn loved a giant woman living on Staffa and he needed the Causeway to bring her back to Ireland.

"The death of Finn is a mystery. One legend suggests that he is not dead but merely sleeping in a cave under Dublin, ready to strike back against Ireland's enemies. The stories and legends of Finn have never been forgotten and he remains one of the most powerful figures in Irish mythology. The Causeway is packed full of folklore but it's an area of basalt columns, some crimson, some shades of gray or black, resulting from a volcanic eruption. Forming a hexagonal shape, most of these columns appear arranged into steppingstones of hills while others jut out into the sea."

They spent time climbing around on the columns that resembled a cobbled road leading into the sea. Glistening puddles of seawater remained in some deeper bowls on the tops of the rocks from the previous high tide. Anne stuck her finger in one, pushing around tiny pebbles. She sat on the rocks overlooking the sea wondering whether her relatives had explored this area or stayed in their small area around Dublin all their lives; her guess was the latter.

She sat for a while, just staring at this marvel which reminded her of the basalt columns they'd seen in Iceland along the southern coastline at Reynisfjara. Imagining a world globe in her mind, she could see how one day they might have all been connected to Scotland, too.

She zoomed her camera in on friends climbing around the rocks like kids. Billy goats came to mind as Dave and Bruce were climbing higher and higher. Anne envisioned a red Coast Guard helicopter zooming in to save one of her Boomer friends, who'd tumbled and broken a leg, or fallen off, or something even worse. She closed her eyes not looking their way again.

Anne politely stifled a laugh while sitting on a bench, peeking down at a woman's open-toed, silvery sandals, certainly not suited or safe for climbing the Causeway.

The weather turned cool and breezy, so several retreated for a hot chocolate at the visitor's center and gift shop. Anne had to remind Dave that the Finn McCool round shield would not fit in his one piece of luggage, and no swords are allowed in his carry-on.

Sue surprised Anne, Jeanine, and Nancy with a sterling silver shamrock, telling them that anytime they wore it to remember their special time together.

Four miles later on the Antrim Coast Road, they hopped off the bus again, this time at the medieval Dunluce Castle, now ruins, the seat of Clan MacDonnell, in the thirteenth century.

Walking across a bridge is the only connection to the mainland. Sue breathed in deeply. "Sure hope there were no sleepwalkers back in the day. It's straight down on either side."

The round towers are in surprisingly fair condition. One wall with several open windows still stands where other walls had already crumbled. This ruin is balanced on a cliff overlooking the sea. Ivy climbed its decrepit sides, likely holding the castle together like duct tape. Several birds were catching the wind drafts above the castle. Anne grabbed the tri-fold of birds and pointed out to Peter a black Sooty Shearwater and Arctic Tern. Along the shoreline were Black-headed gulls so much prettier than theirs in Oregon, rather plain, white, or gray.

Perched on the cliff's edge, the earliest features are the two large drum towers about 30 feet in diameter on the eastern side, both relics of a stronghold built here by the McQuillans after they became lords of the Route. They were displaced by the MacDonnell clan after losing two major battles against them during the mid-and-late sixteenth century. Later the castle became the home of the chief of the Clan MacDonnell of Antrim, and the Clan MacDonald of Dunnyveg from Scotland. The cannons from a wrecked ship were installed in the gatehouses and the rest of the cargo was sold, the funds being used to restore the castle.

They explored a few rooms, small nooks and crannies, and the free info guide explained where to find a drawing of a medieval ship scratched into the castle wall, and how they used the steps to climb onto their horses. The steep drop-offs on the backside of the castle provided views straight down to the sea below and stunning views up and down the coastline.

They heard an odd chicken-like cluck, cluck. "A chicken around here?" Sue stood behind Anne, hearing the same sound. Then they heard an even odder, creepy whine. Turning in a complete 360, Anne located the noisy culprit. Peter opened the pocket guide on *Birds of Ireland* and pinpointed a photo of a Short-eared owl. The auburn and cream-speckled owl peered down at the trio. Her yellow beady eyes glared at them. The two-foot tall bird nervously stepped side to side.

"It's okay. We're harmless." Anne talked in a soothing voice to the bird.

"You think that bird understands you?" Peter put the guide back into his jacket pocket.

"Well, Peter, we *are* in Ireland and it's common knowledge that some birds and animals understand human language, so why not?" Sue always stood up for Anne, no matter if she agreed or not. It was a sisterchick thing.

Two small feathered heads popped up and down in the nest that was firmly tucked into a corner of a retaining wall. "Ahh, that's why she's fidgety," Anne observed.

Local legend has it that at one point part of the kitchen, next to the cliff face, collapsed into the sea, after which the wife of the owner refused to live in the castle any longer. Americans prowled around the still intact newer kitchen next to the manor house. They could see the oven, fireplace, and entryways into it. In the eighteenth century, the north wall of the residence building collapsed into the sea. The east, west, and south walls still stand.

"Don't get so close to the edge!" Linda yelled at Anne who leaned over, trying to see if she could see any puffins nesting in the craggy cliffs.

Down the road, they reached the cute town of Portrush. Homes are built along the roadway, the only thing that separates them from the sea. It's all about the ocean in this village where businesses provide fishing, water sports, and seafood restaurants. Most homes are stark white with shutters accented in different colors to give them some extra zing and personality. Anne could see why it boasted being the most popular seaside resort in Northern Ireland.

Vehicle loads of people carried arms full of bright, cheery sunflowers from Causeway Sunflower Field near Bushmill. She felt like she'd stepped into Van Gogh's sunflower painting like the one that hung in her parents' home for decades. The flowers sat on top of sturdy green stems standing about five feet high stretching toward the sun. Their sun-like look with brilliant yellow petals, also known as rays, were obviously popular.

In County Antrim, they stopped at the Old Bushmills Distillery. The distillery uses water drawn from St. Columba's Rill, which is a tributary of the River Bush. They are proud to advertise their steadfast commitment to "their own way for over 400 years," as well as the oldest licensed whiskey distillery in the world. Bushmills whiskey, well-known for centuries of producing the finest Irish whiskey, started up in 1608, which is proudly printed on the label.

Most men in the group, along with some women, stood around bistro tables with whiskey samples ranging in tone from brown to gold from bottles of Black, Prohibited Recipe, The Original, Single Malt aged ten years, Single Malt aged 12 years, then 16 and 21 years, assuming that was the finest of all.

Anne saw another woman drinking a nectarine beverage in a martini glass and couldn't resist asking what it was and what it tasted like. "It's a Shelby Sour, and quite refreshing. They use their Special Prohibition recipe, an orange liqueur, some lemon juice, simple syrup, and then this orange peel for garnish. Try it, you'll like it."

"I'll have what she's having, please."

Linda asked, "Do you have anything like a mint julep?"

"Oh yes, actually ours is called a Royal Ascot using our

Prohibition recipe, simple syrup, some bitters, and 5 mint leaves. It's served in an old fashioned cocktail glass."

The five mint leaves had her. "Yes, please," she nodded.

Jeanine chimed in, "What's in a Belfast Derby?"

"It's our Original whiskey, with pink grapefruit juice, freshly squeezed lime juice, agave syrup, and some bitters and served in a cocktail glass."

"What's one more favorite?" Nancy inquired. The ladies tended for the frou-frou drinks, with just a little whiskey.

"The Gold Rush with parts of our Original, lemon juice, honey, 4 sprigs of fresh mint, not just leaves, and a lemon wheel, on the side."

Sue, low on her daily caffeine intake asked, "What about something hot?"

"Two choices for you. Our Red Hot Toddy combines Red Bush, simple syrup, ground cinnamon, and whole cloves with a cinnamon stick on top of the glass coffee mug. Of course, we offer classic Irish coffee, too."

"I'm low on coffee today so I'll do that, please."

Jeanine commented to her sister, "Don't I recall your doctor suggesting you cut down on coffee?"

"Coffee is vital for survival. Dinosaurs didn't have coffee and look how that turned out."

"Okay, let's order one of each and share sips." They stepped outside away from the humid, smokey interior, and created their own tasting of Bushmills whiskey, their way.

The attentive waiter overhearing and sympathizing with Sue's coffee plight, delivered a tall glass mug of black liquid immediately. She smelled the deep flavor and uttered, "Hello darkness my old friend." She took several gulps then rested her head in her hands and muttered, "Give me a minute... I'm waiting for the coffee to kick in." Her circle of friends burst out laughing. "Cheers" and "Sláinte" were repeated by each as they clinked a variety of glassware before their first sips of Bushmills whiskey blended drinks.

Two decades. Astonishing, Anne thought. *Where did time go?*

Anne queried Peter, "Does everything seem brighter to you?"

"Well, 20 years ago the border had been open only several months and even though it wasn't guarded, the stations were still installed. And there had just been the bombing."

When they arrived in Derry, well known for its political history, they were greeted by a large vibrant hot pink, free-standing wall that reads, "You Are Now Entering FREE DERRY." It meant something very important back then.

As they drove by the Craigavon Bridge, Anne saw the statue of two men she recalled from their first visit. April explained that the inscription reads "Hands Across the Divide," and told them that the bronze sculpture, one Protestant and the other Catholic, with arms outstretched to each other and their hands almost touching but not quite, symbolizes the spirit of reconciliation and hope for the future. One side wishes to form a united Ireland, while the other side wants Northern Ireland to remain in the United Kingdom. This has been the main conflict behind The Troubles, or the Northern Ireland conflict that started in the 1960s.

At first glance, Anne noticed red, white, and blue painted curbs, identifying political parties. She recalled their first visit decades earlier to guard stations which were used to hold men carrying guns but were now empty. As they had negotiated the Derry wall, a local guide explained as much as he could about the history, politics, and feelings of both sides of people living there. Derry is the one remaining intact walled city in Northern Ireland and the last walled city to be built in all of Europe.

They had toured City Hall and entered a church where they had lined up with quiet, somber locals to sign books of condolence for the Omagh fatalities.

She recalled how later that day they had checked into Bushtown House Hotel and Country Club. The hotel is set in mature woodlands on the outskirts of Coleraine. Standing closest to the receptionist's desk, Anne had smiled at a grumpy middle-aged man as she and Peter were the first of the tour group to check-in. He did not smile back. She quickly considered there could be a good reason for his abruptness, most obvious the bombing. She focused on him and kindly said, "Hello. We are glad to be here."

He replied in a curt Irish accent, "Are you brave or stupid?"

She felt instantly testy, but instead replied, "How about curious and naïve?"

Then he warmed up for whatever reason, half smiled, and added, "I thank you for not canceling your reservation and plans to visit my country. We are not all like those who have created such an erroneous reputation for us." They would hear many people during the next week thanking them for coming. She kept asking herself how had two decades had flown by.

Half watching a rugby match on TV and pacing his small smoke-filled apartment, Seamus felt confident that he remained in Fay's good graces, yet not so with Wrenna. She hadn't even replied to his last text about Wednesday. Calculating what he should do to soften her up, he called a florist and contemplated sending a dozen roses to her apartment until he heard the price. "I'll do six," he stammered.

Well, that's a first, she thought when she read the card signed Seamus. Nothing else, just Seamus. She had many words for him: self-absorbed, arrogant, know-it-all, macho, probably narcissistic would cover his personality traits. This gesture caught her off guard. She thought back about their recent encounter since their school days and how she became slightly interested in him. He made her laugh and they shared a common love for animals. He'd told her if he had an acre or two he'd have dogs, goats, and maybe a llama. She switched her thoughts back to his controlling macho attitude that she saw far more often than this kinder side.

He read Wrenna's text.

> Thanks for the pretty roses.

> Looking forward to Wednesday.

> Maybe.

He huffed around, wondering, *what does she mean MAYBE?* A mug shattered against the wall. *What's wrong with that woman?* He'd never had any problems with any others. *Probably just wasted 25 quid on her.*

The Americans checked into the City Hotel Derry where they would stay for the next three nights. The view out their 5th-story room was of a roundabout with four beds of rosy flowers creating an outer ring on the grass, and the inner circle of ivy columns surrounded by a ring of yellow flowers. Off to the right stands the impressive sandstone, neogothic-style Guildhall with a clock tower, and to the left, the pedestrian Peace Bridge stretching across the River Foyle.

At Browns in Town, she read the restaurant had received a prestigious award-winning Michelin recommendation so she expected it to be spendy. Surprisingly it was not, and she and Peter shared bruschetta and split a giant slab of shepherd's pie. A perfectly balanced meal. Each bite of minced beef in dark gravy topped with creamy, crispy mashed potatoes tasted flavorful. She'd read that the authentic Irish version uses lamb. Anne was particularly grateful that this version used beef and didn't have peas. She hated cooked peas.

Famous bully bread in Northern Ireland, also called soda bread elsewhere, could be one of the most delicious baked products Peter had ever tasted. He'd consumed many slices probably equivalent to several loaves on this trip. The simple combination of flour, buttermilk, and baking soda wasn't difficult to make, but Anne had read that cooks concede you must have "the knack." She felt quite certain she did not. She'd also learned some foods and beverages tasted extraordinary because of the ambiance and not to be repeated at home. She tried several experiments that didn't measure up and vowed they'd have it when they returned to that special location.

And there it was again, those three stupendous words, Sticky Toffee Pudding, this version with toffee sauce and vanilla ice cream.

"I'm so full but…"

"I'll eat a few bites," but Peter knew he wouldn't get much, probably all of the vanilla ice cream though, his favorite and not hers.

That night they watched the sunset like a kaleidoscope, turning the river shades of apricot, peach, yellow apple, and carrot as the white lights of the Peace Bridge, buildings, and churches flickered on. He slipped his arm around his wife as they watched the water turn to indigo in twilight.

Twins Mauve and Moyrah checked into the hotel around 10 p.m., getting a later start than they anticipated.

"It's like Ayden can't do a thing without me," Moyrah whined. "He needs to get a life other than work and me all the time. I wanted to see Anne for dinner but he can't even boil an egg."

"And who spoiled him all these years, dear sister?"

She rolled her spirited but soft eyes. "You're right Mauve, but now it's getting old."

CHAPTER SIXTEEN

Not seeing Moyrah for 20 years, she and Anne hugged for an entire minute, Mauve guessed. "Okay you two, sit down." Moyrah slid a box over to Anne.

"This is from Mam. Since they couldn't see you, she wanted to give you something. And of course, there's a story. But open it." Anne lifted the pink top of the box to discover elegant, shell-shaped mini cakes, the top half coated in dark chocolate with chopped pistachios for an indulgent flare. Her perplexed eyes were as big as saucers. "What are these?"

"When they were in Spain last winter they took a train to France for a week as one of Mam's dreams had always been to take a French cooking class. Not just cooking, but a pastry class. Dad was thrilled as he has quite a sweet tooth, especially for baked goods. This class was on making Madeleine cookies—that's what these are," Moyrah explained.

"When they got home, Mam modified and perfected this sponge cake recipe for her own version, adding Irish Whiskey and chocolate with a splash of coffee. We all got to enjoy her cast-offs during her trial-and-error phase. She created oodles of flavors, let's see... cardamon, which was okay, saffron, orange, and honey tasted delicious, but these are surely her finest. She baked them before they left for Iceland the other day."

"I'm honored, and they look scrumptious. I'll take them to our room and hide them from Peter."

April benevolently invited Anne's cousins to join the tour. The group wasn't surprised to meet another one of Anne's family and were thrilled to spend more time with Mauve. She'd made close to 30 new American friends with offers of homes to stay in on their next visit.

That day a local guide, Mo, took them to see the court-house constructed in the Greek Revival style. Next they saw St. Columba's Cathedral which occupies the highest point of land within the walled city and was consecrated in 1633. Mo laughingly told them he'd be the only Iranian-Muslim Irishman they would meet in Ireland. His Iranian father married his Irish mother and he grew up in Northern Ireland. He and his wife were raising three children, including a son with special health needs. Their talk included the dilemma of Brexit and the concerns about what that could mean for healthcare for their son. Also, his wife's parents often provided childcare and only lived 15 miles away, but on the other side of the border. If the border crossing were to be reinstated, this would make travel and work much more difficult. He did not want to take a step back in time.

The seventeenth Derry Wall is the largest ancient monu-ment in state care in Northern Ireland. It has the longest, complete circuit of ramparts of the remaining 30 walled towns in all of Ireland. There are four original gates to the Walled City: Bishop's Gate, Ferryquay Gate, Butcher Gate, which stretches across a street, and Shipquay Gate, the entry point to the commercial part of the city. Three others were added later: Magazine Gate, Castle Gate, and New Gate.

On the wall at Guildhall Square, Mo talked about historic buildings, churches, and architecture including brick chimneys on rooftops, and the cannons at the Double Bastion by the Verbal Arts Center. The Londonderry Guildhall is a majestic sandstone building and the meeting place of the members of council.

Depending on what Mo thought the group should see and enjoy, they hiked up and down the dry moat around the exterior and up around the top of the ramparts which provided an excellent elevated view to see the city. Scattered among the buildings are huge murals.

Two brothers and a friend illustrated events of The Troubles on walls lining Rossville Street. They saw many political murals drawn to commemorate the events and educate those who didn't live through the struggles.

THE PETROL BOMBER. This mural is the oldest and most famous dating back to 1969. Done in black and white, a boy is wearing a gas mask to protect himself while he holds a gas bomb. The boy's eyes stare dazed from behind the obstructing visor through which the teenager is trying to see. In the background are uniformed riot police and smoke rising from crumbling buildings.

BERNADETTE features Bernadette McAliskey, a social Republican activist addressing a crowd with a megaphone in her hand. A woman is squatting, holding a shield resembling a garbage can lid, and a boy behind her with a shield in one hand and a metal rod in the other. A bulldog stands alone, with burning rubble in the background, and a male holding a handkerchief over his nose and mouth next to a young boy. Bernadette received a prison sentence for initiating and participating in a riot. She would later be elected to Parliament at the age of 21.

Another mural along their tour is called DEATH OF INNOCENCE. This is a mural of Annette McGavigan, a 14-year-old girl killed in 1971. The mural is near where she died. A British soldier killed her while she stood at the side of the road. She is dressed in a white blouse with a green tie that matches her skirt. In the left corner is a butterfly with the top half painted light blue and the bottom is orange.

THE PEACE MURAL, portrayed on a wall at the end of a building, is an outline of a white swirling dove painted over colored blocks. The dove is a symbol of peace and Derry's patron saint, Columba. The dove emerges from an oak leaf. The squares are equal on all sides representing the equality of citizens. This one promises hope and a bright future.

There are other murals such as BLOODY SUNDAY COMMEMORATION, THE SATURDAY MATINEE, THE RUNNER, and many more around Derry. Whether political, optimistic, celebrating the city, or merely artistic, each holds special significance, Mo explained.

He suggested they make a point of seeing The Derry Peace Flame which is one of 15 peace flames around the world. It's Northern Ireland's only eternal peace flame in a city that strives for harmony. The flame is inside a small park beside the Guildhall in the middle of town.

He shared truthfully about his country's struggles, prejudices, and hopes for the future. When he asked if anyone had been to Derry before, Anne told him they had visited 20 years earlier and they'd come to Northern Ireland a few days after the Omagh bombing in August, 1998. She also explained her cousin's story of almost being in the market that afternoon.

Mo took in a little gasp of air and instantly had tears in his dark soulful eyes. He told them that his best friend's son had been in that market and died in the bombing at age eight. It was something he'd never forget. "Me either," Anne told him. They bid Mo farewell and thanked him for his honesty and insight.

Sue pointed across the street. "Coffee break! There's a Costa Coffee." After their previous Costa experiences, all were now pros at selecting exactly what they wanted.

One of Anne's favorite things was people-watching. Airports provided lots of entertainment. But she had discovered coffee shops and bakeries were prime viewing zones. She heard the squeak of hinges that could use some WD-40 and noticed something blocked the sunlight. A man had to duck as he came through the door, drawing everyone's attention. The place turned quiet.

"I've seen more meat on a cheese sandwich."

"He looks like it's been far too long between meals."

"He's got to be a basketball player. Maybe even famous."

The ladies' conversation bounced around discussing one of the tallest men most had seen. Like NBA star-tall.

A woman breezed through the door with two shopping bags draped over her left arm.

"They must be siblings. She looks like a fashion model, only without the glitz. She's gotta be minus size 0." Anne whined, "I was born bigger than her."

"I'd love about four inches of their height." Sue sounded whiney just like Anne.

Anne was not at all disappointed with today's observing strangers and contemplating their lives.

Mickey pulled out his phone and texted his boss.

Missed him again today, boss. will hang around his work and follow him. Don't want to do anything where people might see me.

I'm beginning to doubt your skills, Slick Mick u better prove yourself.

Furious, Mickey hit the dash of his truck, swearing every word he could think of. He hated all the stupid names Eamon would call him like Tricky Mickey, Hick Mick and Sick Mick. Sleazy Seamus couldn't be worth all this trouble. "I'll show that scumbag."

The tour group stopped at Craft Village and perused many handmade items by local artists. Two shelves lined with three-tiered cakes, similar to wedding cakes, showcased a baker's handiwork. Something else caught Anne's attention while meandering—a closed ebony door on a building. Of course, there was nothing unusual about a closed door, but hanging on a nail was a brass ring with four large brass keys. It certainly seemed like an open invitation to her. She was tempted to try each key in the door, but better judgment prevailed.

Next, they saw a house with a perfectly crafted thatched roof with two swans made of straw or thatch, facing beak to beak, resting on the rooftop with their necks forming a heart. They read the sign on the door. "You are welcome to take Irish dancing classes."

"I haven't seen either of you dance. Do you?" Anne nudged Mauve.

"It's a fallacy; not *all* Irish dance like you see on TV or in brochures."

"That's pretty much Riverdance and people who've drank

too much in bars." Moyrah laughed heartily. "On the other hand, there are plenty of wonderful dance competitions using the traditional Irish dance steps. The form-fitting dresses with stiff skirts and long shelves that the women wear are lovely with Celtic knot work, embroidery, and sparkles. Men wear dancing trousers with a button-down shirt and sometimes a vest. Take in a show if you can. It won't be absolutely traditional as those performers originally wore ankle-length dresses, or blouses and skirts, while male dancers wore shirts with kilts in the Irish clan plaid or long coats, shirts, vests, and calf-length pants with leggings."

"Oh my, a man in a kilt. Be still my heart." Anne let a spontaneous moan slip.

"Okay, Cuz, settle down." Mauve shook her head laughing.

Moyrah confided, "I dated a man for several months who always wore a kilt, and he…"

"Enough. No details about what was or wasn't under his kilt," her twin teasingly scolded.

"More! More!" Anne wanted details.

That evening they drove about 20 miles to dinner at The Stable Restaurant, originally the Bushtown House horse stable. Peter reminded Anne, "This is where we stayed the last time but we didn't eat here."

The original stone walls with arches, furniture, and antique knickknacks remained, giving the sense of its traditional character and warm farm-feel charm. The dark wood beams against the creamy ceiling showed off the crystal chandeliers nicely. Historically crafted plates lined the plate rail at the top of the walls displaying different scenes, a stag, and flowers. The restaurant is well known for using fresh local produce, dry-aged beef, and fresh fish caught daily from the Atlantic. Anne needed to go no farther on the menu after seeing Langoustine pasta.

The green beans tasted as if they'd just been plucked from the garden. Others reported that the beef was flavorful and cooked just right. Each bite of the pasta with buttery miniature lobsters tasted scrumptious. Different grains were used in making the dense bread. For dessert, the ice cream tasted like it had been hand-cranked ten minutes earlier the old-fashioned way.

Since she hadn't seen Moyrah since their first meeting 20 years earlier, Anne wanted some firsthand details. Anne had followed her cousin's children growing up and took a special interest in the two young girls, Wrenna and Fay, who were now 26 years old.

Two decades later, her cousin Moyrah appeared only slightly different, certainly a few more wrinkles although with no silver strands in her hair, but it was still difficult to tell them apart. She noticed a few silver strands in Mauve's hair when they were in Dublin but would never say a word about it.

Moyrah blurted out, "Anne, you don't look any different than when I first met you. Are you coloring your hair? It's so attractive and light but I do see some paler shades."

Anne joked, "You know that anybody over the age of 50 has some lighter tones, dear cousin." She teased her cousin who continued to color her hair to keep the "natural ginger" with no silver in sight.

"I can't tell you enough how much I appreciate you coming to Derry to see us. And an entire day with you and Mauve again." After sharing more personal information like Moyrah's menopause saga, and her husband Ayden's job that he hated, Anne could sympathize with the menopause issues.

Mauve had sailed through apparently with no ill effects. "Lucky you," her sister complained as Anne nodded.

"Now, what about Fayanna?" Anne asked.

"Em," her mother started, "she loves working with seniors, like her grandparents and that age group. She's taking elder law classes online through a college. Maybe helping with legal issues, too. She has a true tender heart. But I worry about her. She seems, em, naïve or gullible sometimes. She's not made the best choice in fellas either."

"Are the girls still tight?"

"Aye, even though living in different towns not far apart. You won't believe it," Mauve laughed, "they still insist on the Christmas tradition of matching pajamas, a late-night chick movie, sliders, and now adult beverages, not just hot cocoa."

Anne butted in, "Remind me what sliders are?"

"Sometimes we call them 'wafers' but it's a slice of ice cream sandwiched between two flat wafers."

"Ahh right, we call that an ice cream sandwich. Usually, it's ice cream between two cookies—your biscuits. Oh my word, wouldn't shortbread biscuits with chocolate ice cream be delicious?"

Moyrah nodded and added, "That's actually Fay's favorite."

"I knew I loved that girl for many reasons," Anne observed.

"They are both working today or would have come to greet you."

"That's fine. I feel like I know them well because you've both been so terrific about keeping in contact and sending photos. High school, then graduation, and Wrenna's college graduation pictures were so wonderful, especially seeing you all in them. I appreciate knowing about your sons, too, Mauve, even though I am pretty partial to your daughters."

"I'm sure sorry about your father, Anne." Moyrah slipped her arm around her cousin. "Will your mother cope alone?"

"Thanks. It was a great relief to me and my brothers when our parents sold their larger home and moved into a senior living community. They have access to all sorts of care and when the time comes, apartment living with meals included, even a nursing home if worse comes to worst. We will look after Mom as long as she can stay in their home."

While sipping tea the silence felt thick. Anne saw the sisters glance at each other and Moyrah elbowed Mauve.

"Peter, do you mind if we borrow Anne? Girl talk, you know."

"No problem." He slipped away to another table of friends.

"Cousin, we've got something, em, actually a story that we've decided to share with you. Only Brennan and me, and Moyrah and Ayden know this, and one other, our family doctor, Doctor Kennedy, but he passed a few years ago. We've both discussed this for hours on end and for some reason, we feel drawn to speak with you about this. Maybe for some wisdom or answers, we don't know."

Anne sat in silence. She had a sudden piercing headache as if a red-hot wire had been pushed in through the center of her forehead, one she had experienced twice before when she'd heard secrets revealed. She hadn't even blinked as her cousins bounced back and forth with a story that didn't shock her but hurt her heart for a myriad of reasons. Her somewhat sad eyes brimmed with tears for her cousins.

When the twins stopped, the normal matter-of-fact Anne softly uttered, "Are you going to tell your daughters?"

"Em, that's what we wanted your opinion on. We are uncertain." The twins looked at each other than at Anne.

Anne's immediate questions followed:

#1. "Why is this coming up now in your lives?" Both shrugged their shoulders.

#2. "What good would it do?" No answer came from her cousins.

#3. "What do you want to accomplish by sharing this information?" Again, silence.

#4. "Did you speak with your doctor about it before he passed?"

"Yes, I did and he advised we keep to our original decision to not tell anyone," Mauve replied.

Finally, an answer, Anne thought to herself.

#5. "If your daughters should find out, will they resent you?" No answer.

#6. "Are you prepared to carry this to your graves?" Silence.

"Em, what do you think we should do?" Moyrah stared right at her American cousin.

"Oh no you don't. This would take some real time to think through. I don't know anyone who has gone through what you are telling me, so I'm not the one to share advice or an opinion. I have no expertise on this at all. This is your story and I promise I will never speak of this unless it's with you two."

"You have raised some thought-provoking questions. We will leave it as is. For now."

"Maybe when they turn *turty*," Mauve added. Anne chuckled, her cousins assuming she'd lost it temporarily.

"Sorry, thirty, turty, it makes me laugh. Bad timing on my part."

Their conversation bounced about more surface-level things, jobs, new hobbies, upcoming travels, the general decline of US politics and morals, and world issues.

"I've about had it at home. Can you adopt Peter and me?" Anne sort of joked.

"Well, at least you don't have Brexit and debates and drama of the Eighth Amendment, an abortion referendum. Our greatest pickle is the Irish border," Moyrah noted.

Mauve shook her head. "Wrenna told me she watched the news all weekend when almost seventy percent of people backed repealing the constitution that effectively banned abortion. We discussed it at length as Wrenna told me, it's simple mam — my body, my choice. That's what most believe. The decision is between them, their doctor, and their god. It does seem blacker and whiter to the younger generation who are not as deep-rooted in religious or moral baggage."

Mauve shifted in her chair and bent in closer. "Now we have a gigantic domestic issue, a housing crisis, and pathetic photographs of a woman and her six children being forced to sleep in a guard station overnight. There are about 10,000 people recorded as homeless. How did that start and where does that end?"

Moyrah sarcastically added, "And guess who's visiting next month? The Pope. Not sure what type of reception he will get. I just read that your president is coming in the fall and there are already widespread protests."

"Lucky you. Ahh, well, the grass is always greener on the other side, so they say. Apparently not so different than us."

Anne stood gazing out the window seeing a full moon as bright white as the streetlight on their corner at home. In bed, reflecting on the day, the Derry murals, along with their discerning guide Mo, and the cousins' news flash, it didn't surprise Anne that she couldn't get to sleep.

CHAPTER SEVENTEEN

The next morning, Anne peeked out to see bright sunshine and the clock on the cathedral showed 7:06. After their final breakfast and hugs and tears with the cousins, the travelers set out to see more backroads, heading even farther north.

Parting wasn't quite the sweet sorrow as from their first meeting 20 years earlier but it felt heart-wrenching for Anne. She loved her cousins who lived a continent away. Fortunately, it had become much easier with texting, FaceTime, Zoom, and other options of communication. When they needed to hear each other's voice, they called.

Bill maneuvered through tiny burghs of eight to ten homes while driving along the Inishowen Peninsula and Malin Head. The scenery of craggy rocks and lush hillsides that slid into the teal tide, and zillions of sheep with black heads and legs could have been a photo shoot in *Travel and Leisure* magazine. This was their first sighting of so many sheep with the infamous black faces.

"These are the most common sheep in Ireland and believe it or not, called Scottish Blackface. They are a hearty breed and have adapted well to the Irish environment and land and we will see them all over roaming the hills and valleys. Have you seen Shaun the Sheep, the hilarious Claymation character? Check out Shaun and his cousins on YouTube or Facebook."

One parcel of land had a crop that gave the impression of a sea of blue. "Is that a linseed field?" Anne asked April.

"It's called flax or the 'wee blue blossom' here and produces a colorless to yellowish oil obtained from the dried, ripened seeds of the plant. In the mid-1700s, this region had a great number of flax mills. It was an important crop during the eighteenth and nineteenth centuries, too, when linen production was a major industry.

"See the yellow field in the distance? It's not sunflowers but canola, also known as rapeseed. You probably use canola oil for cooking. A number of small farms around Donegal and Northern Ireland grow and have selective distribution in much of the country. It's a strong market and growing rapidly. You can find bottles of it at farmers' markets and garden festivals.

April continued, "Further out, see the red on the hilltop? A field of poppies. Notice in that direction, the land that appears tan or cream? That was either barley, oats, or wheat that's recently been harvested. It makes an extraordinary pattern, doesn't it?"

"Like a massive bedspread or quilt." Jeanine poked her sister, Sue, sitting across the aisle. "I wonder if the ladies at that church where you live, you know the ones who have the big quilt sale every year, could make something like what we are seeing, these dazzling Irish landscapes. I'd sure buy one."

Sue nodded. "That's a fabulous idea. You know, Dave's sisters Sheila and Estelle, are expert quilters and have been part of First Lutheran Church Quilters forever, like charter members. All of the women are so talented. Dave and I must have ten quilts ourselves and have gifted dozens more. I gave Anne one with ivy, cardinals, and other winter birds on it last year for Christmas. I'll ask them if they'd ever done anything like this."

April explained that Cionn Mhálanna, or Malin Head, is a region still in County Donegal. It comprises an area north of the Black Mountain and there is no specific point that details the location of Malin Head on the peninsula.

Stopping for a stretch and fresh air on a paved path to Hell's Hole, they viewed a cavern with waves thundering against the steep rocks some 2,300 feet below. Anne could taste the salt in the air. Atlantic Ocean breezes touched their faces. Gulls crying to each other along with the crashing waves were the only sounds. Flourishing grass disappeared when reaching the jagged rocks that dissolved into a black sand beach.

They passed a small home painted white with a thatched roof and a ruby door, ruby-trimmed windows with matching geraniums overflowing from ruby wooden boxes, and a cherry red wagon wheel by the front door.

Pulling up to another vantage point, Banba's Crown, before seeing the sights, Anne knew where her group of friends and husband would be heading before anything else —to the mobile espresso bar, actually a tricked-out extended white van. The sign read "Coffee, Cappuccino, Latte, Mocha, Hot Chocolate, by Caffe Banba, Ireland's most Northern and Extraordinary Coffee Shop and Bakery, in Ballyhillin." Turns out this unique treat stop was one of two mobile coffee shops run by a husband-and-wife team who make all the home-baked goods, and a barista makes the specialty beverages surprisingly fast. Most businesses in this area pridefully have the words "Ireland's most northern" or "northerly" in their name.

Anne took a photo of Bruce and Nancy, Dave and Sue,

Chris and Jeanine, and Peter all smiling with their scalding brews. Their backdrop was a rocky bluff overlooking the white-capped waves on the cobalt sea. Greg and Linda were already off seeing the sights.

Sue pointed, "Are those llamas?"

"No," April answered, "actually alpaca. They are friendly, marvelous animals, and great for treks. The guided tours take people off the beaten path with incredible scenery and views."

"Certainly people don't ride them?" Jeanine was curious since they raised horses.

"Oh no, you trek with alpacas across the mountain tops," April assured her. "Granted a little bit scary on the climb but the guides are terrific. Think of a guide dog but instead a guide alpaca."

"I would love to do that next time," Anne poked Peter. "Or climb with alpacas when we return to Machu Picchu." He just stared at her, exactly the response she expected. She didn't dare laugh but she sure wanted to. Any references to Machu Picchu, even though a spectacular experience, reminded him of how sick Anne got, not from altitude but the Norovirus, which included two Peruvian doctors in their hotel room for three hours. Then he caught it on the flight home.

"When we return? Been there, done that, for me."

"Is that a climber on that sheer cliff face?" Anne gasped.

"Oh yes. There are plenty of adrenaline and extreme seeker tours, plus climbing tours." April answered.

"No thanks," Chris mumbled.

"With you on that," Dave stated.

***

Mickey saw Eamon's name on his phone. He swore.

> Did u find him?

> Tracked him to Farren's, he's been given your reminder loud and clear.

> He knows what's going to happen if he doesn't come through in 3 days.

> Aye and I put the stuff u gave me in his beer. He'll b feeling bad soon.

> Good, he knows I'm serious about 10 on Saturday or he's a dead man.

Sitting in the van, normally self-assured, Seamus told himself to stay with his plan. If he admitted it, he felt unnerved by the surprise altercation in parking lot with Mickey, Eamon's volatile right-hand man. Seamus knew full well he only had three days left to come up with the $15,000 he owed Eamon for gambling debts and some drugs. It wasn't his fault he got hooked on greyhound racing, or for that matter cars, motorcycles, horses, or anything else he could bet on. His stomach throbbed, alternating between that and searing pain. He wondered if it was the breakfast from a food truck that morning, then realized it was probably due to stress. He ran his hands through his dark hair noticing his head felt tight like a rubber band stretched tightly.

His last encounter with Eamon hadn't gone well, especially when Eamon called him "boyo." Seamus saw red and about lambasted that condescending, patronizing Eamon, or would have except for two haughty bodybuilders standing beside him for protection. He hated that word "boyo." His father had called him that when he was upset or disappointed in his youngest child, which occurred frequently. "Come on, boyo, smarten up," he'd say or, "Do this boyo," or, "You can do better, boyo," always making Seamus feel even more useless.

Everyone thought Doctor Kennedy was so perfect and wonderful all those years, but his son felt differently. Eamon didn't need to send that eejit Mickey to remind him he had three days left. Then, all of a sudden, Mickey handed him the bottles of beer like they were best mates. *He's wacko, too,* Seamus thought to himself.

The plan. *Stay with the plan,* he repeated to himself tipsy after chugging down another beer. Full of himself, Seamus planned to surprise his girlfriends. Plural, *girlfriends.* He had been clever enough and believed the cousins hadn't discovered that they were both dating him. The infrequent dates with Wrenna probably didn't make her official girlfriend status however, as he'd spent much more time with sweet Fay. He'd pulled a fast one over them. Truth be known, they looked so much alike, it was his mistake calling Wrenna by Fay's name early on. In school, he could never tell them apart and they'd pulled off a lot of tomfoolery that they'd gotten away with.

When he called Fay Wrenna one time, she laughed it off saying they had confused people all their lives. Fay admitted to him that she and her cousin had done plenty of shenanigans over the years, confusing teachers and friends, thinking nothing of it. He relaxed assuming he could get away with a random slip-up.

Between work, juggling the girlfriends, and his gambling habit, he was exhausted. And dating had become more expensive. They all had to come to a civilized agreement. Who would be fortunate enough to continue dating him? He would choose Fay.

In his grand scheme, he would nab the *Star Wars* helmet

from the bar, as part of his grand reveal. He figured they'd think it a hoot.

At least *one* girl seemed excited to get his invitation to the bar. He hoped the roses worked on Wrenna. Sweet Fay had taken time off work several miles away. She'd finally introduce her fella to her cousin, she texted him. He loved Fay the most.

The foreign visitors' next stop was at the well-known Farren's Bar, "Ireland's Most Northerly Bar since 1825" posted outside the building. They laughed when seeing on one end of the building a large, round jade Yoda, from *Star Wars* fame. On the other end of the building was a large, green-painted golfer, Rory McIlroy, who harkened from this area and is always a favorite of the locals.

Milling around the outside of the bar and homes clustered together, in the distance they could see Ireland's most northerly lighthouse, Inishtrahull, just off the coast. It looked lonely by itself. Homes are well kept and the one with a marine yellow front door and window trim popped from the otherwise white houses. A matching house appeared almost the same but with Aegean accents. An empty clothesline sat stationary except when the breeze moved the wooden clothespins.

Before the bar opened to the public, the tour group was given special access and greeted by friendly staff and a young man named Hugh, who escorted them around and provided a little history as he passed around some drink menus.

The bar is done in warm dark wood with dozens of mugs hanging overhead on hooks. Racks held bread loaves, cans of peas, sacks of flour, boxes of sugar, and other staples. At the back of one room a stove radiating warmth is positioned in the center surrounded by cushioned benches and chairs.

Star Wars memorabilia is proudly displayed since the final movie, *The Last Jedi*, was filmed in the area. *Star Wars* ships, Jedi pictures, posters, Guinness wall murals, pictures of famous people, and sports teams are prominent. Another popular object is a large white shoe autographed **Forcefully Yours, Mark Hamill,** aka Luke Skywalker. Linda got to hold it.

A Storm Trooper's white helmet is available for anyone to put on. While Dave drank coffee, Sue hustled to the front of the bar and tried on the helmet. She started the parade of all donning the well-recognized movie icon standing in funny poses. Bruce returned it so other patrons could have ample opportunity. Anne hoped for Yoda's green or Darth's red lightsaber, but nope, not one.

After placing multiple beverage orders with Hugh, Linda mentioned that they were drinking before 11 a.m.

"What a way to start a day," Nancy laughed.

"It's after five somewhere," Bruce gladly pointed out.

"Relax, you're on vacation," Sue chimed in.

"You need to make up your mind because Hugh will be back soon with the first round. Do you want an Irish coffee?" Peter glanced at his wife.

"Make it so." Anne raised her hand with her finger pointed at Peter.

"Uh, that was *Star Trek*. Captain Jean-Luke Picard said that."

Hugh carried in a tray of tall glass mugs of Irish coffees and other beverages to his American guests who gathered around him like ducklings. He brought several extra coffees for those previously undecided. They all lifted their glasses and said "Sláinte."

At a cozy table underneath pictures of sports teams, Greg

drank a Coke, his favorite, and Linda sipped a spiced hot beverage. Nancy also had one—warm mulled cider with a quarter of a thinly sliced lemon floating on top garnished with four cloves. It smelled delicious. By now they each had their drinks and were even more talkative.

Fanning herself with a plastic-coated menu, Anne puffed, "I'm either having a hot flash or I drank that Irish coffee way too fast."

"You're supposed to sip it." Her relaxed husband sat back in a comfy chair after having several swallows.

"Thanks a lot. You could have told me that before I gulped it down—I don't normally do whiskey, well, not before this trip anyway. I need some air. I'll be back in ten minutes. Keep sipping your drinks," she said still fanning wildly, with friends Dave and Sue sitting next to Bruce and Nancy.

"I'll come with you," Sue stated.

"No, relax, it's breezy and somewhat nippy out there."

"I thought it would be warmer." Used to central California temperatures, Nancy wrapped a shawl around her shoulders.

"September in Ireland. Who knows?" Dave remarked.

Seeing an exit sign, Anne stepped out the back door, and outside she took a deep breath of fresh air seeing Yoda, who still seemed out of place. She chuckled strolling to the edge of the grass where she scanned a path and then stepped down. *Ohhh, this is steeper than it looks*, wondering if she had the time to continue. Her inner self yelled, *Go!* Her worried mind nagged, *Best not.* She stepped down carefully.

Anne loved spending time along any beach—she wasn't picky—she just loved the ocean; the crystal clear water, the sounds of lapping waves, and the smell of salty air. It reminded her of her childhood and many family trips to the beach. A withdrawing wave created the familiar sound of pebbles tumbling in the ebbing tide. A brownish vermillion shiny stone caught her eye and she bent down to pick up what she assumed was an agate that she considered one of Mother Nature's treasurers, like a mini-Christmas gift from the earth. Holding it up to the sun, she noticed whisps of amber, apricot, and crimson ribboned throughout the quarter-size nugget and recalled her childhood days hunting rocks with their neighborhood rockhound, Fred. "This is carnelian," she proudly exclaimed with no one but a gull close enough to hear.

Not only did she collect agates from anywhere she beach-combed, she wanted to find just the right rock to take home to her brother, Max. He had specifically requested one from Ireland, a country he hadn't visited yet. He collected rocks, too, and she always took him one or two from their travels. Peter had created a rock garden that curved around the base of a stone wall in their backyard for her expanding collection.

She scattered a pile of pebbles with her foot, being careful not to get her shoes wet, and bent down to nab a green jasper with threads of white throughout. She knew that according to rock lore, it was a powerfully protective stone, perfect for her adventurous younger brother.

Except for the "peep peep" call of a black and white bird with a long crimson bill and legs that she recognized as an Oystercatcher, barking seals on rocks farther down the beach, and some squawking sea birds, it was just her and the sounds of the sea. She searched the water hoping to spot a whale, then turned to search the holes in the bank for puffins but saw none.

The silvery sea foam created a pattern like the lacey curtains she'd seen in many decorative windows in picturesque houses with colorful doors and thatched roofs. Several waves pushed her back toward the bank and this was not the time to get her shoes wet with a drive back to the hotel. Her time allotment about up, the brisk breeze and sea air had accomplished what she wanted, simply to cool off.

Fay approached her cousin who sat cloth-drying clear glass mugs. Wrenna glanced up. "Hey, grand to see you. I'm delighted to have a couple of days with my favorite cousin."

"Me too, and guess what? I'm meeting my boyfriend in a few minutes and finally going to introduce him to you."

"Em, so am I. Well, a fella I've been dating a few times. Supposed to meet out back."

"Now?"

"Aye, 10:45."

"Let's go together." The cousins scooted down the narrow hallway that mostly employees used and slipped out the back door.

Standing in the grass overlooking the beach on the clear sunny late morning, Wrenna began, "Tell me about this fella you're seeing."

"He's a dreamboat but works long hours and too hard. He drives a truck for a distillery."

Stepping out of his van hoping the piercing in his stomach would stop, Seamus hurried in the front door of the bar, nabbed the white helmet, and rushed down the back hallway and out the rear door noticing Hugh busy with guests scattered around the bar. Seamus slowed his pace and sauntered toward the women. Hearing movement, both turned around from the hypnotic motion of the ocean as a person wearing the Storm Trooper helmet approached.

A large squawking bird caught Anne's attention in the direction of the bar. Looking up, some sand blew into her watery eyes and stung like heck. Blurry-eyed, she took a double take. *What in the world?* The white Storm Trooper helmet and several people? It would have been more of a surprise if she hadn't already seen the helmet in the bar.

"Now that's just plain weird," her words carried away in the wind. Anne rubbed her half-closed eyes and turned with her back to the wind. She turned back toward the beach where she longed to stroll and spend more solitary time searching for agates and listening to the surf and birds. She knew it would be harder getting back up the hill then down.

"Not funny, Seamus."

"Oh, come on. Just wanted to surprise you both. Lighten up, ladies."

"What are we both doing here, Seamus?"

"Well," he started proud of himself. "I got to the point where this is too confusing and honestly exhausting, so I figured we need to decide who I will continue to date."

The cousins studied each other. "He's your boyfriend?" Fay questioned.

"Not really. We've only gone out a few times." Wrenna answered really peeved with herself.

"He's been *mine* the last six months."

A fire in the base of each girl's stomach ignited.

"Lassies, er', ladies, no reason fighting over me," Seamus smiled, totally mistaking the tone of their voices. "I do like this a lot though. I'm sure we can work this out to satisfy all of us." He sniggered, slurring his words.

"You're drunk."

"I've had a couple of bottles, aye, maybe earlier than usual. It's like I'm seeing double, oh wait, you're identical cousins," slurring his words even more. He tried to wink at Fay but both shifty eyes blinked instead. "But now you see, I've gotten myself into a little situation and need some help."

"What kind of *situation?*" Fay muttered.

"Financial. I'll pay it back when I can."

Fay scrutinized him. "How much this time?"

"Only 15,000."

"What do you mean *this* time?" Wrenna saw Fay shrug her shoulders.

"Are you daft?" Wrenna exclaimed flabbergasted, a question that could go to either of the two.

Fay, softening at his pathetic plight, stood silent while still bewildered about the dating revelation. "I don't have any money to give you. I am barely making ends meet working at the senior center."

"You can take out a loan at the bank." Outraged, his unblinking bloodshot eyes darted back and forth between two sets of the fiercest, fearless blue eyes he'd ever seen. Almost identical. Side-by-side, he noticed Fay's had a bit more of frosty green in hers. And instantly angry.

"Gombeen!" Fay sneered, not speaking Irish often she had used the word meaning "worse than a jerk" a few times in the past. She saved the Irish version for emphasis and drama and it was certainly appropriate for this occasion.

"Okay, okay, come on now, girlies, calm down. Let's think about this," Seamus seethed inside. "How about your folks? When they have to hear what I've got..." he spouted arrogantly.

"Now we're "girlies?" Don't call us that, ever! The state of you... you bleedin' shite," Wrenna hissed.

"You chancer!" Fay exclaimed.

Wrenna reached for her cousin's right hand, fingers intertwined, their grip tight. Fay's hand hurt; her cousin's grip remained firm. Just like in elementary school and like many other times when nothing could come between them. Certainly not this lying lout.

With his vain ego, Seamus had assumed the ladies would have a grand row over him. He never thought they'd get this worked up over his request for some financial help. His entitlement and narcissism came from early childhood spoiled by his parents and had been enforced by other women who had swooned over him.

"What do you mean you won't help me get the money?" his temper became volatile. When he heard words like "chancer" and "gombeen" coming from sweet Fay's mouth, he guessed his Irish luck had run out. Probably any Scottish luck, too. *Maybe Noreen or Shaleigha could help.* He was deviously already thinking ahead.

"I didn't want to have to resort to telling you something… I'll be sharing some information I happened on in my father's offi…" anger streaming from his mouth.

"Bugger off, Seamus!"

"I'm not surprised at you Wrenna, not forthcoming… with anything." With an evil snicker, "Frigid witch. But Fay, my darlin' colleen, we shared some grand times, didn't we love?" He felt a stabbing pain in his gut and his face turned ashen. He clenched his stomach.

"Don't you darlin' me," Fay shouted, "and don't you ever talk about our times together. Ever. What's wrong with you?"

"Stomach hurts." He coughed repeatedly.

"Too bad," Fay replied sarcastically as Wrenna said nothing.

Like a solid wall of female fierceness, they stepped toward the trickster they both instantly hated. Wrenna felt a flaming energy like lightning coursing between her and her cousin.

Her Irish temper had always been on a slow fuse, Fay's much quicker as an adult. But Wrenna's right hand had balled into a tight fist. Faster than she ever imagined herself, she lambasted Seamus in the nose.

"You..." Seamus blurted out as one hand cupped his bloody nose and he raised his other hand to strike her. Already off-kilter, he stumbled backward over a small log where several had been placed in a row creating a barrier alerting people to the drop-off. Both women watched like in a slow-motion movie, as he tumbled in backwards summersaults in the low foliage until he stopped midway.

"Ouch. That hurt but was totally worth it." Unclenching her fist and rubbing her hand, she noticed a dab or two of blood and wiped it on her white apron. She snatched the helmet off the ground and using her apron, cleaned grass from an edge.

"He can just lay there and think about what he's done." Wrenna's outrage was back in check.

"I hope you broke his nose and blackened an eye. No, I really hope he dies. No man does that to us," Fay huffed.

"No, you don't but I'm glad he'll be sore and bruised. He'll learn his lesson not to toy with us. And drinking this early, what an eejit."

"What did he say? Some gibberish but I didn't catch it. Something about his dead father?"

"Poor Doctor Kennedy is probably turning over in his grave. Seamus is so drunk or on something. He's got the brains of a sparrow."

"We will never speak of this. Ever."

"Agreed."

Returning through the same door, they calmly retraced their steps. Wrenna placed the Trooper helmet to its rightful place on the shelf. She coolly stepped back behind the counter and then ambled to the kitchen to help Rafferty chop vegetables as Fay calmly set off to the bathroom. Wrenna poured a pint for her cousin, both outwardly unaffected by the entire episode.

Anne glanced up to where she thought she saw something out of the *Star Wars* movie. Nothing was there. "Gotta be that Irish Coffee." She checked her watch. "I need to get back up that hill. Shoot. I've got two minutes, I'll never make it that fast," she said, speaking to a nearby gull.

Climbing up the trail wasn't nearly as effortless as coming down. The gulls and other seabirds created a cacophony that startled her so much that she stopped halfway, turned, and took a photo down the beach at the stunning setting.

A few steps farther in the brush she heard a noise, guessing it to be a shy creature like maybe a hare which is larger than a rabbit and very common, or a cute hedgehog. Curious, she stepped into the bushes about knee-high. Seeing a person lying face down she hollered, "Are you okay?" Louder this time, "Hey! Can you hear me?" The person lying in the brush didn't answer.

I can't believe this. Getting no response, Anne sprinted as quickly as she could uphill, which admittedly wasn't very fast. She panted reaching the flat grassy area around the corner of the bar, pushing open the front door. A whoosh slammed the bar's door closed. Bent over at her waist trying to catch a breath, she tried to blurt out to Hugh, "There's..." Taking another breath, "There's somebody..." Still bent over, side throbbing, she finally got it all out. "I was down on the beach... there is somebody in the brush about halfway down the hill." She took a sideways glance to where she'd seen the trooper's helmet earlier. It was sitting in the exact same spot. She heard water splashing in the kitchen, the fizz of beer, the clinking of glass mugs, the creak as someone came through the front door; her senses were on high alert.

Anne glanced at a woman sitting on a stool drinking a pint.

Anne blurted out, "Fayanna?"

"Aye?"

Anne noticed another familiar face behind the bar. "Wrenna?"

"Holy Mary, mother of God, cousin Anne?" Wrenna blurted out.

Anne backed up into a chair, almost falling. Both women ran to their American cousin.

"Mam mentioned you are on holiday but didn't mention you would be here." Fay hugged her and whispered in Anne's ear, "Did you see anything?"

Anne peered into her unreadable fearless eyes. Releasing Fay and sensing something amiss, Anne answered, "No. Just spotted a body in the bushes."

Wrenna wrapped her arms around Anne and in a low voice she enunciated her words distinctly, "Family first, cousin Anne."

Several minutes after Hugh called the Carndonagh Garda Station located three miles away, a white 4x4 Hyundai Tucson pulled into the bar's parking lot. The conversation between Detective Sergeant Morgan Graham and Garda Michael Devlin on the short drive down Malin Road included the possibility of needing assistance from district headquarters, Buncrana Garda station, southwest across the peninsula about 30 minutes if traffic wasn't heavy.

"Let's see what we have going on first before contacting

Buncrana. Hopefully just a drunk teenager," DS Graham mentioned.

"Or clumsy tourist," Devlin blew his nose. "If it is we may need to contact National Ambulance service and the fire brigade to be on standby. They might prefer Mountain Rescue get involved."

"Again, wait and see. Getting sick?"

"Allergies this time of year, sir."

Hugh met the guards outside and pointed to the path down the hillside. "The American who detected the person is inside." Both guards scrambled down the bank, taking a few items with them. The man wasn't breathing nor had a pulse.

"I recognize him. We were in school together. Seamus Kennedy." DS Graham motioned with his arm. "Devlin, you stay here and start taking some pictures with your phone. Weather might change before assistance arrives. Check his wallet and take photos of everything in it. His driver's license will have his address. Be careful where you step, might be evidence in all this brush. I'm going to the bar to speak with the person who first saw him and see if anyone happened to notice anything. I'll phone Buncrana and tell them what's going on. They can decide on the removal process since it's a precarious location."

DS Graham entered the bar glancing around. He heard laughter in surround sound and did a quick count of around 30. The place was full of merry American tourists. His intensely sharp blue eyes locked just an instant with a flash from his past as Wrenna's curiously soft eyes were locked on his as well. She noticed Graham's eyes were the color of blueberries in their family garden. Odd she should remember the color of his eyes, she thought.

Hugh recaptured the guard's attention, pointing at Anne who had not moved from the chair she landed in after speaking with Wrenna and Fay. A guard dressed in an official yellow and navy uniform introduced himself to Anne as Detective Sergeant Morgan Graham. Anne's heart thumped and her skin suffered wave after wave of goosebumps. She had a flashback to her childhood, to the first time she saw Deputy Tall-Dark-and Handsome, Clayton Malloy, at the headwaters of the Metolius River. It was love at first sight with the deputy, 15 years her senior. She thoroughly enjoyed seeing a man in uniform, but not under these circumstances.

Anne told her brief story to him. She had learned to keep her comments short and not ramble in these situations. She provided her name, age, and where she lived. "I was walking along the shoreline"— here she swallowed and wondered, *do I or don't I?*— "and when returning up the hillside, I heard a rustling and noticed someone laying in the bushes. He or she didn't respond. That's all I know."

"Time?"

"About 20 minutes ago."

"10:50 a.m. then?" he asked as he wrote in a small notepad.

"Right," Anne answered as she checked her watch.

"You didn't notice him on your way down the hill?"

"No."

"Did you see anyone else outside?"

"No."

"Did you see anyone else on the beach?"

"No."

"Okay, thank you. Please write down your phone number, email, and physical address. We will contact you if we need more."

Peter joined Anne who sat with the detective, while their group of friends were involved in a conversation.

"Poor Anne, not another one. She is going to get a serious complex." Linda shook her head back and forth.

"Or think she's jinxed," Nancy added.

"No, she won't. She's not superstitious," Sue added.

"I think she believes in fairies and ghosts," Jeanine noted.

"But who doesn't?" Nancy added.

"Uh, me," Dave mumbled as everyone scrutinized him in disbelief. "How many bodies is that now? Like eight?"

Sue socked her husband in the right arm, "No way and the first one doesn't count since it was her entire family when they stumbled upon the body in the headwaters of the Metolius River. She was only 13."

"Then she and Peter were on that glacier outside of Juneau." Bruce took another drink of coffee.

"Right. Mendenhall Glacier, where she noticed a boot in the snow, that just happened to be attached to a body down a crevasse," Jeanine added as she moved over by Chris.

"Were any of you on those infamous trips with them?"

"Nos" came from the circle.

"So, then they traveled to the Galápagos Islands and onto Peru and Machu Picchu. Linda turned toward Greg. "We toured a couple of years after they did. She didn't find a body there but did happen to be taking pictures and didn't realize she'd gotten a sequence of murder on her camera. So that doesn't count either because she didn't exactly find a body."

"Well, it sort of does since she had the proof." Greg nudged his wife.

"More recently though was the Danube River cruise where, as it turned out, she'd had several encounters with the man that would be killed, and she did discover his body."

"Right, but she didn't know he had died."

"And she befriended the supposed killers."

"Do you remember Casey and Cathy, their friends from Salem? They were on the Mendenhall Glacier trip and the Danube Viking river cruise. They got to know the *murderers*, too. They were all fooled. Another friend, Julie, too." Sue explained.

"We love Julie and have been on a few trips with her. Other longtime friends, Mike and Kathy, too. They were in Alaska for that first shocker and on the Danube cruise. And Mike's parents camped with Anne's family and were there at the same time the family made that find. So that's almost three times, and they all travel together frequently along with Phil and Sharon," Nancy added. "Bruce and I have met them all on trips, too."

"It's been a rough year for those two," Dave said, looking at their best friends. The foursome had known each other for over 25 years. They'd met when Dave and Sue lived in Salem for some years before returning to the Seattle area. "Peter's father passed away five months ago and now Anne's. Then this episode. Jinxed, I'm telling you."

"If you say that one more time… she is not jinxed, cursed or a magnet. Just the wrong place at the wrong time," his wife scolded him.

"So we know it doesn't happen to friends she's traveling with," Linda reminded them.

"That's a relief." Chris chuckled.

"Not yet anyway." Dave drank the last drop of coffee. "She's like Angela Lansbury in *Murder She Wrote.* Everywhere her character went, she discovered a body."

Sue looked around the group of friends, "Anne is not Jessica Fletcher nor has she found bodies on a weekly basis. Just one every five years or so. Or three."

Dave went on to correct his wife, "Well, wasn't it just …"

"This topic is closed. No more discussion, do you understand me?" Sue glared at her spouse.

"I'd go anywhere with her and Peter. They are great to travel with. Anne organizes everything so I don't have to think about a thing and they are easy-going, which you have to be when it comes to travel. And think about all the trips they have gone on where nothing like this happened.

Australia, New Zealand, Canada, all over the Caribbean, throughout the Mediterranean, most countries in Europe, even Russia on a Scandinavia cruise, plus the Nordic countries. They've been to over 40 countries with only four, maybe five, wrong place, wrong time." Anne's loyal BFF, Sue, set everyone straight.

"We've been to Iceland with them, too." Linda sipped her drink.

Greg sat down. "Don't forget that incredible day in Greenland, too."

"Right. Us, too." Bruce moved next to Nancy.

"Well, I guess we have been all over with them and nothing tragic has happened. Until now." Dave focused on where Anne and Peter were sitting with the guard.

"You'd better mind your ps and qs," Sue warned. "You could be next."

"This is our first trip abroad and I appreciate how she sent all the reading materials, answered dozens of questions, and is the leader of our pack." Jeanine coughed after a sip of the laced, potent coffee.

Sue chanted quietly, "We love Anne! We love Anne!" Then they all burst out in nervous laughter.

Anne turned in the direction of hilarity just in time to see her friends high-fiving each other, clueless what caused such camaraderie.

Hugh thought he was whispering quietly enough to Wrenna. "Word is the guy down the bank is dead."

"Really? Dead?" She sucked in a large gulp of air searching for Fay, "Are you sure that's what you heard?"

"I overheard two guards talking. They are calling for extra assistance."

This is not what I wanted to hear, Anne thought to herself. She watched Wrenna speaking with Fay whose expression was unreadable.

"Anne. Anne? Are you okay?" Sue sat in a chair by her best friend reaching over she rubbed Anne's arm.

"It does look like you've seen a ghost." Nancy sat down on the other side of Anne.

"A bit stressed and probably just tired," was her answer, knowing what she'd overheard, *the guy is dead.* "Maybe some air... I just keep running the episode like a video in my mind."

"I sense you need a hug. Stand up," Linda ordered.

"Oh, okay—oh, it's happening, okay, we're hugging."

Releasing herself from Linda's grip, "No, no, I need to hug you for at least 30 seconds to calm your sympathetic nervous system. I learned this from my friend and massage therapist, Heather."

"Uh-huh." Anne's phone chirped.

"Don't look at your phone. Okay, breathe, Anne."

Anne heard Sue say, "The guard is speaking with your cousins. Pretty official like,"

"Seriously, I feel like I'm gonna vomit."

Linda quickly released Anne saying, "It's okay, I've got a bag in the bus. Nurses are always prepared for anything."

Anne noticed the guard approach Wrenna who became engrossed in a conversation with the handsome officer.

"You gonna say Hi?" she quipped as he reached out his right hand to Wrenna. Just as soft as ever he remembered.

"Sorry, uh, you look different. Not bad different. Good, different," his voice soft spoken, clearly unnerved. "Not that you looked bad the last time I saw you." She could tell he felt very uncomfortable and wanted to giggle, but instead, she smiled up at him, her being four inches shorter.

"It's splendid to see you, Morgan Graham, em, Detective

Sergeant Graham," she reached out touching his left arm. *She's way too relaxed*, he thought, and, *here I am sweating.*

"What have you been doing with yourself the past several years?"

"Graduated college, a bit of this and that. And you? I expected to see your name on billboards by now as Ireland's most famous rugby player."

He laughed loudly. She'd always made him laugh easily. "I love the sport and mam always told me I was running around the garden with a rugby ball before I talked. But after two concussions, each shoulder dislocated, and knee ligament injuries, the collar bone fracture determined my fate. I chose law enforcement instead. I much prefer detective work over patrol."

"Is a detective needed here?"

"Not sure yet, depends on if it is determined suspicious or not."

Anne knew true love when she saw it and whether these two recognized it or not, they were in love. Was he the one that Mauve mentioned Wrenna was dating? No, it's clear they haven't seen each other in some time. *I'm totally flummoxed.*

"Can you step outside with me?" Graham put his hand on Wrenna's lower back.

"Em, sure Morgan," using his first name, "but I am working." To him, her voice sounded as sweet as honey.

"Please."

"Hugh, I'll just be outside." He gave her a thumbs up. Morgan had always enjoyed the way Wrenna pronounced his name, MorGan, with more emphasis on gan.

"Did you cut yourself?" he checked, noticing a blotch of smeared blood.

Wrenna scrutinized her apron, "Aye, cut myself chopping vegetables for the stew. Didn't even need a bandage."

"I didn't want others to hear but do you remember Seamus Kennedy from school?"

"Of course. He was a pian san árse to everyone."

"He's the one down the hill. Did you see him in the bar often?"

"I've just been here the past two months. He's not a regular but he does deliver product from the distillery."

Morgan couldn't get passed how stunning Wrenna appeared, long thick wavy auburn hair, it had darkened since school, and fair complexion with a few freckles. He recalled how he'd told her a face without freckles was like a sky without stars. Her peachy high cheeks, rosy full lips, and familiar blue-green eyes, and how contented he felt around her.

But today he stood there sweating. *Oh man, just like in school, I'm a dunce around her.* He had an enormous crush on her for two years in high school and they dated more than just a few times. He recalled how they attended the senior dance together and what transpired afterward at Rossy-longan Forest, a park with thousands of trees and soft grass.

After the summer she was gone, off to college, and slacked off on returning his emails and texts. She'd moved on apparently.

Wrenna noticed the dots of perspiration on Morgan's forehead. Her hands felt clammy. She had a major infatuation, too, and that summer had been magical to her. She would have married him in a heartbeat except she didn't want a life with a professional athlete. She couldn't see farther down the road with him. It had been easier just not to answer him and let him go than explain it all to him. He'd made it abundantly clear where his priorities were with his upcoming profession.

All sorts of memories enveloped both, looking a little sheepish at what had occurred between them eight years earlier. He glanced down at the ground as she gazed off in the distance.

He removed his two-tone yellow and navy jacket and she noticed how handsome he appeared, especially in the light blue shirt and navy pants. Off came the hat. "Whew, it's a warm one today."

Just the opposite, she'd slipped on a coat and bundled up due to the breeze.

Peter and Dave watched the officer rope off the area below with bright yellow tape.

Graham paced in the parking lot waiting for assistance and replaying the entire encounter with his high school sweetheart. When Sergeant Doyle and Cadet O'Neill from Buncrana Garda arrived, Graham filled them in on the situation.

Peter overheard him tell the newcomers, "He'd be alive most likely if he hadn't hit his head on the rock. It's probably what stopped his fall or he would have tumbled another 50 more feet to the bottom."

"Doubt he would have survived a 100-foot-fall."

"ID?"

"Aye."

"Who is he?"

"Actually I recognized him from school, Seamus Kennedy. His family moved from Scotland in elementary school. For some reason, he acted entitled. Maybe because his father was one of the local doctors. Doc Kennedy never had airs but his son did. He acted likable and flirty with girls and mean to smaller lads. Almost a Dr. Jekyll and Mr. Hyde personality. I'm pretty sure he works in the delivery business, driving a truck for one of the distilleries. Lost track of him years back.

But there is a company van." Graham gestured toward the vehicle in the parking lot.

"You think someone pushed him off the edge?" Doyle stepped to the edge.

"A fairly dark subject for such a stunning view." Pensive, Graham turned from gazing at the water, directly at the other man.

"What's your take on all of this?" the young cadet probed.

"I don't have any opinion yet, it's too early."

Three officers lumbered down to the body, one with a camera. While Devlin interviewed people in the bar, Graham, Doyle, and O'Neill volleyed back and forth in conversation. Doyle had five years of seniority over Graham even though their rank was sergeant.

"As I mentioned, I know him from our school days, as well as a woman who works in the bar and her cousin who is visiting," Graham began.

"Will your past be an issue?" Doyle asked.

"No sir," Graham assured him.

"Any contact with these three since your school days?"

Graham shook his head. "Just random with the victim. I saw him probably a year or so ago at the race track when I was there working an undercover sting. He wasn't part of that case. But I did pick up that he was deep in debt."

"You know, there are many victims in a death, murder especially. But guards can't let emotions cloud the investigation." Doyle sounded like a counselor.

"Right, sir." Graham took a side glance at O'Neill.

"What's this Kennedy fellow doing here?" Doyle probed.

"He drives for a distillery and Farren's gets regular deliveries. The van is half full of product."

"His face is bashed. How would that happen in the bushes?" Doyle sought more answers.

"I can sure smell beer on him. He'd had a few already this morning," O'Neill added.

"Why would he be back here if he had deliveries to make?" Doyle pressed on.

"Maybe he needed to take a leak," O'Neill speculated.

"Phone?" Doyle inquired.

"Retrieved and bagged," Graham jumped in.

"Could you unlock it?"

Graham shook his head back and forth. "No such luck. But I'll have Devlin try some other combinations. He's exceptional with this sort of thing. O'Neill, ask Hugh if he has CCTV. If he does, let's see if Devlin can establish a timeline, since we don't have any witnesses."

"Devlin already checked sir. There is one camera out front that works, and one on the side, but not in the back." O'Neill replied.

"Grand," Graham replied sarcastically. "Radio him to review it when he's done with interviews and contact me if he finds anything interesting."

"Copy that."

"Any next of kin?" Doyle asked.

"I'll handle that. He has an older sister as I recall. I knew her from school."

"Detective Sergeant Graham, please come to the Bar office," squawked his radio. Graham stood over Devlin sitting in a swivel chair, together viewing the camera footage on the laptop in Hugh's office.

"Hugh arrived first at 9:42 a.m., followed by two male workers. Lad's name is Rafferty, he works in the kitchen.

Second is Brian, the bartender. This woman parks and enters the door marked 'Employee's Only' about five minutes later."

Graham watched the screen as Wrenna pulled up in a '90s Fiat, then chuckled. "That's her mother's old Punto. Wrenna has always been frugal."

Devlin glanced up at his sergeant over his reading glasses. "Oookay… then there's a van from Yellow Bird Bakery. The guy unloads and takes items into the side door. He's gone, then ten minutes later, a second female arrives and goes in the front door."

"That's Fayanna, Wrenna's cousin, who is staying a few days with her." Devlin peered again over his reading glasses at his boss, which Morgan noticed for the second time.

"What, Devlin? Are you implying something?"

"No sir, Detective Sergeant sir. Just seems you know a lot about these two women," he observed, teasing his normally private and somewhat shy superior and friend.

"Proceed."

"Then this distillery van arrives and the victim gets out. He doesn't go anywhere. See how he's pacing around? At first, I thought he was making a delivery but it's more like he's waiting for someone. Another van arrives and this guy gets out and marches up to Seamus all puffed up. See? Oh, notice there is no writing on the side of the van. Look how he gets right in Seamus' face. Yelling and waving his arms. Now catch this. Shoves Seamus against the side of the van."

"That's interesting. This is when I wish lip reading would be taught during training," Graham chuckled.

"Actually, my cousin has a friend who is deaf and she learned lip reading to communicate with her friend."

"Good to know. We may need that type of assistance."

"To me, it seems that Seamus takes it and doesn't do anything. Then watch this, the guy goes to the cab of the van and hands Seamus a bottle of beer which he downs in seconds. The guy has one also. Then he hands Seamus another one. Like best pals all of a sudden."

"Okay, so that explains the beer smell on him."

"Now this. The guy pats Seamus on the back, all best friends like. Then he drives off. Few minutes later, we've got Seamus going into the front of the bar and that's it. Must have gone out the back door. Turns out there are two ways out, one the employees normally use which is a narrow hall-way, and one that patrons can use."

"No 'Luck of the Irish' here. Why no footage?"

"Hugh told me he hasn't replaced the camera that broke off in a wind storm last year. It had been mounted above the back door." Devlin sneezed three times.

"So we don't know if anyone left through the back door?"

"Right. The blooming flax is killing me," before two more sneezes.

Even though young compared to many older more experienced guards, Graham learned to trust his gut, and his gut was telling him this was suspicious.

"This adds an entirely new dimension that raises more questions," Graham observed.

"The guy in the unmarked van?"

Graham shrugged his shoulders. "Broad daylight, some wind, a drunk, and a fall. Sounded uncomplicated enough. Now we need a lot more answers. I think we need the coroner to do tox screens. Probably need to review phone calls and texts. I'll run it by Sergeant Doyle, too."

"We don't have his passcode and the touch ID doesn't work. The phone is probably too old. A subpoena will take some time but I'll send the request in. I'm going to try some different combinations like you suggested. Maybe his sister will know?"

"See if they can rush it for us."

Sergeant Doyle recognized Graham's commanding voice

on his radio, "Sergeant, after watching CCTV footage, it's my opinion we should contact An Garda Síochána."

"Copy that. Call and explain the situation."

He turned back to Devlin. "Time to call in the big boys. Ask for Inspector Murdock. And keep trying to unlock that phone."

Jeanine approached April, "Do the Irish use the word police or gardaí?" pointing to a white SUV with the word Garda on it. Others huddled around for her answer. April noticed a cadet watching the process and approached him.

Cadet O'Neill joined the group. "Here's some of history that I learned in classes last month. Organized policing in Ireland can be traced back to the early 1800s. A county constabulary was a uniformed police force formed on a regional basis. Before this, there was a basic police force known as The Peace Preservation Force. The Irish Constabulary, later to be known as the Royal Irish Constabulary (RIC) and the Dublin Metropolitan Police (DMP), were established to replace the county constabulary.

"By the early 1900s, around 11,000 men were stationed in about 1,600 barracks. There were widespread attacks on the RIC on their barracks and on patrol. Following the Civil War and the truce in 1921, the RIC disbanded and a new police force, The Civil Guard, was formed by the Irish government. The DMP merged with another group, but I don't recall what they were called. The Republic of Ireland has one national civilian force called 'An Garda Síochána,' meaning 'Guardians of the Peace of Ireland.' Their functions include crime prevention, detection, and investigation, as well as national security, road security, and community policing. We are unarmed and uniformed and divided into regions, both geographical and by specialization."

"So you are a garda, singular, and gardaí is plural?"

"Correct. Garda Cadet since I am in training. But most don't call us police or garda but guard. But sometimes police."

"So if we say 'guard' we are fine? What type of training is required?"

"Yes, guard is accurate. I trained for two years spending some time at Garda Síochána College in County Tipperary. There I studied duties, did physical exercises, drills, swimming, and first aid followed by a major examination. After one year on the job, each Garda Cadet returns to Templemore for a one-month refresher course which I will do soon."

"What types of deaths occur around here?"

"Greg!"

"What? I'm just curious. It seems so quiet and peaceful."

"Normally it's boating and water-related incidents." O'Neill answered.

Anne whispered to Sue. "Looks like he's not a day over 16."

"What are you gravitating towards? Patrol? Investigation?" Peter inquired.

"I am very interested in forensics but will need to have many years of experience like this before I would ever reach that level."

They all heard "O'Neill" blaring from his radio with instructions to fetch three tarps. He ran to the SUV, opening the back door full of supplies and equipment.

In one stop her world turned partially upside down. Again. Still sitting in the same chair, she didn't even want to think about her past encounters but she couldn't help it. It all started when her family discovered a body in the headwaters of the Metolius when she was a teenager. She tried to close that compartment in her mind, but the door remained stubborn and wouldn't shut all the way tight.

She felt a bit... what did she feel, actually? Certainly out of sorts. But also befuddled about the presence of Wrenna and Fayanna at the bar at the same time. Except Wrenna did work there.

"Poor Anne." Nancy had really spoken to herself.

"Why poor Anne?" a woman on the tour from North Carolina lowered her voice.

"Mysteries and incidents."

"What in the world are you talking about?"

"Maybe Peter or Anne should tell April about her other 'discoveries' over the years." Dave turned to Sue.

"For what purpose?" She felt instantly protective of Anne.

"What good would that do?" Linda snapped equally as defensive.

"Well, word is bound to get out about her past dealings with..."

"At least it's not ghosts," Linda cut in the conversation.

"You know that Irish saying, 'Who keeps his tongue keeps his friends.' Think about it." Sue drank the last drop of her second Irish coffee.

———

Assured they would be able to reach their discovery witness, there turned out to be no need to keep Anne. She hadn't touched anything or seen much.

Guard Devlin circulated through the bar, asking if anyone had been outside earlier or seen anything to shed light on the incident. Since the bar had opened early for the tour group instead of normal hours at 11:00, it had only been their group around to start with. And they had all been inside listening to Hugh share about the bar, history, and famous Irish movies like the comedy *Waking Ned Devine*, the biographical period drama, *Michael Collins*, and the narrative memoir *Angela's Ashes*. Only Anne had gone outside to cool off.

During Fayanna's questioning, she reported her cousin told her they were opening the bar early for a tour group, and suggested she come by before they got too busy. Fay would be staying with her cousin for a few days.

"Did you know your cousin Anne would be there?"

"No. My mam told me Anne and Peter were in the country on holiday. but I had no idea she'd be here today. Purely coincidence."

Wrenna's version matched Fay's. The cousins were in sync. She didn't know Anne would be there either. She hadn't seen her in 20 years except through photos from her mam.

Devlin took a double take after speaking with Wrenna and then to Fay, thought he was seeing double. In his notes he scribbled: *Identical cousins or twins? Ask Graham.*

"We need to catch the noon news, even if it's the last five minutes," the woman yelled at the cameraman tapping her watch. With her irrational expectations along with being scatterbrained and ungrateful, he was about to quit. He'd been driving like a madman on the narrow roads trying to avoid pedestrians, bicyclists, and hares. He would have laughed at the scenario but figured he'd get fired by the temperamental fake blonde who he didn't care much for. Neither did anyone else for that matter.

The TV news van from Derry skidded to a halt, as the two jumped out; the driver grabbing a camera and the blonde holding a microphone. She mumbled something to a man in a uniform who pointed to the inspector who had arrived just 15 minutes earlier. Normally a five-hour drive, Murdock had arrived by helicopter landing at the local elementary school where O'Neill picked him up. Only minutes earlier standing over the deceased, Murdock removed his hat and moved his right hand making an invisible cross touching his forehead, chest, and shoulders. O'Neill glanced sideways at Graham who wasn't surprised. He knew Murdock to be a devout Catholic.

"I look like a disaster but get me on now!" Trying to straighten her windblown hair, she adjusted her clothing in time to see her cameraman countdown with his fingers, three, two, one, then pointing to her.

"I'm Meegan Hennessy reporting **LIVE**. Our station is the first to report a suspicious death behind the popular Farren's Bar at Malin Head. I am joined by Inspector Thomas Murdock of An Garda Síochána headquarters, all the way from Dublin."

"What can you tell us about the death?"

"A man was discovered this morning around 10:50 a.m."

"Discovered by who?"

"An American tourist."

"Who is he?

He ignored the question, "At the moment, the guards are at the scene. The body is still there, so details are quite sketchy at this point. We are still waiting for the arrival of our forensics people from headquarters to examine the scene."

"Can you tell us what happened?"

"The body was lying in the bushes about 50 feet below."

"Does it seem like he could have survived this fall?"

"Unlikely."

"Was he pushed?"

"Don't know. It's way too soon to know anything."

"Can you speculate on the reason for death? On drugs?"

"I don't speculate. Again, it's way too soon to know anything. How did you hear about this already?"

"I have my sources. How long has he been dead?"

"I told you he was discovered around 10:50."

"You did, but how long has he been dead?"

"I don't know. One of the aspects the pathologist will be reviewing."

"You're from Dublin. That's hours away. Is this a case that warrants a person of your status to come all this way? Does this mean this death is a murder case?"

Murdock didn't feel the need to answer everything in detail but thought he'd give her a tidbit. "Many times we use aircraft for transportation rather than the roadway system, especially for weather reasons and traffic issues in general. This time of year is tourism. I happened to be on my way back from another case when I was contacted about this one. So I wasn't that far away to begin with."

"Fine. But you're not giving me any case details. My viewers expect information and I need answers for them." Her slow burn had picked up a faster pace.

"You know everything that I do at this point. We will hold a press conference when we have actual facts." Murdock turned his back on the irksome reporter. He had little regard for the press and this included her. She had a reputation of embellishing the truth to benefit her own career and the questionable morals of the television station's hierarchy were despicable in his book. He would not contribute to her less than accurate reports. *Will they ever learn?* He knew the answer to his question.

———

With all the excitement of the TV interview happening at Malin Head, on the bus Anne stared out the window at hundreds of sheep. In one field the sheep that had been shorn were sprayed with a strip of red. All sorts of things were floating around in Anne's mind like questions in bubbles in a cartoon. *How did the person in the bushes fall? Most likely drunk. At least I didn't know him or see him fall. How did he die? Were the girls involved?* She suspected she'd hear more from one of the cousins via text since both daughters were in the bar. Sitting in the front seat by Anne, April now heard Anne's version of prior episodes with the deceased from around the world.

Splotches of sunshine-yellow shrubs brightened the hill-sides lifting Anne's spirits. She asked April about the flowering bushes that resembled Scotch Broom at home. April explained that it's similar but different. Gorse is a shrub with spiny green prickles and a family of plants in the pea family. Gorse is sometimes called furze. Broom is a large shrub of heaths, open woodlands, and coastal areas.

They passed a field with dark green waxy, oval-shaped leaves and Anne asked, "Some type of leaf lettuce?"

"No, it's the tops of sugar beets, a crop grown all over the island. They will be harvested later this month." This time Bill answered.

Returning to Derry, they stopped for late lunch at a favorite restaurant that April knew they would enjoy. April hoped Primrose on the Quay would cheer Anne up. It had a sign on a wall inside that read "Purveyors of Primrose Fine Irish Foods original recipes."

The eye-catching pastry display drew the attention of Sue, Linda, and Anne. A "confetti cake," as it is called, had five layers with each layer a different color. A watermelon-colored layer started the masterpiece, followed by mandarin, lemon, and lime, ending with teal. It was frosted with smooth yellow icing, with elongated sprinkles scattered on the side. The bottom and top were lined with teal flowers. The top had more sprinkles, dotted with more flowers. Anne took a few photos hoping one of her nieces would make it sometime for a family gathering.

The lunch lived up to its fine reputation but the best entertainment were the hamburgers delivered to Dave and a second one to Chris. The look on Dave's face read, "How in the world am I going to eat this?" Under the top bun sat a fried onion ring, a layer of lettuce, another fried onion ring, and then a half-inch thick beef patty. Including the bottom bun it totaled at least ten inches high. Both men rose to the occasion and devoured their burgers.

Anne selected a Fentiman's botanically brewed ginger beer (like ginger ale at home but with much more ginger flavor), and a bowl of tomato basil soup because she knew what she wanted next—a Millionaire Shortbread bar for dessert. She had come across these delectable delights in England some years earlier. A combination of decadent ingredients: a shortbread base, and a layer of gooey salted caramel, topped with a thin layer of unsweetened dark chocolate. The first luscious bite brought back wonderful memories of their adventures in England.

Conversations at meals normally recapped their day, what was coming up, or mundane issues like laundry. Today anything about Malin Head was avoided. At this point in the trip, washing clothes, particularly underclothes, by hand in the hotel sink had become tiresome for most, and burdensome for one procrastinator in particular who hadn't kept up with his wash. He mentioned cotton items would take too long to dry. Anne reminded him he could use the hand-held hair dryer on the wall in any bathroom if the items hadn't completely dried overnight. He whined that he had several pairs to wash that night and she suggested that, for efficiency, when showering he wear all three pairs at one time. Wide-eyed nodding heads agreed with her newly introduced travel philosophy, but Anne never heard if anyone actually tried it.

While others in their group were finishing their delicious lunches, Peter, Anne, and Dave were loitering outside when they came upon a Dulux Decorate Centre, a paint store. Dave had worked his entire life in the industry. He was a marvel at applying paint and phenomenal at combining colors. "Come on, we have to go in," Anne demanded.

Dave easily struck up a conversation with the store manager. Anne picked up some samples because she had convinced herself they needed to transform their new home's front door into a bright eye-catching color the minute they got back. Dave narrowed it down to three choices for Anne and Peter's home, considering the weather, heat, and angle of the sun.

Despite the distraction of the yummy lunch and paint samples, Anne was more than curious about what could be transpiring at Farren's. Especially with her younger Irish cousins. She would stay out of it, just as she would stay out of the situation Mauve and Moyrah had told her about just the night before. Had it only been 24 hours?

Anne texted Mauve.

Have u heard from Wrenna?

No, why?

Have you seen the news?

No, why?

Body found behind Farren's.

by Wrenna?

Me

Oh Anne r u still at the bar?

No, on our way back to the hotel in Derry.

I'm texting W now.

Not far from their hotel, Peter and Anne moseyed along the riverfront toward the Peace Bridge. The River Foyle is clean saltwater not far from the sea. Central to the city, the river is a peaceful spot with wide walkways and fencing, lined with dozens of large overflowing baskets of bright fuchsia, all with minuscule purple daisies and small white flowers. Fuchsia blossoms reminded her of two-tone layered swirling skirts. Anne couldn't resist the temptation to gently squeeze a ruby bud to hear the pop. It was a naughty childhood fixation that her mother didn't particularly appreciate, but it sure was fun, similar to stepping on a puffball from an oak tree. She thought about her mom and dad. And her Irish family. Goodness, the bees were loud, like buzzing filled her head. She shook her head back and forth and noticed even more flowers, ruby with white, tangerine with yellow, pink

157

with blue, scarlet with purple, and many more varieties. She didn't realize there were so many types. Anne typed notes to herself into her phone and took many photos of the more extraordinary fuchsia. She had a few varieties in pots on their patio at home but would now be on the lookout for more unique types in the future.

She heard, "Pssst!" and glanced at Peter who gave her a c'mere look. She moved towards him and saw what he was alerting her to. Seven hummingbirds were sharing one plant. "We've never had seven hummers at our feeders at any one time at home."

But something didn't look quite right to her. "Peter, I don't think they're all hummers." With closer examination, he agreed and searched the bird tri-fold pamphlet. "Anne, get this, a few of them are probably hummingbird hawk-moths sometimes called hummingmoths. Listen, they even make the same humming noise."

Stepping in closer, Anne could see sable with white patches on the side of one's abdomen. The insect clearly didn't care she was eyeing its body. Its forewings were sandy with darker crosslines and hindwings the color of goldfish. They watched it dive head first, deep into a petunia that was scattered among the fuchsia.

The hummingbirds were larger than the moths and a lime green bird with indigo under its wings zipped between two pots. A broad-tailed hummer with its scarlet throat and snowy chest zoomed back the forth. The sun made its top florescent green.

"Look at the rusty one flying upside down. It's a lot like our rufous variety at home." Peter ducked as it whizzed around his head. Anne attempted to get a few photos but nature's winged jewels were too speedy.

People were on the water riding in paddleboats, canoes, and kayaks in a serpentine pattern with mallards, two large cranky white swans, and a territorial graylag goose that didn't want to share his space at all.

As they got closer to the Peace Bridge, the two structural white arms heading in opposite directions from each other grew bigger. They symbolize the coming together of both communities from the opposite sides of the river, the Protestant Waterside and Nationalist Bogside. The bridge stretches from Guildhall, in the city center, to Ebrington Square on the other side. People sat and some reclined on benches and watched the rambling river while many stopped to chat. One young man strummed his guitar. The bridge is over two football fields long and 13 feet wide making plenty of room for its curved footpath, track, and cycleway and all the people with their pets on it.

Anne noticed a woman with two dachshunds, one with creamy white long hair and the second, a wire-haired with its coat of multiple colors. Each dog took multiple steps to her one, their short stubby legs going as fast as they could. The long-haired one obviously had gone far enough, sitting down in the middle of the bridge, stubbornly refusing its person's command, "Come. Come."

Anne was partial to any wiener dog because she and her brothers, Max and Will, grew up having two traditional smooth-haired miniature red doxies, Duke I and Duke II. Anne smiled as she remembered theirs had a propensity for digging and their German Shepherd-sounding loud, deep barks alerted the family to anyone close to the front or back doors.

Reaching Ebrington Square, they intercepted Dave and Sue, and the four wandered around a former military square and barracks that transformed itself into a public space with sitting areas, flowerbeds, coffee carts, ice cream stands, and a space for multipurpose events. There is a statue of a soldier with a rolled tent balanced on his right shoulder with his right hand and a large duffle bag in his left. Scanning across, Anne centered Derry Guildhall between the arms of the Peace Bridge for a memorable photo and added another postcard in her mind.

Back across the grand tribute bridge and meandering around the hotel neighborhood, they came upon an art gallery that was up a flight of stairs. Sue and Anne had to go mainly because the staircase was unusual and amusing, each stair a different color. Starting at the bottom, Anne stepped on stairs of teal, cream, melon, lime, navy, pink, light gray, yellow, charcoal, cantaloupe, cherry, light blueberry, aqua, and purple like grapes, reaching the top to the delightful gallery with handmade jewelry, enamel painted sheep, watercolors, even fridge magnets. Both supported the local economy as best they could by purchasing a small green plaque that read, "A best friend is like a four-leaf clover: hard to find and lucky to have."

Anne read her text from Mauve.

> Girls know the deceased & attended school with him. Don't know much more, they r fine.

> Those poor girls.

> Poor, you, too.

> Ummm, not my first rodeo.

> Not funny, Anne.

> I know, it's not. But what else is there but humor sometimes?

Winding their way back to their hotel, the four friends stepped into the impressive Guildhall, originally named Victoria Hall. Not just a church, it is an exhibition hall featuring informative history of Derry. Along the corridor, they saw superb views of the majestic painted windows next to tall plaques retelling the history of this building and the region. There are displays of old books, and one ancient map shows details of what the region looked like in the past. Not only are the stained glass windows remarkable but there is an impressively large statue of Queen Victoria.

Guildhall has the second largest clock face in the British Isles, second to Big Ben in London. The building is made of Dumfries sandstone, marble oak paneling, ornate ceilings, and incredible stained glass windows. Anne perked up recognizing Dumfries sandstone. She pointed it out to Sue and told her that it was from Scotland, a mere 20 miles from where these sandstone quarries lie close to her ancestors' home in Sanquhar. Sue confided that she felt deep down she had Scottish roots and would be doing a DNA test to confirm her suspicions. "Let's do Scotland together one day!" Sue exclaimed.

"Absolutely, sisterchick," Anne was on cloud nine.

Serving in his official capacity, Detective Sergeant Graham heard the doorbell ring inside the house and footsteps racing to the door. A young lad answered, looked him up and down, and yelled, "Mam, there's a giant guard at the door."

Wiping her hands in a towel, the petite brunette had an apprehensive look on her face.

"Yes?"

"Good evening. Are you Sorcha Kennedy?" Graham asked, even though he recognized her from their school days.

The woman answered, "Sorcha Kennedy O'Sullivan."

"Mrs. O'Sullivan, do you have a brother Seamus?"

"Aye, younger by three years." She let out deep breath. "What's he done now?"

"I attended school with him. I recall both of your parents are deceased." This time he heard her inhale and exhale then release a sad sigh.

"Correct. Excuse my manners, please come in," she said as he followed her and sat down on a cushy gray sofa. "Oh, I remember you from school. I was ahead of you and my brother's class. You were a big rugby player. What is this about?"

This was the most unpleasant part of his job and he hated it. "I am very sorry to tell you but Seamus died this afternoon from a fall behind Farren's Bar at Malin Head."

"Oh, I thought you were going to tell me he'd been murdered or something else."

The toddler who answered the door stuck his head around the corner, and Sorcha scolded, "Brayden, go be with your father and stay put."

"Why would you think he could be murdered?" Graham asked very curious.

"He texted that he needed some money to pay back some hefty debts, money I didn't have nor would have given him if I did. He's always been trouble. My poor parents never understood how he got that way, he's not like them at all. Or me. You know, I can remember when he was born even though I was just three at the time. They treated me like a princess, then when Seamus came along he was treated like a king. The baby and a boy. They spoiled him but they did me, too." Graham didn't interrupt or ask any questions. "But as he grew up, he seemed to think they owed him. He always asked them for money and if they said no, he'd steal it from mam's purse. And they never did anything about it. He felt entitled and for the life of me, I don't know why. He'd be a great study for a psychologist. He's made some dreadful choices and I just assumed one day those choices would catch up with him."

"Currently, we have little reason for suspicion."

"Good, easier that way I suspect. If he fell, was he fluthered? It seems any time I saw him he was. He drinks, well, drank, way too much."

"We haven't gotten tests back yet but he smelled of alcohol."

"He did do some drugs, too, but not around us. That was another reason for needing some money. Sometimes he was so naïve thinking he could make some fast money by doing stupid things."

"Anything specific come to mind?"

"Actually any type of betting at the races. But one time he told me he dropped off an old fishing tackle box, a guy paid him $200 and told him not to open it. I asked him what he thought was in it and he didn't care, just easy money."

"Again, I am sorry for your loss."

"Do I need to go to the morgue or anything?" She sat still but her hands were trembling.

"Aye. Officially, we do need a relative to ID his body even though I already have."

"I can do that tomorrow. Tell me, does he appear horrible? I can't see him if his head is bashed in. I'd have to send my husband," her voice wobbly.

Graham could sense the news was sinking in. Her only sibling was dead.

Gently he replied, "No, actually he looks okay except for a broken nose. He hit the back of his head on a large stone on the side of the hill that probably stopped his falling quite a ways. But you can send your husband if you prefer."

"I'll decide tomorrow, if that's okay." She brushed a tear off her cheek.

"Sure. A funeral director can help with arrangements. If we have any more questions about his past or need any statement from you beyond what you told me, could you come to the station?"

"A funeral. Right. I don't really know any more than I told you. I haven't seen him in probably a year. He did drop off an X-box for my Brayden, for his third birthday. Who gets a wee lad an expensive, over-the-top gift like that? I must admit, my husband enjoys it though. Gosh, it's just me now with both dad and mam gone and now Seamus. I feel like an orphan." She started to cry.

Graham pulled a cotton handkerchief from his pocket. "I'm very sorry," he said, handing it to her. He bought them by the dozens and always carried a few along.

Sorcha's husband had been standing out of view in the kitchen and arrived at just the right time to surround his wife in his arms. He reached for Graham's contact information printed on a business card. The young lad opened the door letting the guard walk sadly into the night.

As Graham finished his time with Sorcha, everyone in Anne's party planned to go across the street to the Exchange Restaurant. Peter suggested staying in and Anne gladly agreed.

We're doing room service. C u tomorrow.

164

Totally understand. Hope U can get some sleep.

Sue replied to Anne, adding three purple heart emojis and a mossy four-leaf clover.

"What do you feel like having?" Peter read the menu from Thompsons Restaurant in the hotel.

"Comfort food. Do they have mac and cheese?"

"Sorry, not on the menu."

"Could you share the burger with me?"

"Sure. Chips or onion rings?"

"Both and ask for tartar sauce, please."

"Got it."

"Oh and check for dessert. You know what."

"No Sticky Toffee Pudding. How about chocolate crème brûlée with Chantilly cream, shortbread biscuit, and strawberry jam?"

"Story of my life... I *suppose* that will have to do." He felt relieved to see her smile.

Peter turned on the TV just in time to catch an inspector named Murdock in the middle of an evening press conference with a female news reporter.

"The rock stopped his fall and was most likely the cause of his cracked skull. Some of the wounds could be from the vegetation. He had head and facial injuries," the official stated with no inflection in his voice.

"Any idea how long the man has been dead?" a woman shifted back and forth from one foot to the other. Her nasally voice grated on Anne nerves. Plus that, she needed her dark roots touched up to match the rest of her bleached blonde hair. Anne was not in a particularly great mood.

"That's one for the pathologist. Formal identification will have to wait before we can release any more details."

Inspector Murdock abruptly turned and walked away before the reporter could ask another question.

———————

Wrenna chuckled as she read her cousin's text,

> I'm done with men.

Fay added a frowny emoji. She sat in her comfy chair crying her eyes out. She didn't know exactly why. Either the Seamus episode or her decisions picking the wrong men.

———————

Anne soaked in the bathtub while they waited for room service, trying to guess what might be going on in Malin Head. Wearing a hotel bathrobe, 20 minutes later as she dipped a second onion ring in the tartar sauce, her thoughts were miles away.

"Penny for your thoughts," Peter's words mushed while eating fries.

"Maybe a silver dollar, and even then probably not. The cousins shared some family issues with me last night. They've got some decisions to make. Or not."

"Anything you can do to help?"

"Not likely. I suspect they just wanted somebody else to know and I seem safe enough almost 5,000 miles away."

"And then there's today." She appreciated his sympathy.

"And then there's today." Her tone sounded somewhat dejected to her husband.

"Contacted your brothers and Peggy yet?"

"I am going to text Peggy in a bit. She won't believe it. Well, maybe she will. After growing up camping together at the Metolius, then when she and her husband Rich were on the Alaska cruise and the Mendenhall Glacier incident, she'll believe it. I think I'll wait to let Max and Will know. Not like they can do anything, and I certainly don't want Mom knowing and worrying about me. They all have enough to deal with right now."

"Don't forget Clay," Peter added. "He'll want to know. Fortunately, we don't need any assistance in this one."

"Well, we never have needed his or Will's help on any of these foreign episodes. I might delay emailing Clay until we're home. Last I heard the family is doing more traveling abroad since he retired... again. This time he's really done with law enforcement."

"Or so he says. I can see him volunteering or as a consultant as long as he can breathe," her husband added.

"Very true," Anne remembering him decades earlier at the Metolius River incident, and then their fortuitous encounter in Juneau decades later when Anne came upon a body on the glacier.

Daylight vanished and on their final evening in Derry, the Peace Bridge shone brightly, bathed in soft lights. To the right stood the darkened Guildhall, except for the clock and tower, both awash in pale light.

Peter, normally the sound sleeper of the two, noticed his wife tossing and turning most of the night. Was it from the onion rings, the body incident, or her Irish family's woes?

CHAPTER EIGHTEEN

Mickey swore when he awoke to read Eamon's text. *It's 5 a.m.,* he said to himself.

> **What did u do?**

> about what?

> **Seamus, you eejit!**

> What r u talking about?

> **He's dead.**

> No way. he was fine when I left. how do u know this?

> **Inside source and he's dead. u better hope it's not traced to u or me.**

> Won't b. no writing or plates on the van.

Mickey, normally sure of himself, lay in bed trembling.

That morning Anne woke before her phone alarm buzzed. They'd be getting an earlier start than usual for a full day of touring. Peter was still asleep and she didn't want to disturb him but thoughts niggled her brain to full consciousness. She glanced at the clock, 5:16. She patiently waited until 6:30.

"I'll turn on the morning news to see if there is anything from Malin Head." Peter closed the drawer after taking out a lightweight sweater.

"Fine, but I can't watch it. I'm on a need-to-know-only basis. You tell me if it's necessary."

"Got it."

It was a little hard not to hear the same female reporter with the grating voice, "I'm with Inspector Thomas Murdock on the discovery of a body by an American tourist. People are wondering whether the region's first murder in living memory has meant that life there has altered forever."

"This area is open-minded, there's always an ebb and flow of new people coming in. I think anywhere near the water keeps you fresh. You can't become stagnant where there's an ocean outside your door," the inspector gazed contemplatively at the water.

The reporter peered quizzically at the philosophical inspector now a nature lover. "Em, okay... there are all kinds of rumors swirling around."

"The local people grew up with the local legends and myths and lore. There are lots of standing stones and stone circles. Copious mythology..." Murdock seemed deep in thought.

The reporter butted in while pensive Murdock took a breath, "I think people are desperate to find a safe, quiet place to live."

"Aye, including lots of sets of blow-ins. Mostly the artist community, some yachties, hippies, and dope smokers." He looked directly at the reporter.

"Inspector, back to the death at Malin Head."

"We have a very determined team on this."

"An experienced team?"

"Enough said."

"Thank you, Inspector Murdock." The reporter uttered her words sarcastically. "I will keep pushing for answers and keep you informed," she said, glaring directly into the camera, defiant cat green eyes flashing hostility. "I'm Meegan Hennessy reporting LIVE and will be back with any late-breaking reports. Inspector, when will you release the name of the victim?"

"Soon."

Murdock sat in Doyle's office with Graham in attendance. "I am returning to Dublin but am available when you need further assistance. You've got some ground work to do but I suspect we will be involved soon enough."

Peter read a short article in the local newspaper about the incident one day later.

The body of a man was discovered Wednesday morning down an embankment behind Farren's Bar in Malin Head. Identification will be announced once the next of kin have been notified. A guard cordon remains in place while forensic examinations are carried out as part of the investigation.

"An investigation remains underway in the area and guards are in the early stages of establishing exactly what happened," Detective Sergeant Morgan Graham stated.

Peter handed the newspaper to Anne.

After a final full Irish breakfast, they checked out of the hotel, loaded the bus, and headed south. Stopping for road construction, passing through four unadorned roundabouts, more minor construction, another roundabout with flags of different counties, and circling another seven roundabouts with a few hearty vibrant red poppies sprouting from rocks and gravel. Anne exclaimed, "I'm glad I don't get car sick like I did as a child."

Sue sat next to Anne on the bus. "Well, what have you heard?"

"Really not much to go on. Sounds like they could use some help."

"Anne, you are not suggesting that you get involved in a criminal investigation, are you?"

"Well, you can't possibly expect me to just sit idly by and do nothing. I encountered him. I have an obligation." Anne feigned a serious facial expression.

"Is that how you felt about the many bodies you've stumbled upon over the years?"

"Many is an exaggeration, Dave," Anne snipped.

Sue turned to Peter across the aisle, "Are you really going to let Anne attempt to solve a murder?"

"She's a capable woman." Peter teased Sue who was truly concerned about her BFF's involvement. "Besides, we know that she is incapable of sitting on the sidelines."

"So true. I bet that you already have a working theory." Sue turned toward Anne.

"I don't." Actually, she really did. However, she would stay on the sidelines.

April announced that although they were ahead of schedule, the Manor House telephoned saying they were behind due to a team of tournament golfers running later than expected. She and Bill hatched a plan that she hoped the group would love. "It's a really fascinating place that we don't get to explore much because of scheduling. We're taking you to Marble Arch Caves."

"Did she say caves?" Peter turned to his wife.

"She did."

They pulled into Marble Arch Caves, set in the foothills of Cuilcagh Mountain, subterranean caves formed over 340 million years ago and not far from the town of Enniskillen, where they'd be spending the night.

Peter's face drained of color. "It's okay." Anne patted his knee. "I'm not going down there either." Dave overheard Anne's comments and remembered why Peter wasn't going anywhere near caverns underground. He leaned across the aisle to Chris and Bruce, "Peter had a traumatic experience some years ago with caving in England. You'll have to ask him to tell you about it."

Neither Dave, Sue, Chris, Jeanine, or Bruce had any desire to go through caves, sinkholes, or anything subterranean ever, so they joined Peter and Anne for a drink at the Marble Arch Café. "You might need something more potent than tea." Anne felt for Peter recalling how he appeared when he had emerged from the caving fiasco.

"Well, start talking you two. Something about England."

"This is Peter's story, he can tell you."

"But you do the preliminary story, while I fortify with strong tea." Anne could tell he found it somewhat more humorous than years earlier.

"Here's your cup, sir." A perky server placed the steamy drink in front of him.

"I'll try to do the *Readers Digest* condensed version."

"Since when do you do anything condensed?"

"Shush. Okay, short or long version?"

"Long. We need details and have plenty of time." Jeanine took a long drink of a lemonade.

"Before our first trip to Ireland, we flew in a week early to see our friends, Howard and Pearl. They lived not far from Oxford and we'd get to their house after visiting the southern region first. After 15 hours of travel plus gaining a day, enduring customs, luggage pickup, and shuttling to a rental car lot, we climbed in a medium-sized manual transmission rental car. We drove 270 miles south on the opposite side..."

"Wait, wait, wait," Peter interrupted, "there's more to the car story. It was a cute little number; however, it wasn't just the driving on the opposite side of the road. The steering wheel was on the other side which means the manual gear shift was on my left and I'm not left-handed. As I recall, even the shift pattern was the opposite. A triple whammy and not an easy transition."

"After no sleep for over 15 hours?" Bruce shook his head, a bit surprised at his Type A friend, Peter.

"Not our brightest decision."

"Anyway," Anne continued, "we're driving south on the motorway, like a six-lane freeway at home, around and around the roundabouts. I had pages with the printed MapQuest directions.

"Cornwall would be our final destination as Part One of our adventure. We had been fascinated by the area since watching a 1970s British drama series shown on Masterpiece Theater on PBS. *Poldark*, the name of the series and main character, depicted the difficult tin and copper mine industry during the late 1700s.

"Sometimes the roadway narrowed, usually not much wider than one car width with no shoulder, nor were there lines painted in the middle or sides. Since there weren't signs indicating a suggested speed limit, Peter dillydallied through the back roads slower than I would have preferred.

"I had done research in finding accommodations on the water and came across the Don & Shirley Pengilly Bed & Breakfast, boasting beautiful sea views over St. Michael's Mount. The address sounded as charming as I imagined the lodging would be: Castle Nook, Turnpike Road, Marazion, Cornwall, population 1,208. The Pengilly's children had grown and they converted one bedroom and added a tiny bathroom for rent.

"Shirley welcomed us in a charming Cornish accent. She escorted us to a room that had a double bed, dresser, and a chair and as promised, a view of St. Michael's Mount, surrounded by water looking like an island.

"She invited us to sit in the dining room where she presented hot tea in floral china cups with a pitcher of cream and cubes of sugar in a matching oval bowl. Usually they had scones for their late-morning break but she had observed that Americans enjoy them anytime. She suggested we try her homemade preserves from their garden berries. She placed a small bowl of something puffy and white and Peter asked if it was whipped butter.

"'Clotted cream,'" I answered. Anything with the word "cream" sounds delicious to him. Spooning the thick cream onto the halved scone with a spoonful of strawberry preserves, Peter's first bite resulted in repeated sounds of umms in appreciation of faux American strawberry short-cake. This tasted hundreds of times better. Slightly embarrassed, I asked her what exactly clotted cream was. She told us clotted cream is a slowly thickened cream that is neither airy nor sweet.

"I told her that our whipped cream is as light as a cloud and bright white, and sweet. She had tasted our whipped cream which was much too sweet for her and noted that theirs is thick enough to spread and tastes more like milk.

"Peter told me we needed to find this cream at home. He had all sorts of ideas for it—on pancakes, waffles, muffins, biscuits, breads, and my pumpkin bread. Then he suggested maybe I could learn to make it like Shirley does."

"And my dear wife glared at me then as she is right now." He grinned at the memory.

Anne proceeded with the story. "The next morning Shirley told us we should begin our day by going over to the Mount with the tide being low. So, the Mount isn't an island after all. Stones create an elevated walkway across the sand with the water parted on both sides. She told us to be mindful of the incoming tide or we'd be wading back waist-high in water.

"Royal visits to the island have been captured in time by casting the actual footprints of visiting kings and queens. We saw the bronze casts of Queen Victoria, Queen Elizabeth, and Prince Charles, set among the harbor cobblestones. It rises from the waters of Mount's Bay and perched on top is an embattled castle, originally a Benedictine Priory built in the twelfth century. From 1660 until the present, it has been the home of the St. Aubyn family.

"It was an easy stroll across and up to the castle. Inside we were able to wander through the living quarters of the Captain of the Mount. A private sitting room with over-stuffed chairs and polished tables and The Armory contained sporting weapons and military trophies from various wars. The Library, formerly the family's breakfast room, is the oldest part of the castle. There were more smaller rooms, secret dark passages that I made clear I wasn't treading down, and a small cheery church with stained glass windows.

"From the North Terrace, there are views of Marazion and the beaches. The South Terrace has a small walled garden containing subtropical plants not often seen in England. I remember the palm trees, too. At first, I thought it was jet lag, I mean who expects to see palm trees in England?

"Then just as Shirley warned us, the tide came in and we watched the brave (or stupid) people on the walkway knee-high in seawater. We took the boat taxi back and meandered around the small town lined with palm trees, orchids, stone buildings, and colorful doors with tourists in shorts and tee-shirts enjoying the coast."

Peter stood and stretched saying, "That afternoon we trekked to Penzance on Mount's Bay, the most westerly town in Cornwall, and stopped at Merry Maidens, a Bronze Age stone circle where 19 girls turned into stone for dancing on a Sunday. Down the road, we reached Minack Theatre, an ancient Greek-style theater. Below on the beach, we saw sunbathers, surfers trying with little wave-action, and palm trees. Palms grow here due to the warming influence of the Gulf Stream with waters from the tropics. The coastline turned out to be as rugged, just like we'd seen in *Poldark*. We nosed around an old tin mine."

"Standing at a sign, Land's End, we gazed at the seafoam water below dotted with islands. It was sooooo stunning," Anne interjected. "After dinner, we stayed up long enough to see a vibrant mosaic of fiery oranges and purples reflected on the bay."

She continued, "The next morning we stayed off the scary motorway and four hours later, we arrived in Winchester where we lucked into the Best Western Royal Hotel. We figured it only appropriate to see Winchester Cathedral, stunning but probably made more popular by the Beatles song. We stopped at the marble stone in the cathedral where Jane Austen lies beneath. I read the entire tribute and told Peter that it was lovely but it didn't mention what she's famous for, her writing. Peter was probably correct saying maybe that's because she wrote anonymously in life. Jane's headstone had more fresh flowers than all the other memorials.

Anne rambled on, "At three o'clock we arrived at the home of Pearl and Howard who lived in Abingdon, a small town not far from Oxford, where Pearl worked at Mansfield College at Oxford University. She and I met through our mutual work when Pearl's college had hosted my Willamette University College of Law alumni travel groups for several years."

"So this is all before the caves, right?" Chris swallowed some coffee after a bite of pastry.

"Yep." Peter was still sipping tea. "She's doing a lead-up to the big event."

"We got up the next morning because they were taking us on a road trip. We saw the ritzy Somerset district on the way to our overnight accommodations. We were stunned as they drove through the gates into Banwell Castle and checked in at the hotel. The Gothic revival castle, built in the late 1800s, sits on 21 acres of grounds and gardens and is furnished in a Victorian style. They booked us into the Master Suite with a four-poster bed with a canopy. Oversize wooden doors opened onto a veranda overlooking the gardens.

"We sat outside in the sunshine watching chickens, turkeys, and peacocks roaming the gardens with an occasional romping red squirrel, and lots of birds entertaining us while sipping tea, eating crustless sandwiches, and devouring sweet cakes and pastries."

"Don't you love how she tells a story? I feel like I'm right there with her," Jeanine cut in.

Anne gave Jeanine a grateful smile as she'd been told by others, like her brothers and sometimes her husband, she tended to be a bit wordy. "That afternoon we drove to the Wookey Hole Showcaves and Papermill where we saw how paper had been carefully created during Shakespeare's day. Putting on helmets, we trekked into the Great Caves, famous since the Roman times. The Cathedral Cave is brought to life by an atmospheric light and sound show.

"Peter stood by a full-size Roman warrior in complete uniform of gold and scarlet. Evidently, 2,600 years ago the Celts were farmers who lived in or near the entrance to Wookey Hole Caves for over 600 years.

"The stalactites and stalagmites were formed over extremely long periods as water slowly dripped from the roof of the caves. One single column reached all the way from the ceiling to the floor of the cave."

"*Dr. Who* had used this as a film set." Peter jumped in when Anne took a breath.

"Dinner reservations had been made by Howard, and that evening at the castle we were the only ones there except for a group having a birthday party for one of the adults in the family. They were eating and drinking and having a very merry time.

"We had a delicious dinner in a 'dimly lit' dining room. Dimly lit is important here. About the time we were finished with dessert, I picked up my purse and placed it on my lap because I thought we were leaving. One of the men in the party group came over to apologize for their noisy frivolity and offered each of us an after-dinner drink of brandy. A large glass, much larger than a wine glass, with about a half-inch of mahogany liquid appeared, and I was instructed only to sip it. This would be my first (and last) sip of brandy.

"I sniffed it first which caused my eyes to water and I sneezed really hard. Everyone laughed except me because I thought a contact lens from my right eye popped out. I wore hard contacts, and although rare, it could happen. Before I overreacted, I carefully ran my hands over my blouse hoping to catch it there. I hesitantly informed the other three what I guessed had happened and before I knew it, we were each on all fours gently touching the carpet under the table where it was dark. Very dark."

"Yuck. Carpet in a restaurant?" Sue rubbed her fingers together imagining what could be in or on a restaurant's dining room carpet.

"Exactly. I darted to the restroom thinking maybe it had slipped down into the lower lid. Those who have ever worn hard contact lenses would know exactly what I mean. In the dimly lit restroom, I couldn't see a thing. I returned knowing I'd just have to see out of my left eye or wear my pop-bottle thick glasses for the upcoming three weeks. I alerted the dining room staff of my predicament.

"When we returned to our suite, I poked around my poor eyeball looking underneath my upper eyelid, down in the white part at the bottom of my eye, all in a dimly lit bathroom with a 40-watt bulb. The entire place was dimly lit. I used our mini-Maglite, holding a flashlight in one hand while trying to pull down my eyelid with the other hand. My eye hurt like heck. Giving up, I tried to sleep and not obsess about it. In over 20 years of wearing contact lenses, I'd never, ever lost one. And I didn't have an extra pair with us because they were expensive. No more thinking about my lost contact, I'd just deal with it. But it still hurt.

"The next morning while enjoying a delicious breakfast, the staff reported that they carefully had cleaned up and did not find my lens. The breakfast at Banwell was fit for a queen and king with steamy tea, biscuits, egg and meat options, assorted fruit and juices, delivered on fine China with coordinating placemats in a lapis and white design."

"Ready? You're coming up soon." Peter nodded.

"So, Howard told Peter he'd set up an adventure and we were heading there next. In a short time, we arrived at Cheddar and the home of Cheddar Showcaves & Gorge. Some say it is the origin of Cheddar cheese. Poor Peter had no clue what was about to happen to him, and that would scar him for the rest of his life."

Peter began with his rendition, "Howard had booked a caving expedition for us without consulting me. Normally this would have been about the last thing I would ever do. I'm not fond of close quarters and darkness. Howard thought it sounded like great fun.

"While waiting for our check-in time, we had a few minutes for a cold beverage sitting outside at a café. Howard had a headache and asked Anne if she had any tablets; we say pills. Anne had a few generic brick-colored ibuprofen pills in her small makeup bag in her purse and saw three loose ones that had sunk to the bottom of the small clear clutch. This part is better from you, Anne."

Anne went on saying, "One pill appeared weird, being a strange color. I nabbed it gently, pulled it out, and there, adhered like glue to the rusty-colored pill, was my blue contact lens. When it popped out of my eye the night before it dropped into my purse that I had placed on my lap. Safe and sound. We were all astonished as Howard blurted out, 'Well, you certainly live the *Life of Riley*.' Then I had to tell him my maiden name is Riley."

Peter started again, "So we disappeared, getting ready for the expedition. Of course, I didn't know what I was in for, so I had dressed in khakis and a polo shirt that I'd also be wearing for the next couple of weeks."

Anne interjected, "So Pearl and I on the other hand were far more interested in the glassmaking demonstration, crafts and engravings, and spending some money. We were to meet our husbands at a designated time and place a few hours later. We knew our time had come to an end so we waited at the exit area of the cave experience. Out staggered Peter as pale as I've ever seen him, clothes filthy even though they had coveralls on. Poor guy, unsteady on his feet. Then we heard the entire story. To this day, when Peter repeats the harrowing adventure, it's as if no time has passed."

The story bounced back to Peter, "Ya, well, The Timeless Cheddar Cave brochure was full of information I read while waiting, like what was provided, a helmet, lamp and coveralls and small groups are taken into these areas by an expert caver. What I didn't read was we would ascend then descend into three chambers on our hands and knees, slink through body-hugging drippy walls using only the small helmet light to illuminate directly ahead of us, then down a flimsy 40-foot rope ladder before crawling the fourth chamber. We all stopped after climbing up the side of a wall, and the only thing I heard was people sucking in air and the drip, drip, drip from stalactites. The air was thick with humidity and hard to breathe. It felt like an eternity in darkness. I did wonder more than once what would happen if any poor soul had a medical emergency underground.

"The brochure mentioned the words 'total darkness.' I couldn't even see my hand in front of my face. Nobody exiting smiled the way they were shown in the color promo-tional materials." Peter sighed and drank the last of the tea.

"Before bed, Peter, never a pill-taker, took some ibuprofen just in case. Pearl washed his clothes three times then we threw them away when the Cheddar cave dirt didn't come out. It was not a souvenir he wished to keep," Anne added.

Sue noticed Anne's face change when she mentioned Pearl. "You miss Pearl, don't you?"

"I do. Sometimes I can hardly believe she is really gone. I

knew she was deteriorating with random health issues along with Alzheimer's, but to go at 71, that was a tough one. She was such a kind soul. I'm blessed that we had many delightful adventures together and the times they would come and stay with us usually over winter holidays are precious memories now." Sue wrapped her arms around her melancholy sisterchick.

Their England and Peter's spelunking saga concluded as a portion of their group surfaced from their tame caving experience.

Graham heard his cell phone indicating a text. It was from Devlin.

> I'm in his phone. U were right, he used his birthday. And u r going to want to c what I am reading.

> Copy that. b there shortly.

A short distance later they arrived at their accommodations. They were eager to get there because it was a manor house and was highly regarded, plus full of history. The Manor House in Enniskillen is a nineteenth century estate located on a secluded lake in the westernmost part of Northern Ireland.

Anne giggled like a little girl when seeing The Manor House. "Now this is a WOW property," she heard behind them. Matching granite lions on the right and left greeted them as they marched up the wide staircase to the entrance.

The outside was stunningly elegant with its well-manicured lawn, though not quite Downton Abbey but close. Their large suite faced a multi-tiered fountain. Lounging rooms were extravagantly decorated, yet comfortable and welcoming.

Anne turned on the TV, hoping to catch some news about the mystery of the body incident. Inspector Murdock had contacted Sergeant Doyle, instructing him to talk to the media, sharing only the victim's name and not much more. He was talking to Meegan Hennessy, the same female reporter.

"The deceased is Seamus Jamie Kennedy, age 26, of Derry. Our investigation is progressing steadily. We set up an incident room with a team assembled to work this investigation. Everything is being studied and documented."

"It's her again, Peter. That obnoxious reporter," Anne said loudly so Peter could hear in the bathroom.

"What type of evidence have you rooted out, Sergeant?" The reporter poked the mic in his officer's face.

"That's confidential."

"Why all this for a man who could have just fallen off the edge of the bank?" she probed.

"It is unlikely he fell on his own accord."

"Why do you think that?" she questioned.

"Intuition."

"Facts?"

"That's a given. I try to keep my eyes riveted on the facts." His eyes were actually set directly on the gorgeous reporter. He wondered why others thought she was bothersome. Afterall, she was just doing her job. Just as the guards were doing their job; being vague.

"No first impressions? No forensic insights?" She pushed further.

"That's confidential." Gorgeous or not, the interview was getting tedious and he wanted it over. He contemplated asking for her phone number but thought best not to, at this time anyway.

"Are you stalling? What are you not telling the public?"

Doyle was miffed now. "No, you're right, there is one more thing."

"Oh good."

"It's because of people like you, television shows, and two-hour movies that everyone thinks forensic technicians are magicians. Do you know that it takes at least ten hours to properly document, identify, and collect evidence from a crime scene? And this isn't the only case overworked techs are working on."

She shook her head back and forth.

"No? Not a surprise. It takes three or four times that when we're working outside. Do you know the difference... do you have any idea what a crime scene technician actually does?"

Not wanting to show her ineptitude, she deflected, "Sergeant Doyle, you know, locals are talking."

"Small town. Big gossip. This isn't a TV program where conclusions are decided in one hour."

"Whoa-whoa-whoa, that's all you have on day two?"

"I will contact you when we know anything more."

"Thank you for a riveting interview." He'd already turned away, completely missing her sardonic remark. Dropping her voice to a whisper, she addressed the camera directly, as if speaking to a confidant. "The only guard who would speak to me, albeit anonymously, confided they would be pulling out all the stops on this investigation. However, he admitted they have had no experience with a crime of this caliber nor of any serious crimes at this level. Most of the injuries or deaths in this area involve the sea. Reporting, I'm Meegan Hennessey, with more updates to follow."

———

The Watergate Bar at the Manor House was decorated in dark warm woods, soft lighting, and well-worn wing-backed chairs along with a sofa that, when Anne sat down, she sank so low she feared she might need assistance getting up. A young man approached them. "Cheers. What can I get for you?" A round of smooth Bailey's Irish Cream over ice appeared five minutes later, courtesy of Nancy.

They had dinner in the Belleek Restaurant starting with vegetable soup and a melon plate. Anne selected Atlantic prawns, while Peter had the stuffed loin of pork as their entrees. A scoop of custard the size of a tennis ball with a round flat piece of monogrammed chocolate with a snowy M on the top with a side of berry compote and a spoonful of unsweetened whipped cream was the perfect end to a delicious dinner.

After dinner, they wandered around the palatial house seeing marble columns, a grand ballroom, the stately drawing room and massive sparkly chandeliers, Cellar Bar and Restaurant, floor-to-ceiling windows, alcoves with statues, and fresh floral arrangements in antique vases, all darn impressive. Down one corridor seeing two extra-large chairs, fit for a king and queen, each took turns sitting in and taking photos of each other. A glass of wine might have had something to do with their giddiness along with being unaccustomed to such opulent surroundings.

While Peter was sleeping, Anne couldn't. She texted Mauve who now was well aware of what had transpired having heard from Wrenna that afternoon.

Anything new as far as the body incident?

Hit his head on a rock that killed him. under investigation.

Why? didn't he just fall?

Don't know.

Anne couldn't sleep. She thought about the look in Fay's stern eyes at the bar when Wrenna whispered, "Family first." It was dark enough for her but *probably* too quiet she thought, peeking at the glaring two-inch numbers on the clock, reading 2:45 in the morning. She sent a quick email to her brother, Will, asking how he thought their mother was doing, as well as how he was, too. She finally fell asleep while waiting for his reply.

In her dream, someone played an accordion, and another person a violin, or maybe it was a banjo. A stranger moved around the room jostling and bumping into people, muttering questions. He approached Anne in a threatening voice, "I just wouldn't wanna see you getting hurt or anything. Will you just leave it alone? This death was an accident, nothing mysterious." She woke up and pulled the covers over her head.

CHAPTER NINETEEN

Anne read a brief email response from Will that they were all doing the best they could, their mom was holding up, and he was grateful for the busy work of the memorial service that would be held two weeks after Anne and Peter returned. Anne's heart ached. She missed her dad and felt guilty she wasn't there with her mom. She had moved in with her mom two weeks before her dad passed, driving her back and forth a couple of times a day, cooking, just being there with her, alternating overnight stays with her dad, switching off with her brothers.

The tour group had breakfast in an elegant room surrounded on three sides by windows overlooking the immaculate grounds. Breakfast consisted of a full Irish breakfast and a variety of pastries. At each place setting were three butter patties delicately creating a flower pattern.

Stepping carefully on the fishing dock, they noticed several expensive boats tied up along the pier of the pristine lake. Sheep were grazing on the hillside across the way. Peter could have stayed several days, especially with WIFI and a fly fishing pole.

Chirp. Chirp. Anne couldn't help but peek at her phone. She read a lengthy text from Mauve about Wrenna.

> She told me she had dated the dead man a few times and was going to break it off the day he died. But Fay was dating him longer, like 6 months, and smitten. Neither knew the other was dating such a gombeen.

> Gobsmacked! Do the guards know this?

> Don't know.

> Do you think they will find out?

> Yes.

Departing under a canopy of cushy tree limbs that brushed the top of the motorcoach, April provided verbal enlightenment and musical entertainment on the bus ride. Anne wiped tears away from her misty eyes thinking about her dad and gazing at the rolling hills. When the famous traditional song "Danny Boy" by The Irish Tenors played, she used up six tissues.

They drove around hillsides blanketed in colors they'd seen a lot of already: green of grasslands, beige from tracts of reaped grains, and blue and yellow meadows of oil crops. Then through a village where a grandmother was pushing a tram down the sidewalk with a golden retriever prancing perfectly in step, passing one home displaying a Canadian maple leaf flag along with the Northern Ireland flag, seeing spired churches, ancient cemeteries, tall white wind turbines, fishing ponds, and zigzagging streams.

Inspector Murdock sent the coroner's preliminary autopsy report to Sergeants Doyle and Graham.

Name & age: Seamus Jamie Kennedy. Age 26.

Time of death: Between 10:20 and 10:50 a.m.

Cause of death: Head injury by blunt force trauma due to hitting a rock.

Alcohol and possibly drugs likely contributed to the fall. Some preliminary tests are showing a type of poison.

Note: This could go either way, accidental or not. Toxicology report due in three days.

Murdock called Graham. "Any idea why he'd have poison in his system or how it got there?"

"The guy in the unmarked van in the parking lot gave him two beers."

"We need to talk to that guy. Find him."

"And the victim was in serious debt according to what I've read on his phone texts," Graham added.

"Possibility of suicide now. Hmm. Very complex. Get those beer bottles tested, too." Murdock ended the call without saying goodbye.

Wrenna opened the door and saw Graham standing there. "So soon?" she thought to herself as they'd just had their first date the night before. He viewed her seriously, "I need you to come down to the station for an official interview."

"What? Why? What's wrong?"

"I can't go into that here. Please come with me."

Graham held the door open as Wrenna stepped into the garda station. Her saucer-size eyes locked with her cousin who was exiting an interview room. No one noticed each had slightly raised clenched fists.

Chirp. Anne read,

> Phone records indicate a history of calls guards r checking into.

Why is that important?

> With Wrenna and Fay, much more from Fay. Interviewed for 3 hours about her relationship with Seamus. Wrenna's time was shorter. They r searching for a man named Mickey who the girls never heard of.

Oh my.

Anne was glad for a diversion from the Malin Head saga strolling the square and was elated for a designated shopping time; retail therapy was overdue. Donegal sits on a charming harbor with a spotless beach, and stone ruins including its own castle, abbey, churches, railway, heritage center, gift and specialty shops.

She would have been having lunch with the cousins; however, since Anne had spent time earlier with Mauve in Dublin, and then Moyrah in Derry, things changed. Boy, had things changed. But now she had time to shop until she dropped.

Along the trip, Anne and Peter had been watching for

some type of artwork to take home as a memento that would always remind them of the special time with Dave and Sue, Chris and Jeanine, Greg and Linda, and Bruce and Nancy. Something depicting Anne's roots. She surmised her family had sheep and worked hard on a farm. So, it seemed meant to be when they noticed at Triona, the Donegal Tweed Visitor Center, two eight-foot-long woolen runners about one foot wide that she could hang together on a decorative ladder propped against their bedroom wall.

They observed how wool is woven on a large loom. Each square of material was knitted in a different color in a herringbone weave—teal, jade, olive, berry, pastel pink, and finally purple, the color of heather. Each has flecks of cream and white in the yarn, softening the colors to a muted hue. A clerk offered to ship them along with three open-weave scarves Anne purchased for her mother, a sister-in-law, and herself, thus preventing additional bulk in her already stuffed suitcase. It was getting heavier by the day.

Reporter Meegan Hennessy read the press release she pulled from the fax machine. "Seamus Jamie Kennedy, age 26 of Derry deceased. Guards noted that the autopsy report will not be made final until a toxicology report has been completed. Cause of death likely head injury by blunt force trauma."

CHAPTER TWENTY

The following morning they set out for Connemara, yet another day through stunning farmland and tall timbers before stopping at Cong and another very old Celtic cemetery. Some motion or a sound captured Peter's attention. He heard a high-pitched, sharp kek-kek-kek and watched a bird with slate-gray on its back and carroty striped underparts, broad wings with a long tail, hover, then dive down and snatch a small rodent or bird from the ground, undoubtedly a meal for the raptor's youngsters. As it ascended, Peter could see its bright yellow eyes. He had always enjoyed bird watching and knew it was some sort of bird of prey. The pocket guide revealed a sparrowhawk.

Anne stood overlooking a perfect river curving through grassy banks jam-packed with shrubs and trees and a well-worn red boat just waiting for someone to use it for fishing. She recognized a merganser. They had this breed at home, too, with its cinnamon-colored head, long, narrow rosy hooked bill, and blue-gray body, being followed closely by her mahogany and ivory ducklings in a disorganized row.

Two had a free ride on momma's back and the other five paddled as fast as they could.

With wide open range where cattle and sheep roamed without fences sharing pale green rye grass, they stopped at Abhainn Oirimh in Gaelic or Errif River, where a low two-step waterfall had what appeared to be root beer water flowing over it, not the sparkling blue they'd seen elsewhere. Workers were harvesting peat, also known as turf, not far away. The dark peat influenced the color of the river like glacial melt did in the Alaskan rivers.

April explained peat has been an invaluable source of heat and energy throughout Irish history. It is an accumulation of partially decayed vegetation called peatlands, bogs, mires, moors, or muskegs. Peat moss is the most common compo-nent in peat, although many other plants can contribute. Peat is harvested as an important source of fuel in certain parts of the world and has been harvested for centuries by a method known as "cutting."

It was found to be an alternative to firewood for cooking and heating throughout Ireland and other parts of the European continent. She showed them historical photos of men and women with flat-blade shovels. Peat is thick, muddy and when cut, looks like dark earthen bricks. These sods were stacked on one another in a formation that allowed the dry summer air to pass through. After drying for a week or two the bricks were carried from the bog in baskets or nets. To save labor, donkeys and small horses were used to carry the turf back to the farm where they were stored in a shed to keep them from getting wet. The fuel creates a thick smoke.

They drove by house after house that used thatch instead of shingles on their roofs. One white home had a bright scarlet front door with matching window trim, flower boxes with the same color geraniums, and a neatly trimmed thatched roof.

While in County Sligo they stopped at Drumcliffe—Yeats country! They visited the protestant church where William Butler Yeats likely would have attended. A sacred place, they spoke in whispers. He had been a pillar of the Irish literary establishment and was not only a famous poet, he helped start a theater and also served as a senator of the Irish Free State. They came across his gravesite in another quaint churchyard. On the flowerless, plain square stone read the words: "Cast a cold Eye On Life, on Death, Horseman pass by W.B. Yeats."

Once again, well-worn from centuries of weather, Celtic crosses of various shapes and sizes stood reverently at the head of plots. Dainty wildflowers lent colors to brighten the grayness of the stone monuments representing hundreds of years of families.

That afternoon on the highway navigating an artfully adorned roundabout with circles of bright fuchsia pink begonias and watermelon-red chrysanthemums, they arrived in Galway, a city of around 50,000 people.

Peter and Anne recalled their first visit 20 years earlier. Some in their group had been assigned to stay at the Graduate Bed & Breakfast, an interesting name for accommodations. Some stayed at a hostel downtown.

Anne confessed, "I still don't know why we were lucky to stay in the quieter B&B. Remember how that night after dinner we listened to live music in that bar? It was infectious. One couldn't help but move, tap a finger or a toe, or just get up and dance. And you overheard a few people around us speaking in low voices about something that had happened that afternoon in a smaller town in Northern Ireland, about 100 miles from us."

"And we went to bed that night hearing the international news from home that President Bill Clinton was in a predicament as a young female intern accused him of improper behavior. Good grief, what a mess and embarrassment," Peter said, shaking his head.

"And those horrid twin beds with the plastic cover under the sheets? I woke up sweating and they crunched anytime we moved." Both were laughing about it now.

"It seems like yesterday, Peter. Remember how departing that Sunday for the day of touring, we picked up other members of our group who stayed at the hostel downtown? Our tourmates were awake all night because of people in the streets expressing their rage and sadness and most in the hostel crying and protesting over a horrific bombing the afternoon before. In protest, students staying at the hostel opened and slammed doors all night. Poor Rebecca and her dear mother, Marty, told me about the night and being frightened themselves not understanding the goings on. Half of us were clueless about what our travel mates had endured.

"Then our tour guide told us the devastating news that at 3:10 p.m. the day before, a 500-pound bomb packed in a car had been detonated with a remote trigger in Omagh, about three hours away in County Tyrone, Northern Ireland. Reports were they only knew it occurred in a busy Saturday market and dozens had been killed. He said that glass, bricks, and metal tore through the crowd on the street as a fireball swept out from the epicenter. Twenty-one people were killed instantly, some of them were never located, because of the force of the blast. A main water line under the road ruptured. Some of the dead and badly injured were washed down the hill. More than 300 people were hurt. It took hours to hear accurate news, but those early reports were grim and heartbreaking. It still hurts to think about it," she said teary.

"I didn't think that it was far from where Mauve and her

family lived. You unfolded the laminated map and spread it out over our laps pointing to the village where they lived circled in red, about an hour away. And Mauve told me they went to a Saturday market each week or so, that's why I thought the name of the town sounded familiar. Then the panic about them and trying to contact them. I remember we were very concerned."

Peter added, "Remember how the bus driver and guide both acted subdued, nervous, and even scared? Nigel tried to divert our attention and took us to a Fairy Circle."

"Wild ferns, purple thistles, and bluebells popped out where they could around rocks and mounds reaching for sunlight without a care in the world. What a somber day." Anne looked out the window.

"You tried hard to find one of the little shadows, or fairies or whatever, with no luck," Peter chuckled.

"Yes, I did but darn it."

"Then we stopped at The Burren, that limestone plateau, and wandered around the rugged rocky area of Dolmen Tombs, those megalithic tombs from 2000 BC. We learned a lot about glacial retreat, moraine in the form of rounded boulders, meltwater flow, and much more. That was really cool," he recalled.

"I remember the many types of wildflowers. I took pictures of a bright magenta flower squeezed between two flat stones. A dainty purple orchid stood out among the grasses and then a golden butterfly, with wings as if dipped in black paint, flitted past. Mother Nature at her finest."

"Wasn't it around there that we spotted a family of foxes and had been warned to watch out for badgers and herds of feral goats?" he asked his wife.

"You're right."

Anne remembered how she felt during their first visit. She had a difficult time grasping how the violence could continue decade after decade in such a seemingly civilized country. She didn't know what to expect after reading so much about The Troubles. But her first time in Ireland she was shocked that people were just like her, not horrible monsters. They drove modern cars, lived in homes, attended church and shopped in modern stores. How were they so different from her? How could some harbor such hatred for people they didn't even know? How could they commit such an unspeakable act?

Coming down from her condemnatory pedestal, she recalled how an anti-government militant and his co-conspirator bombed a federal building in Oklahoma City three years earlier, killing 168 people, including 19 children and injuring about 700 others. She also couldn't comprehend how a person could take a gun and kill bystanders, people with whom they have no connection who were in cafeterias, office buildings, concerts, schools, restaurants, post office buildings, and workplaces. *Violence is violence no matter what country you are in*, she thought.

In 1994, in his autobiography *Long Walk to Freedom*, Nelson Mandela said, "No one is born hating another person because of the color of his skin, or his background, or his religion. People must learn to hate, and if they can learn to hate, they can be taught to love, for love comes more naturally to the human heart than its opposite." Anne hoped that was true.

"Remember how we returned to the bed and breakfast in Galway, and after dinner the kind owner let you use her phone to call Mauve?"

"It rang and rang with no answer. I was a nervous wreck. Then the owner offered her computer for me to use and said I could check it in the morning, too. I composed a quick message to her. The next morning, I headed to the B&B office finding a one-line message from Mauve.

I have a story to tell you but we are okay. See you soon.

"Then Roy announced to everyone that your cousins were fine. And it was an enormous decision, go or not to Northern Ireland, or Plan B, stay in the Republic because of the bombing. And the entire group thought we should go ahead as planned. Twenty years ago seems like a dream. Where did the time go for us, Anne? And here we are again. New day. New era."

"I was so excited that day and could barely stand it. After all those months of emailing back and forth then finally meeting two of my third cousins."

She remembered the day like it was yesterday. Driving through a large village in County Fermanagh, they drove across the Erne River and into the Belleek Pottery parking area. Anne felt like a child on Christmas Eve, eagerly anticipating something but not quite sure just what. They were in Northern Ireland and part of the town crosses the border and River Erne into County Donegal.

Mauve and Moyrah had told her they felt equally as nervous and excited as their American cousin. Their surprise for Anne was that they brought their six-year-old daughters, cousins, glued together at their hips. These girls were close, close, close. Fortunately, they only lived a few streets away from each other. And their parents wanted to meet her father's cousin from America, too.

The cousins agreed to meet on the upper mezzanine in the Belleek Tea Room. Anne had done her homework and knew Belleek China is composed of Parian porcelain which makes it famous for its thinness. Holding it up you can see light through it, with an iridescent surface. It's covered with a creamy yellow glaze that suggests it's wet if you touch it, a bit like mother-of-pearl. Anne had been given a small vase and bowl from an elderly friend who was downsizing. She was the only one Sally knew who would appreciate it, having Irish roots and going there.

Anne hadn't quite trampled others on the tour bus or elbowed her friends out of the way, but by now everyone on the tour knew about the recent family discoveries, and the story of Anne's Irish roots and what was happening this very day. When she stepped off the bus her anxiety melted away as she gazed at the tranquil River Erne. She about ran to the Belleek Visitor Center hardly noticing the "Established in 1857" plaque, ready to bound up a flight of stairs to meet her cousins. But the doors flung open as she approached and both of her twin third cousins wrapped her in their arms. As they hugged, people stopped by saying "Hello Mauve," or "Greetings Moyrah." It became humorous, 35 strangers greeting them. Mauve giggled, "Does all of America know about us?"

"Well, at least this busload along with how I became a Riley."

"Anne and Peter, meet our parents Patrick and Keera O'Riley."

"You kept the 'O,'" Anne's left hand instinctively covered her heart.

"Aye, that we did, Lass."

"I really love being called a Lass even though I'm way past that age group."

All were teary as Peter snapped candid shots. Although they would complain later about their ugly cries, they didn't care about sharing their emotions, maybe because they were Irish, or maybe because that's just who they were. "No apologies. Emotions show you care," Moyrah sniffed.

All were talking over each other until Anne noticed their young girls watching intently. Mauve hadn't mentioned she had twin daughters. Anne knew of one daughter for each sister. "So, who are these lovely girls?" Anne joked.

She couldn't get enough of hearing the Irish brogue. When her sweet little fourth cousins said their names, Wrenna and Fayanna, she dropped to her knees and gave both girls a big hug. She couldn't help seeing how these two cousins were identical but how could that be? Mauve and Moyrah were twins but how could they each have a daughter that looked so much alike? "My goodness, you girls look so much alike; you could pass as twins instead of cousins."

Fayanna sort of moaned. "We hear that all the time. I'll show you our differences. My ears are larger," pulling up her hair in a ponytail fashion, "and Wrenna has a birthmark on the back of her shoulder. Wanna see?"

Anne burst out laughing. "No, that's okay, I believe you." She didn't notice when the twin sisters glanced at each other, sharing knowledge that only five people knew including their doctor.

"First, are you okay?" Anne noticed a sling on Mauve's left arm and couldn't miss the steer-strips on her cheek.

The Irish cousins all talked again at one time about what happened to them four days earlier when they arrived in Omagh to shop at the Saturday market as they often did.

"Mammy got hurt when she fell back against something cement," Wrenna sniffled, reliving it.

"I'm fine, honey, you know that's what the doctor told me. Nothing is broken, just cut and sprained. I thought it was only my cheek being gashed but my arm was wretched."

"How terrifying for all of you," Anne commiserated. "I can't even imagine."

"Our friend Emma who we buy lots of cool things from is fine. She'd left early because one of her children got sick."

"The news is horrifying and 29 lives were lost, needlessly taken. This must stop." Defiantly, Moyrah pounded the tabletop.

Fayanna sniffled, "I think we should say a prayer for all those families."

Mauve added with a wink, "We've sent lots of extra prayers heavenward the past few days. Of course, dear, you go ahead."

Right there at the table, all bowed their heads as six-year-old Fay prayed to God to take care of all the babies, children, mothers and fathers, and grandparents along with guards and firemen.

"That's so kind, Fay. Thank you," Anne said. "A point of clarity, please. I've heard the Irish refer to mothers as mammy, mam, mummy, mum, mother, and mom. What's the difference?"

"It's simple really. In Ireland, most of us call our mothers mam but anything is fine, even Ma is used part of the time. Mum is common in Great Britain and used more in Northern Ireland," Moyrah explained.

"I've heard some friends even call their mams by their first names, it's commonplace," Mauve added, "but I prefer Mam."

"Mammies never change," young Fayanna held her cousin Wrenna's hand.

While others on the tour shopped, the family talked nonstop except when sipping tea. Peter took photos.

Even though it was their first meeting in person, the women felt like they knew each other well after email communications over the past several years. Still, there was lots of chatter about their families, jobs, hobbies, and favorite things the girls enjoyed doing, and preferred classes in school. Fay's was music and Wrenna's was science.

Anne did need to purchase a few items, Christmas gifts for favorite friends and a favorite Riley cousin, Patti, at home. Her cousins joined the shopping spree. "Honestly," Mauve told Anne, "this is so close to our home but until

April when the border opened, I had only been once in my life."

Anne purchased a Belleek classic, a *Bless this House* ornament in the shape of a front door for their Christmas tree. In addition, she snagged several round ornaments with five shamrocks daubed around the outside with an Irish Blessing written in green script with gold lettering.

"Oh, these shamrock-shaped ornaments are perfect! I need five of those. I left plenty of room in our luggage for purchases like this."

On the way out, with more hugs and tears, the cousins promised to keep in touch, and hopefully, well maybe, the Irish family would someday visit the Oregon family. Anne promised a party if they did. Wrenna, the more outgoing of the younger girls told Anne, "Wait cousin, Fay and I have something for you." The almost identical cousins linked arms and recited, "May you have many blessings and wherever your path may wind, may every day that's coming be the bright and happy kind."

"They've been practicing for weeks," their granny smiled.

Both little girls, extremely proud of themselves, gave Anne one final hug. Moyrah slipped a box into Anne's hand and whispered, "Open this later and know Mauve and I have one now also. Remember us when you look at it."

Anne cried even harder. For whatever reason, she felt a kinship with these two women. She didn't know that even though sporadic in communication over the years, the distance would melt away when they were together.

Two decades ago, Anne sighed.

That night in their hotel, sports matches dominated the TV channels, but at 11 o'clock they caught an interview from

Malin Head. The woman reporter's hair was blowing in the breeze, her scarf about ready to fly away.

"Sergeant Doyle, this is the first murder in this area for nearly 100 years. On Wednesday a body was discovered by a tourist from America down the bank behind Farren's Bar in Malin Head. Do you have anything to share with our viewers about the process and what is happening?"

"The deceased is Seamus Kennedy, long time resident of the area, currently residing in Derry. Where every investigation starts, you start with a clear mind. You have no preconceived ideas. Because if you do, it's wrong. It's the evidence and the intelligence. That's what directs you in a certain way."

"I've heard some locals refer to you as the Donegal Poirot."

"It's rubbish. Poirot was a well-paid man. I am not," he guffawed.

"What more can you tell us?"

"An outdoor crime scene is a very difficult area to retrieve evidence. We detected many sets of shoeprints, obviously tourists admiring the stunning view. The fingerprint expert would have taken whatever fingerprints were available. His results produced nothing. We then focused on the possibility of DNA evidence. No indication of other people in the area, except the witness on the beach who saw nothing but noticed the body. With blunt force trauma, the blood most likely will be the victim's own. We are awaiting the toxicologist report that should be available soon."

"Thank you, Sergeant. Can you add anything else?" she added truly appreciating the information.

The interview this time was actually going well, so Doyle elaborated, "Unless something happens specifically, most people would find it quite difficult to tell minute by minute what they were doing at a certain time. What were you doing

Wednesday morning at 10:30?" he asked, trying to make his point. "If you're telling the truth, you've no problem. If you are covering up something, you tell lies. Well, we will find out eventually. The investigation is being taken very seriously and is ongoing. We are searching for a person of interest driving an unmarked white utility van." A picture flashed on the screen. It was a direct appeal for anyone with any information to contact them. A blurry video clip from the bar's CCTV showed the van and Mickey. Doyle wondered if now would be a good time to ask for the attractive reporter's number.

Anne typed a text to Mauve.

> Any updates on the dead man?

>> No

> Did Wrenna date that guard?

>> Yes, I always thought they'd get married--all attended school together, the dead man also.

> He's a hunk, the officer, I mean.

>> Plus likable, considerate and has a stable job.

> Let me know if U learn anything more.

>> Aye

A yellow smiley face with a red heart emoji ended their conversation.

CHAPTER TWENTY-ONE

Their second visit to Galway was much different than the first, pouring down rain, vehicle horns honking, and people scampering for shelter. Several decided to skip the walking tour and headed directly for a dry mall where they wandered gazing in local shop windows. In the mall stood a stone three-story round column that housed the Tower Gallery where people could purchase their family crest or name with historical explanation. She did.

"There's a Costa Coffee! I need some serious caffeine," Sue insisted. No one disagreed. They tracked down another Aunty Nellie's Sweet Shop, the same name of the heavenly chocolateria that they heavily invested in while visiting Killarney. This shop had a totally different vibe with colorful walls lined with a massive selection of packaged candies offering everything from Harry Potter frogs to toffee mice, candy canes, and chocolate bars crafted by local artisans. Some handmade chocolates were available but sweets, biscuits, and regional specialties like salted and flavored licorice were the highlights here. She'd never seen so many licorice products: rounds, triangles, coins, diamonds, wheels, balls, and buttons in the shape of herring. She felt like a kid where a little money could go a long way. Her dad loved licorice, so she bought a half pound of buttons in his honor and gave one to each of her traveling chums. This made up for not finding Murphy's Ice Cream. Slightly.

Morgan called Wrenna and one hour later they sat together in a café drinking iced coffees. "Let's clear the air," he nervously began. "I don't want the Seamus investigation to interfere with whatever it is we have going. It's taken us too long to find one another again." In the light, he noticed her dazzling eyes came across as bluer than usual. Maybe the ocean or the sky.

Her eyes sparkled, "I agree."

He leaned closer to her. "Love makes the world go round but beer makes it go twice as fast, especially when it's been poisoned."

"What?"

"Coroner says the poison was foxglove. Grows wild in Kilternan. It's popular in gardens, but not dangerous in small amounts."

"How do you know that?"

"Not the first time plants and flowers have been used in poisons. We are not going to speak of this again until the investigation is closed."

He noticed a teardrop on her cheek as she glanced down at her drink. His heart melted.

Anne heard her phone chirp. Mauve again.

Don't know anything except there was poison in his beer!

Good grief!

Heading farther south as they negotiated a roundabout, Anne noticed in the center of the circle a boat with splotches of cinnamon paint remaining. The creaky old thing at one time held one, maybe two people in a river, certainly not a moody ocean. In its retirement, it served as a flower container filled with poppies, snowball white, scarlet, and a couple of blue ones, the shade of blueberries. She had seen blue ones in Scotland and knew they were uncommon. She enjoyed checking out the decorations in roundabouts which varied from weeds and wildflowers to manicured grass and sculpture gardens.

They stopped for an opportunity to experience the daily life of a traditional Irish family at Rathbaun Farm, not far from Galway. The farmer named Fintan skillfully sheared a sheep in three minutes flat. Peter guessed that years of experience and hard work made it look effortless. Sue asked if the local weavers used the wool for the sweaters, scarves, and other woolen items. He explained that they were woven here but then wool is also sent to China where it's fashioned into a variety of garments and sent back with labels that read "Woven in Ireland." Rarely did one find something woven and then made in Ireland.

Fintan shared the daily chores of a rural farmer. While showing them around, his sidekick, Ted, arrived to help with the next demonstration. Ted, the Border Collie, a valuable member of the staff, displayed how he rounds up the sheep from various corners of the field. All the animals did end up in the pen with Ted gently corralling them in. One, maybe a comedic and famous cousin of Shaun the Sheep from Scotland, wasn't exactly cooperating, but Ted was patient just circling and moving it toward the gate of the pen. There were darling lambs, one white with a black face and another solid black that they were able to hand-feed bottles of milk.

Feeling like they'd accomplished something outdoorsy and now skilled farmhands, or at least semi-skilled, they were treated to homemade warm scones right out of the oven with home-grown rhubarb preserves, clotted cream, and bright yellow butter along with hot tea in English teacups. Frances introduced herself and offered seconds if they wanted, which no one declined. Anne inquired about her recipe and if she could purchase the scone cutters. Anne did purchase a few sets for a special niece and friend at home who she knew would appreciate this souvenir. She felt especially drawn to Frances, that being her middle name, and when she told Frances, she suggested they have their picture together. And that the two Frances's did.

Departing down a tree-canopied, single-lane road they stopped because the Highway Department was doing some repair work. Bill cautiously maneuvered around a man on a bicycle as Anne overheard their skillful driver mumble something like, *ya thunderin' eejit* (her guess was not just an idiot but a really, really stupid idiot) with no shoulder on the road for non-motorized vehicles.

Even though well into their trip, Irish brogues were still hard to understand. She kept her giggles to herself when hearing 'thing' become 'ting' and 'thirty' become 'turty.' She recalled on their first visit some bozo from the southern part of the US, trying to get a drunk Irishman to pronounce 'thirty-three and a third' which sounded like 'turty tree and a turd.' She was getting a little better with names but Siobhán, pronounced *shiv*-awn, still baffled her.

CHAPTER TWENTY-TWO

Anne woke up well before the alarm buzzed. Peter was sleeping soundly and she didn't want to disturb him but thoughts niggled her brain to full consciousness. She glanced at the clock. Numbers glared 6:30. Soaking in the bathtub she wondered what this day would disclose.

Already at the station at 7 a.m., DS Graham read an official report that had also gone to Sergeant Doyle. An investigative team was being assembled to work on the case that appeared to be much more than an accidental death or suicide. Now they were looking at a possible murder since the victim was poisoned. Traces of foxglove were confirmed in both bottles of beer.

However, Seamus's phone was full of texts and some emails about gambling, drug pickups, and more. His death was no longer the priority. He handed the report to Devlin.

"Guess we're out of it now," he told his sergeant.

"Maybe." Graham explained what he meant by 'maybe.'

Well-preserved Dunguaire Castle, a sixteenth century tower house with fortified walls along the shores overlooking Galway Bay was their next stop. The tower is 75 feet high.

"This is really old, 1520. It's not the largest castle we've seen but certainly unspoiled," Bruce observed before heading off to climb a stone wall. From the top of the castle, a green, white, and orange flag stood out straight in the breeze.

The child-friendly footpath complete with emerald-colored cut grass, or maybe sheep cut, led to the arched entrance. Anne imagined it differently hundreds of years ago caked with mud and maybe a few rocks. The castle was constructed by the O'Hynes clan, a prominent family in the area, who were descendants of Guaire, the king of Connacht who died in 663 AD.

Anne read, "Known for its bountiful banquets and storied history, Dunguaire Castle is rumored to be the most photographed castle in Ireland."

What caught her attention when reading the pamphlet was the name Martyn. She read that Richard Martyn, Mayor of Galway lived here until 1642, and the Martyns of Tulira owned the castle until this century. In the 1920s, Oliver St John Gogarty purchased it and began repairs to restore it. He was a famous literary figure and it became a popular meeting place for literary revivalists, like Yeats, Shaw, and Synge. In 1954 Lady Ampthill, the final private owner, set about completing the restorations begun by Gogarty, and then it became the property of the Shannon Group, who continue to occupy the castle to this day. "I've got to tell Nancy at work about this, and her sister Kathy, too. They'll love this. I wonder if they know about their Irish ancestors," Anne asked Peter of her Martyn friends back home who spelled it the same way.

A must-see in Ireland is the Cliffs of Moher. On their first visit, it had been in high winds with not enough guardrails, in her opinion. The famous Cliffs of Moher, rising 650 feet from the sea and about five miles long, were shrouded in mist. There were no fences or barriers and at home they would certainly have multiple warning signs for protecting those daredevils who just had to get as close as possible to the edge. Of course, some daring young man did just that. Anne couldn't watch for fear of what might happen to him, especially with winds gusting around 40 miles per hour. The heavy mist pelted and stung her face like sand when walking along the shoreline. Seagulls and other seabirds were tucked away safely between rocks on the cliffs. The birds were smarter than some of the tourists.

Two decades later the site has transitioned significantly making it easier for tourists to get to the cliffs, or in the opposite direction to the O'Brien Tower. The sun shone so brightly that the normally green grass turned a shimmery silver, moving ever so slightly in the breeze.

She took way too many photos of the magnificent cliffs and felt artsy as she lined up dandelions mixed with wispy blue and white wildflowers at the bottom of the frame with the cliffs, ocean, and sky even with a few gulls in the shot.

This time the weather was perfect with just a fresh breeze. Using binoculars, Anne scanned the rock cliffs for bird life, particularly puffins. She had a fondness for puffins looking like colorful sea parrots dressed in black and white tuxedos, with day-glow orange around their onyx round eyes and bright scarlet bills. She had been fortunate to see colonies a couple of times in Iceland and figured it wasn't likely here because the birds are usually gone by mid-August. But she hoped a few might still be in the area. She identified black and white birds on nests tucked into the rocks and thought she'd detected a few stragglers, but nope, they were gulls.

The café is built into the berm of the hillside and they ducked in for a lunch of loaded baked potatoes and organic tomato soup.

"I wonder how many colors of green there are on this island. Everywhere it's green, green, green with a random yellow, tan, and blue." Sue took another bite of piping hot baked potato.

"I think Johnny Cash had it right when he sang at a minimum Ireland has 40 shades of green," Dave answered.

"What about Johnny Cash?" Nancy joined in the conversation.

"He did a song about Ireland?" Anne couldn't quite imagine it. "He was before my time and not exactly my genre."

Linda and Nancy, already with their phones out, had Johnny Cash belting out "Forty Shades of Green" within seconds thanks to YouTube. His baritone voice and western twang sang about missing the Emerald Isle and its towns. Dingle, Donaghadee, Shannon, Skibbereen, Dublin, Cork, Tipperary, and Shalimar all were mentioned honoring this 40 shades of green land.

Wrenna's phone dinged several times. She read a long text from Fay.

I've met the man of my dreams. He's the grandson of 1 of my favorite residents here. His father was born here but fell in love with a Greek girl decades ago when he was there on a college winter break. His gran seems to think it was just yesterday. She's somewhat confused these days. Anyway, the son stayed and they got married and he stepped right into her family's olive production and shipping business. So Stephanos, one of three Irish Greek children, works in Greece for the family company and travels around the world. That's why he hasn't been able to visit his gran much. Pink heart emoji.

This is the longest text I've ever read from u. We need 2 meet for dinner so u can fill me in more.

Can u tonight or r u going out with Morgan somewhere? I've got so much to tell u about Stephan. He's got dark hair, almost black, and thick, with fair complexion, what a combo. Not tall tho.

Stop. Save some for tonight.

Wrenna added an uncharacteristic emoji, hers a laughing face.

On the road again, a large cobalt and scarlet road sign caught Anne's attention: "Matchmaking Festival, Lisdoonvarna, Willie Daly is the matchmaker. All September. Europe's biggest singles event."

Driving inland they stopped at the well-preserved fifteenth century Bunratty Castle and Folk Park in County Clare. The site is a living reconstruction of the homes and their environment a century ago. The castle has occupied this spot for over one thousand years.

They strolled along Main Street encountering locals dressed in period costumery and sheep nibbling on bushes. They popped into thatched roof buildings like the doctor's house where the parlor was used as a dispensary and for surgeries. Red poppies were scattered around edges of the grass. The pub in the center of the village would have been used by well-known customers. Irish linens, poplin, and woolens are still famous. Sean O'Farrell's Drapery displayed a variety of clothes in the family's rooms upstairs.

Each small town printed pamphlets, handbills, notices, and newspapers in the print workshop with all typesetting done by hand. Cuala Press Prints, established by the Yeats family, are still produced on the premises. The grocery store held all foodstuff as well as imported goods. McInerney & Sons Hardware Factory built tools and utensils. Lastly, on Main Street is the post office. Different types of farmhouses dotted the area from a one-room dwelling of a poor laborer to the home of a farmer rich from the lands, complete with stables and a corn barn. Piles of peat logs were loosely stacked against most buildings.

The large medieval tower house was partially wrapped in scarlet vines with deep green ivy tossed in for an accent color. Six-foot-high fuchsia bushes with bright rosy blooms shrouded the front and around the corner of the castle.

They were warmly greeted at the front door by a woman named Nellie wearing a long velvet dress in multiple hues of green with a bright scarlet short jacket. She wore a hat with a wide ribbon hanging down her back. Inside they saw furniture and décor belonging to both the McNamara and O'Brien Clans, and the secret stairways to the rooftop.

It is furnished with mainly fifteenth and sixteenth century furnishings in the style of the period of the Great

Earl. The main building has three floors, each consisting of a single great room or hall. The four towers have six stories each. A small gate leads to a dungeon, way too creepy for Anne.

Nellie explained that in the Public Chapel are finely decorated sixteenth century stucco ceilings and several precious artifacts including a fifteenth century Swabian altarpiece. Swabian is one of the dialect groups of Alemannic German that belongs to the High German dialect continuum. It is mainly spoken in Swabia which is located in central and southeastern Baden-Württemberg (including its capital Stuttgart). When Nellie mentioned Stuttgart, Anne and Peter knew exactly what she was talking about. Stuttgart is home to the Porsche factory they toured after a Viking River cruise a year earlier.

In The Great Hall, Nellie continued her narration. "This is the original banquet hall where the earl would give judgments as he sat in his Chair of Estate." French, Brussels, and Flemish tapestries hang on every wall. There is an oak cupboard dated to 1570 displaying crockery and cooking paraphernalia. The prominent coat of arms of the reigning family was conspicuously displayed.

Nancy and Sue stood side-by-side scrutinizing swords and other military weapons displayed on the wall. "You know, I must say it's a little unsettling to have all these sharp weapons just out and about."

"This place would be a nightmare to grandchild proof. I would have to put protective covers and safety tips on everything." Both grandmothers shook their heads.

"As we discovered recently, beer can kill, too. So what's a couple dozen spears?" Anne half-heartedly laughed.

There are private apartments in the South and North Solar. The South Solar ceiling is partially a replica of the Tudor style. The North Solar apartment housed the earl and his family. The oak paneling dates to 1500 AD and the table is reported to have been salvaged from the wreck of a Spanish ship. The earl's bedroom includes a magnificent carved bed draped on the top by fabric. A lady's dress lay on the bed. Food was prepared in the kitchen and large turtle shells were used as dishes and covers. And it had its own garbage chute."

After absorbing this seemingly first-hand history lesson from the fifteenth century, Peter could smell pastries baking somewhere. Their noses led them to the Tea Room where they feasted on refreshing tea complete with milk and sugar, and still warm buttered scones with freshly homemade fruit jams.

"Might ruin your dinner," Anne kidded him. She knew he could eat anytime and anywhere, and not gain a pound. *So unfair,* she still thought after all these years.

"Doubtful," he could barely respond with a mouthful of warm scones.

Later that afternoon, they arrived at Old Ground Hotel in County Clare. More scarlet vines accented the outer walls. Baskets of hot pink geraniums sprinkled with small bright blue flowers and ivy were overflowing from cement pots and the baskets under the windows. The entrance was especially striking with a huge fireplace, and off the lobby a large room with overstuffed chairs and sofas for lounging, reading, or just gazing outside.

Returning to Bunratty Castle for dinner, they were in for a treat, especially for those who never experienced a medieval banquet before. Fortunately, they were allowed to use eating utensils, as some medieval banquet venues do not. Heavy crockery cups were full of red wine. A waiter brought a salad of cucumbers, greens, and cold smoked salmon, or lox, as some would refer to it. A hearty lentil soup was served in a bowl with no spoon. Each picked up their bowl and drank, often dipping a dense, multigrain piece of bread in it. Plates of half chicken, root vegetables, and mashed potatoes were delivered by servers dressed in period costumes. Numerous musicians and actors performed while they ate. A warm, layered apple dessert with a crumble topping appeared, but sadly not the Sticky Toffee Pudding that Anne was hoping for.

CHAPTER TWENTY-THREE

Peter saw a road sign to Kilrush. They continued on the N67 and pulled in line behind seven touring motorcycles, some with sidecars. Clearly, Boomer-aged friends were on their holiday together. Bill got the all-clear for their bus to enter onto the three-story ferry and they were free to roam during the 45-minute cruise across the Shannon Estuary, eliminating a 200-mile road trip or at least three hours. They were on the *Shannon Dolphin* gliding through choppy gray water passing two smokestacks that dwarfed a white three-story lighthouse. The *Shannon Breeze*, a sleek single-story candy apple red and white ferry, passed them quickly going in the opposite direction.

Unloading from the ferry at Ballybunion, they were greeted by the familiar blackface sheep feeding in the two fields of different colored grass that gently dropped off onto sand and lapping waves.

Bruce asked about the crops and April explained that most animals eat rye and fescue varieties, fescue being the darker green color and rye almost the color of celery. "See further out, the greenish-gray field? That's Timothy grass.

Then that whitish-pink field way off in the distance is white clover, like you have at home. Livestock eat that, too. It's also an important source of nectar and pollen for bumblebees. And we all know bees are important for our existence. Without them, the world could be a very different place."

They drove by Rinn Na Spainneach (Spanish Point) where weathered summer homes dot the hillside over-looking this pretty-as-a-postcard area. The two-lane road is lined with houses with groomed yards and gardens. In one area surfers were enjoying the waves, even though not big, and there were even a few windsurfers. Passing through towns, they popped out of civilization into meandering hills again sprinkled with relics of old buildings, and crumbling stone walls.

Anne preferred how Ireland used the word 'county' first, then the name. County Limerick, County Clare, County Shannon, County Cork. They lived in Marion County and she wondered what it would take to reverse the words to County Marion. As they headed into a dairy region, hundreds of black and white cows munched vivid green rye grass where some farmland was separated by streams, some fences, and some hedgerows. They saw in the distance a group of standing stones, broken down stone buildings, and little villages with stores and houses with flaking paint, thatched roofs, and front porches that felt cottagey. Some homes displayed flower boxes on their windowsills and pots at their front doors. Occasionally there would be a round satellite TV dish mounted on the side or top of the house.

Before reaching their next stop, Kerry Kingdom Museum, they noticed something quite out of the ordinary in a town called Tralee. "Have we magically leaped to Holland?" Peter pointed at a white Dutch-looking working windmill, and a one-story yellow building, perhaps a homestead, and a white three-bay shop or garage. The door had been painted shamrock green. Anne snapped a photo as the sun created a duplicate scene on the still water.

The topography between Tralee and Dingle flattened out as they journeyed along the west side of Ireland's coast. The patchwork quilt effect from hues of green pastures and tan harvested crops separated by shrubbery was frequent and she never got tired of the scenery. Often a patch was dotted with hundreds of sheep. And sometimes the quilt slipped off the side of the hill into the sea.

Their compact room at Bambury Guest House in Dingle on the peninsula contained two twin beds and a lamp sitting on a small square table separating the beds. The plaid curtains in several shades of blue perfectly matched the bedspreads and the shade on the small lamp. The plaid scheme reminded her of a salad made with fruit: blueberries, blackberries, purple grapes, and plums.

When reviewing the menu outside of Doyle's Seafood Restaurant, the only thing Anne cared about were three words that popped out like planets in a dark sky: *Sticky Toffee Pudding* with butterscotch sauce and butterscotch ice cream. She rolled her gleeful eyes heavenward.

"Oh my word, Peter. Quick. Get in here. I see one table open." Perusing the menu she halted her dinner search at the photo of shrimp, langoustine, or something similar in butter with herbs as an appetizer. That was it for her.

"That's all?" the female server asked Anne.

"Yes, thank you, I'm saving room for my favorite dessert in the world, well UK anyway, Sticky Toffee Pudding."

"Em, I understand perfectly; a house favorite and mine, too."

"Let's do another starter. Tapas plate? Local Glenbeigh oysters? Mango fish tacos?" Peter said.

"Sure, whatever you decide is fine. I'm getting the shrimp."

"Local oysters it is," he decided.

"Super," Anne replied less than overjoyed, but when would oysters ever be better than just plucked from the ocean?

"Wait, can I add to my order, please? I'll have the mixed seafood pasta, too. I should get an assortment of seafood, shrimp, salmon, mussels, local catches, oh yuck, squid, oh well, I'll pull them out for you."

One fresh oyster was more than sufficient for her with Peter happily consuming the other three.

Peter asked, "Remember those oysters out of that fresh-water bay of that tiny town, Mali Ston on Pelješac Peninsula in Croatia? Salty from the ocean influence, so mild, and tender."

"I must admit, those were finger-licking delish. I liked the fresh mussels better though."

Peter's first bite of the brown bread was soft with a crispy crust, and he declared it probably the best of the entire trip. Anne preferred the garlic and sun-dried tomato bread.

He savored each bite of the "Spanish Style" Dingle Bay Fish Stew with lots of chunky fish, flavorful and spicy. Not wasting any bread, he soaked up every single drop of the stew broth.

Each bite tasted even more delicious as she dug through pasta for more of the fresh seafood. "This is absolutely scrumptious!" Anne muttered with her mouth full. Some local folks sitting next to them picked up their non-Irish accents and told them that they'd selected the best restaurant in Dingle.

After three minuscule bites of warm Sticky Toffee Pudding, Peter sat back and watched Anne happily down the rest.

"Well, how does it compare to Scottish versions?"

"Darn close and almost as delicious; I can't complain. I think it's the added butterscotch ice cream that sets it apart."

Afterward, the couple ambled toward town. They passed ebony, old-world streetlamps, Murphy's Pub painted in eggplant purple, John Benny's Pub done in royal blue with two crimson doors with matching window trim, and on a corner was An Droichend Beag, a yellow-brown building trimmed in Celtic green. They heard music coming down Bridge Street.

The lively sounds emanated from a flagstone building with the front door painted crimson and windows outlined in the same color. A plaque read "Headquarters of the Dingle Fife and Drum Band, the Green and Gold Wrenboys, and a place where the history of Dingle Gaelic Athletic Association is revered." They were at the famous O'Flaherty's Pub, where farmers and fishermen plus plenty of tourists were squeezed in enjoying a pint and tapping their feet, trying to discuss whatever was happening around them but drowned out by the energetic band. A guy played his harmonica, another strummed a banjo, another plucked a hefty base, another blew a flute thing, and others had a fiddle and a small accordion. The fellow on the harmonica really rocked as they played a jig that compelled you to move, but by now there was only room enough to stand. The band took a short break to introduce themselves as Kilian, Fergus, Niall, Angus, Rourke, and Caelan.

The man named Fergus told them O'Flaherty's came to be in 1957 after his father, who had been a fisherman, broke his leg and had to give up fishing. Fergus turned out to be the current owner.

Pictures hung on the walls, and the pole in the middle of the bar was obscured with stapled flyers and announcements promoting whatever they wanted. After the delightful hour of Irish tunes and Irish Mules, they moseyed back to their hotel as shadows crept in as the daylight receded and a cascade of coral and amber danced on the water. Peter complimented his wife, "Best Mules ever except the ones you make at home."

"Thanks. I never thought about using Irish whiskey instead of vodka. I'm experimenting when we get home."

———

Wrenna parked her car and noticed the grass was freshly mowed and thought Morgan could use some shrubs and plants. They stood in the back garden of his home on their third official date since their serendipitous encounter at Farren's the previous Wednesday. "He's called Flynn. He's my best pal," Graham hugged the neck of his dog, coal-black except for mahogany coloring on his paws and lower legs. Flynn had his two front paws on the shoulders of his person. "Down boy."

"Oh, you're so handsome, aren't you?" she bent down even with Flynn's face. "I just love Gordon Setters, even though technically they're Scottish, you know."

"Aye, but Irish setters are too common around here. Did you know Gordon Setters are to be exercised a minimum of two hours a day?"

"He looks fit and healthy. How do you do that with your hectic work schedule?"

"Always an hour before work and after."

"And get this, mental stimulation games are highly recommended for the breed."

"What does that mean?"

"I scent a dummy then hide or throw it into a bush and he locates it. I even got a scent training kit on Amazon. We play Fetch which is a great way to burn up energy. Oh, and I bought one of those handball launchers with an extra-long handle."

"Does he like the water?"

"Loves it. Next time let's take him to the shore," intimating next time was a given.

Next time, Wrenna thought to herself, *he's already making future plans.* "Maybe a picnic on the beach with him?"

"Grand idea."

They took Flynn for a long romp before going out. At dinner, Graham explained he'd be working out of town for some time on an undercover case.

Chirp. Anne grabbed her phone.

> Wrenna and Graham have gone on a date or two.

> Really??? Tell me more!

> Aye, seems to be rekindled feelings. I hope it works for them this time.

> My goodness. Maybe something good can come from bad?

That's all Anne could think to reply. But she thought to herself, *I am not getting into other people's business. Let sleeping dogs lie.*

CHAPTER TWENTY-FOUR

Before any others were up, Anne headed out alone in the bright sunshine along the shoreline. Golden gorse with its yellowy flowers were the cause of her itchy eyes. In the distance, the water was calm and she could see where they'd go later that day, toward the Dingle Tower. She enjoyed the solitude of the morning.

Several hours later when the tide was out far enough, several slogged in the damp harbor sand which wasn't easy going. The sand touched the sea and they kept watching for a popular water attraction, a Bottlenose Dolphin named Fungie. As they reached the tower, Anne turned back toward Dingle with the crystal clear water and emerald meadows, taking her breath away. An occasional red poppy dotted the terrain. She wondered if any of her relatives had been in this idyllic area.

They took their time going back on the path through a cow pasture. Friendly black cows seemed to assume the two-legged creatures should be sharing some treats with them. The unprepared humans had not brought anything, so the four-legged friends turned away and resumed munching on boring grass. The only thing they had to watch for were their gifts of cow pies.

As they got closer to town, there were dozens of large chartreuse fishing nets piled with carrot-colored weights tied in various locations. A young man slept soundly stretched out in the sun, probably exhausted from hours of fishing or hours at O'Flaherty's. And sure enough, like pressing the ON button, Fungie jumped out of the water, did an acrobatic flip, and smoothly glided back into the bay. He or she is a friendly dolphin and swims playfully alongside boats. They don't know if this was Fungie II, III or VIII, but she or he has been around for decades.

They wandered along Mail Road past the Alpine Guesthouse and the Dingle Diner stopping at the bright golden and sky blue painted-two-story building of Dingle Crystal on Green Street. It's a family-run Irish crystal company founded by master craftsman Sean Daly. Sean started as a young apprentice in Waterford Crystal and studied for 15 years to become a master cutter. When Waterford Crystal decided to move their production overseas, Sean wanted to keep the tradition of crystal cutting alive in Ireland. So he and his wife moved to Dingle and set up Dingle Crystal.

The shelves were lined with crystal bowls, decanters for wine and whiskey, vases, glasses and tumblers, and stemware, in all different shapes, sizes, colors, and designs.

Anne heard her name from across the street as Sue and Dave were waving at them. They crossed the street and the ladies bolted into Fiadh Woven Design, a tiny shop painted periwinkle, full of Nordic designs and dozens of scarves and wraps, and sweaters in creative designs and darling baby socks. Anne bought a lovely alpaca wool scarf, one side done in several hues of green with dots of navy, and the other side purple with ruby threads. It was pricey but a once-in-a-life-time original gift to herself. Anne guessed that the two sprigs of purple heather in a pottery vase were Fiadh's inspiration.

"Anne! There's a bookstore. We've got to go in." Sue had dabbled in writing some short stories and poetry over the decades but now she was serious about becoming a children's book author. She had published a charming book about Misty, a brave Irish lass, and her fun-loving donkey, Clara. She would be writing humorous scenarios about their rambunctious pugs, Nelson and Spanky, in a new upcoming series.

The sisterchicks slipped in a white door that popped out from the cobalt-painted store called Dingle Bookshop. Anne took a deep breath. She loved the smell of bookstores, sometimes musty, sometimes inky, certainly dusty, and this store also smelled of sweet incense mixed with salty sea air. If she let her imagination run wild like she had in some stores of older vintage, she would use words including woody, earthy, smoky, even decay, since paper is wood and slowly dying, and even coffee, red wine, and sometimes vanilla.

Bookstores were on both women's "must visit" lists. Sue had mentioned more than once she believed that independent bookstores are the cornerstone of civilization. Anne couldn't agree more. Books were displayed in the two front windows. The independent bookshop, just a stone's throw from the Wild Atlantic Way, had been selling books for several years.

Sue made a beeline to the children's section while Anne meandered to the travel then mystery section. She loved a good mystery, maybe something by Agatha Christie. Books lined the walls and were piled on tables in neat stacks.

She came upon a book for Peter about the Dingle Railway and picked out *The Coastal Atlas of Ireland*. She would have purchased several others including *Moonflower Murders*, but stopped herself, knowing she did not have an infinite amount of luggage space. Then she came to the Local Authors section and selected another, *Living Among The Puffins*. Anne had also embarked on her own journey of writing. Her nonfiction stories were about their travels and her obsession with colorful doors. Three were already on the market. Dave and Peter who had been loitering outside became their wives book carriers.

"There's Doyle's," Anne pointed out. "Two nights in a row would break all of our vacation dining rules. Can you do one more?" she asked her husband.

"One more what? Dinner at Doyle's?"

"No, silly. One more shop. I know I'm pushing your limits." Anne and Sue had already stepped into Dingle Pottery with its window a glaring billboard of colorful hand-thrown vases, bottles, teapots, candle holders, oil burners, butter dishes, plates, jars and jugs, bowls, espresso cups, mugs, and more. Anne read that all the products are thrown on a wheel and hand-decorated by artist Hedi O'Neill. Dave and Peter tagged along.

"I'm sure glad I still have room in my carry-on since we are nearing the end of our trip."

"Well, we're still about a week out, Anne. Pace yourself."

"You have room, I peeked. These mugs are fantastic and the swirls of vermilion, cream, and chartreuse with black trim are stunning. I could spend a lot of time and money in here."

"I know you could but I am getting quite hungry."

"There's not one thing that matches. See if you can find two objects in the same colors, everything is so unique. Whoa, check out the tall vase in scarlet, pumpkin, and sunshine yellow outlined in navy with the bright cobalt handle. Oh my word, that teapot with the ruby handle, green spout, aqua lip, and multi-color body. Niece Becky would love that."

"So what is it going to be, shopping queen?"

"Being the practical sort," Anne started, ignoring the feigned coughing from her spouse, "I am going to get one of the butter dishes that will go with any color scheme I have in the kitchen for the rest of my life."

"I'm fading from all this shopping. It's either protein or caffeine. Should we try somewhere new for dinner?" Peter asked. "You know, our, well, *your* made-up motto on vacation, 'Don't eat anything you can fix at home or dine at the same place twice.'"

"Phooey on that, I say back to Doyle's! I want the langoustine. Join us," she said to Sue and Dave.

Still not tired of Irish music, the foursome returned for more entertainment at O'Flaherty's. They joined their friends who had politely pushed their way in, and eight crammed around a table for two.

CHAPTER TWENTY-FIVE

The next morning, prowling around the far western tip of the Dingle Peninsula, a local guide named Mark came to escort them to Dunbeg Fort. It butts up against and overlooks the Atlantic Ocean. It was in the middle of an open field, with homes and farms some acres away. Anne wondered who else had stepped along the well-worn stone path. Mark shared some basic history.

"The Iron Age in Ireland was from about 500 BC to 500 AD. The most significant relics uncovered from this area are the promontory and hill forts. These are unusual monuments with a large stone wall enclosing a large area of hilltop or cliff ledge. On the whole, they were defensive structures, but often a refuge of last resort."

There are few promontory forts left and their tour group were at the steps of one of them, Dunbeg Fort. The wall surrounding the fort is built of flat, layered gray stones and a narrow doorway gives access to the interior. Similar walls are the remains of a roundhouse inside the fort. The interior of the house has a gravel floor, but Mark guessed it had once been a sod floor of the home.

Looking down from a low window, Anne could see from the side of the house how disconcertingly close it was to the cliff's edge. They peered into a small chamber probably used originally for storage. The roof had deteriorated over the centuries. Grass and weeds with white flowers covered berms. A tall square tower remained, and they peeked through slits in the sides of the structure that warriors, when inside, could shoot arrows through to protect their fort. It is small but impressive and somewhat eerie being located on a sheer cliff that juts south into Dingle Bay at the base of Mount Eagle.

One lone enormous tree, maybe a fort of its own for several different types of birds, stood guard. Several birds were from the finch family, but different in color than in the Pacific Northwest. This goldfinch had crimson around its beak that bled down its chest and up toward the crest of its head. One lime-colored bird, Mark pointed out, was a Greenfinch, and perfectly logical. Another had a scarlet underbody with salt and pepper feathers down its back and a solid obsidian head. "It's a Bullfinch." The sparrows were similar but different because of their coloring.

"Gosh, it's been just over a week since Malin Head." Anne chatted quietly with Sue.

"No answers yet, right?

"Umm, not really. Apparently, it's unsolved due to speculation of suicide or accidental death, maybe murder because of the poison, but Mauve says they seem much more concerned about what they lucked into on his phone. Drugs, gambling, and maybe even more."

They continued to mill around, and Anne heard some musical notes floating along with the breeze and wondered where they were coming from. Turned out Mark was also a musician. He sat on a pile of rocks blowing into his penny whistle. It looked like a thin white flute and he explained that the penny whistle is commonly called a tin whistle and is a woodwind instrument often heard in Irish music. This small instrument has six holes plus a mouthpiece and is played by blowing in the air and using your fingers to cover different holes to produce different sounds. He serenaded them with an Irish jig followed by a slower somber song. The melody evoked a melancholy aura in Anne's soul stirring jumbled thoughts of the morning in Malin Head.

Mark shared more insights about the fort's central causeway that provided access to the interior. Only about half the length was recorded in 1854 because much of the western half had already fallen into the sea. The absence of dateable findings created difficulties in coming up with a chronology for the site. A radiocarbon date of around 800 AD from the base of the inner fosse suggests it was in existence in the eighth or nineth century AD, and dates of around 900 AD from the occupation layers in the beehive suggest it was inhabited in the tenth or eleventh century AD. As he imparted his Irish history and wisdom, he entertained them by playing a few more light, cheery tunes on his penny whistle, the melodies to be carried off the rugged coastline reaching far and beyond. The view reminded Anne of the coastline in their home state of Oregon, where the hillside drops quickly into the frothy ocean. White waves beat the shoreline as gulls soared overhead, probably watching to make sure the intruders weren't getting too close to their nests.

Off in the distance were the Blasket Islands, one larger than the others. Mark waved his hand toward the image of a man lying face up. They could easily see why he was named the Sleeping Giant. There are several legends of how this giant came to his final resting place in the ocean. One is that a druid put him to sleep, and another is that he resembles a reposing Finn McCool, who supposedly built the Giant's Causeway they'd seen earlier.

When they reached an area with cell reception, Anne heard a chirp and pulled her phone from her Baggallini travel bag. She appreciated all the compartments and knew where each item would fit perfectly.

Home for a half day from undercover work out of town, Graham asked Wrenna, "What did you get?" as she came out of the chocolate shop.

"Some candy and this exquisite Celtic trinity knot brooch. I always thought that it was linked to Christianity. But the woman in the shop told me that back in the day it meant to honor the triple goddess—the maiden, the mother, and the crone."

"The crone? I'm not touching that," he teased.

"But there's another interpretation as well. The family— two parents and a child," she gazed at him boldly, super-charging his heart rate, impossible for him to miss her meaning.

The bus motored down a lane lined on both sides with blooming wild fuchsia bushes about eight to ten feet high with glimpses of Smerwick Harbour to Gallarus Oratory in County Kerry. Gallarus means either "rocky headland or house" or "shelter for foreigners." Completely encircled by a two-foot walkway, built between the sixth and ninth centuries, it's an early Christian stone church. The entire group fit inside and peered through windows of thick stone. It's one of the best preserved and most iconic early Christian churches. Over 1,000 years old, this small building was constructed entirely from dry stone masonry and is the archeological and architectural highlight of the Slea Head Drive. They saw the Three Sisters and Mount Brandon farther out in Smerwick Harbour. A rock standing about four feet high was etched in early Celtic writing.

As they drove a while longer, they came to Kilmalkedar Church, a Romanesque, early Christian, and later medieval site, that was spread over about ten acres. It is associated with St. Brendan and is thought to have been brought about by St. Maolcethair, a local saint. Even though deteriorated with no roof, it showed every sign of being safe and in fairly good shape.

Outside on the northern side of the pathway that leads to the church, there is a remarkable holed ogham stone that stands six feet tall and three feet wide at the base. There is an inscription carved by slash marks that all mean something. This stone may have been a standing stone with the ogham writing added during the early Christian period. There were several other standing stones with holes and some without.

The Chancellor's house is a rectangular building built on top of a boulder foundation and situated on sloping ground with an incredible view of the Three Sisters and Smerwick Bay. They prowled around and followed a path and steps that led to a kitchen area. Outside of the house were aboveground stones which were vessels or tubs used in cooking. They seemed perfect as a rainwater collector for birdbaths now. Christmassy vibrant green ferns and small bushes popped through any gap they could find, reaching for sunbeams.

Their next stop in Ogham had even more ancient stones from about 300 AD and some of the earliest Irish script. On one tall rock were dozens of straight slash marks that originated from the Ogham alphabet. Anne had purchased an alphabet booklet in a local bookstore and could almost decipher the words. Well, not really, but she hoped so.

She heard a giggle behind her and turned in a complete circle seeing no one close by. Odd but certainly not out of place, they were in Ireland after all, she scanned the area, trying to find the source of the friendly giggle. She didn't, and decided it wasn't something she'd share with Peter or her friends.

That evening some returned to O'Flaherty's for pub grub and entertainment. The room was crowded so many stood at the bar listening to the traditional music. More people piled in to listen. Anne couldn't get enough of it, but Peter did and passed on this evening's Irish entertainment. The noise took her mind off of her cousins, temporarily, anyway. That night she took a half of Xanax, hoping she wouldn't wake for at least seven hours. It couldn't have been more than ten minutes before Anne was in slumberland.

Mickey texted Eamon.

> No sign of guards. I'm done hiding out and ready 2 work.

> Ok, meet me at the dog track tomorrow at noon.

CHAPTER TWENTY-SIX

After a couple of hours of driving, Bill stopped the bus at a small market and they all selected lunch items for an upcoming picnic. There were assorted yogurts, fresh fruits, vegetables, and a myriad of breads, several types of smelly cheese, sticks of cured salami and peppered beef, large juicy strawberries, apples, and grapes.

Standing in the store, April told them that flavored potato chips were created in Ireland. The credit goes back to the 1950s when Joseph "Spud" Murphy hated the taste of plain potato crisps, our chips. Back then the only flavor was salt and you were given a packet of salt that you had to pour over the crisps. Thanks to his hatred of the crisps, he opened a potato crisp company in 1954 called Tayto. He started with eight workers out of a van. One of the workers experimented with different flavors until he pinned down one that Murphy approved of: Cheese and onion.

Peter tried to decide between a bag of Pepto-Bismol pink Prawn Cocktail, a bright blue bag of Salt & Vinegar, a light blue bag of Salt, a rusty bag of Smokey Bacon, a green bag of Sour Cream & Onion, or a red bag of Cheese & Onion.

Hunky Dorys are the crinkle cut crisps with Salt & Malt vinegar flavor and Flamed Grilled Steak flavor in a burgundy bag.

April continued, "Murphy wasn't sure how to market the inventory so he approached the Findlater family, who owned upscale grocery and wine stores. Not only did they sell the flavored crisps in the store, they also sold them to other outlets. Today, Tayto is one of the most widely recognized brands in all of Ireland." Anne selected Salt and Vinegar and Peter Smokey Bacon.

The Americans sat overlooking the lake, munching on their proper Irish picnic marveling that they were there having lunch *on a lake at a mansion*—Muckross Mansion in Killarney. A squatty jar held some chocolate spread called Nutella. At first bite, Anne became hooked on this dippable, spreadable, delectable, chocolate delight. They dunked apples, celery, carrots, bread, and about anything else (even fingers) into this heavenly milky hazelnut chocolate confection. Normally a dark chocolate purist, it was a new day—out with peanut butter and in with Nutella. It would be the first thing Anne would search for when returning home.

Muckross Mansion was hidden in ivy that wound up the walls and chimneys, giving it a DayGlo Rocket Red gleam. Two Irish Wolfhounds romped in the distance. They learned this is an ancient Irish breed of dog, and famous for being the world's tallest dog, dating back to Roman times. They were once used to hunt wolves, elk, and wild boar. Interestingly, their characteristics are their sweet temperament, intelligence, and patience. Sadly, the average lifespan is only seven years.

Side-by-side, Peter and Anne sat on a bench taking in the sights at Killarney National Park with the lake and Aghadoe Heights in the distance. "Yet another idyllic place to live," Anne announced. A group of four were playing croquet on the lawn. "Not quite the same setting as when we play in our backyard," Sue laughed.

Anne's phone chirped. It was from Mauve.

> Lots of texts from others who will b questioned. Dead man not only poisoned but in major debt so now might b suicide.

> This has turned into a real mystery.

Anne typed back the quick reply.

April drew Anne's attention back to the topic at hand. "Thanks to the Queen of Hearts playing the game of croquet in *Alice in Wonderland*, you may have always thought the game was invented in England. It's very popular there, and a favorite of Queen Elizabeth II. Well, that's a wrong assumption. It originated on Ireland's west coast.

"It's believed that the game, which was popular during the 1850s, stemmed from a similar game that had been brought to the island from northwest France. There was another game known as 'crookey,' which was similar to croquet. Some records show it was first played at Castlebellingham in County Louth in 1834 on the bishop's palace garden. But there are no documents that provide any instructions on how the game was played. Evidently, the game spread like wildfire across Ireland, then across England, which eventually led to the All England Croquet Club, later known as Wimbledon."

Mickey squirmed in his boss's office while Eamon expounded on his ineptness and allowing Seamus to die without making payment. "I should take it out of your wages for the next year."

"Boss, it's not my fault as I've told you a hundred times now. He was fine when I left him in the parking lot. That's probably why the guards haven't hunted me. By now they've watched the CCTV footage."

"You better be right. But this isn't over, I just need to think of some way for you to pay me back."

"Sure boss. I'll do some extra weekend work if you need me."

"That's a lot of weekends to make up for 15 grand, boyo," Eamon stated slightly appeased by the eejit's offer.

"Likely until I'm 35," Mickey growled under his breath.

"Try 50. And get me some new customers."

Late that afternoon, the travelers arrived at their accommodations, Killarney Plaza Hotel. After dinner, they were treated to some traditional song, music, and dance by the Gaelic Roots. Just watching them, the audience was exhausted by the end of the performance, and concluded this was undeniably for a younger generation of performers. The step dancing had always been Anne's favorite type of dancing since she'd seen Michael Flatley in *Riverdance* twice after their first visit to Ireland. It was easy to recall the feeling of the beat of dozens of synchronized feet pounding and tapping the floor with a fast rhythm and catchy music. The twirling, leaping, and jumping were truly fascinating, her Irish roots tingling even more.

"We've watched more TV on this vacation than we ever have. I hate the news, and I'm glad we aren't tracking our pathetic news from home," Anne complained back in their hotel room.

"We don't have to check if you prefer not to."

"Leave it on. Maybe there is something new."

"Meegan Hennessy reporting tonight about the ongoing case of Seamus Kennedy, a resident of Derry. Guards have confirmed toxicology reports and a final report by the coroner. The cause of death is head trauma but how it happened is still unsolved. The report reveals marijuana, alcohol, and foxglove in his system. Foul play? Accidental death? Suicide? Drunken state? Or does forensic evidence point to murder?

"This is a good reminder to viewers at home that many outdoor and household plants and flowers can be dangerous for children and pets if taken in high amounts. We will continue to follow this mystery and report when more information is available."

"I guess that was her feeble attempt at a public service announcement about poisonous flowers." Her husband's remark lightened her sudden crankiness.

CHAPTER TWENTY-SEVEN

A pril told them that today's driving route would be along stunning rugged coastline, looping around the enchanting Ring of Kerry, along unspoiled beaches, through picture-postcard villages and impressive terrain.

Before leaving town and comfortably situated in her conveniently high vantage point, looking out the bus window, Anne glanced over to her left, sitting eyeball-to-eyeball with a full-size bronze goat. Actually, it was a statue of a smiling goat with a crown on its head. April laughingly explained that he's a popular goat called The King Puck, and the statue represents the story of a goat which alerted the townspeople of impending disaster. King Puck was wildly popular. Someone had placed a necklace of fresh white daisies around his neck.

Summits of mountains were haloed in clouds but they could still see plenty of pastures and farmland dotted with ponds and lakes and goldenrod gorse. Unique and varied scenery would be the keywords for the day. In the distance, green, yellow, and tan plots on the rolling hills with brilliant sky and a few random puffy white, flat bottom clouds, looked picture-perfect. The only thing dark was her shadow.

At the Killarney National Park, they boarded a boat and sailed through breathtaking lakes escorted by expert boatman Captain Donal. A storm rolled in and when the clouds touched the water, they couldn't even see the shore-line. The knowledgeable Captain Donal entertained them with witty one-liners, stories of the lakes and the national park, and laughed about the ever-changing weather.

Before the day ended, they'd become familiar with the names of places, villages, and forts. Names like: Kilgarvan, the Battle of Callan in 1261, Cloonee Lakes, Uragh Stone Circle, Derrynane Abbey, Ballinskelligs Bay, Leacanabuaile and Cahergal Forts, Coomasaharn Rock Art, and MacGilly-cuddy Reeks. Not likely to ever remember these names, Anne was glad to have the map they'd brought from home.

A stop at the Kerry Bog Village teleports one back to the eighteenth and nineteenth centuries. Two friendly Irish Wolfhounds, who obviously owned this place, greeted them at the front door. One white house had a pistachio front door and matching window trim. Anne loved the front door because it is what Americans call a Dutch door, where the top and bottom open separately. She and Peter had one in their second home and it reminded her of a favorite television series when she was young called *Petticoat Junction*.

Of course, she had to go in. Glancing up once inside, bog scraw, larger than their straw at home, was used to insulate the house during cold winters. Using flagstones made the floors uneven. An iron bed and cot were in one bedroom. Coming out of the Dutch door Anne heard her name and stopped as Sisterchick Sue took her picture. Complete with a thatched river reed roof, this house belonged to the turf cutter. Large families were the norm even though they lived in small dwellings. Outside, above a pile of peat, hung a basket of scarlet geraniums.

Off to the left sat an old nineteenth century Roman caravan. These were used by those known as "traveling people" who navigated the roads of Ireland. A single black and white cob or a piebald horse pulled the caravan. Many families lived in these rolling homes.

The blacksmith, O'Sullivan's Old Forge, lived in the next building. The walls of the forge were thick with the center section composed of loose stone. Several windows helped with good ventilation along with double doors and a large chimney. When a hot horseshoe plopped into cold water to cool, it created billows of steam.

The stable dwelling had been the home of the MacGillycuddy family. This was a typical home with a stable side for valuable animals like pigs, horses, and cows, and their body heat helped warm the house. The family lived on the other side of the residence. Families made their own cheese and butter.

The Laborer's Cottage is considerably smaller and showed a different class among village residents. A man worked in the boglands cutting and transporting turf. There is a neatly stacked mound of peat against the front of the house. The front door and window trim were painted bright yellow and inside is a mud floor. The few windows were small, and the reason given, as in most cottages of this era, was for tax purposes. The owner had to pay higher taxes for having larger windows as light was considered a luxury. This tax started the famous phrase "daylight robbery." Of course, cottages did not have toilets; instead, they used a special pot placed under the bed.

The Thatcher's Dwelling with its thatched roof appeared perfect. Thatchers of this time were in high demand because they were responsible for building and repairing the majority of cottages in their area. Displayed on the walls were teapots, pitchers, plates of several sizes and patterns, lanterns, and other items used daily. This cottage even has an upstairs and a much airier and spacious interior.

Having enough of cottages, tools, and machinery, Anne meandered behind the complex to discover some well-groomed horses munching in a field of dandelions. However, to her surprise, the informational sign told her that these were Kerry Bog Ponies. They are a native breed to Ireland, recognized by the Irish Horse Board. The breed had been dangerously close to extinction in the late 1980s, however, with the perseverance of John Mulvihill and the Kerry Bog Pony Co-Op Society, the breed is back in healthy numbers.

A hazel pony with an onyx mane ambled over as if to say hello. Another cocoa-colored one with a matching mane had all-white socks at the bottom on his sturdy legs. Each had some white from the top of its head down to its pitch-black nose. Petting whichever one came closest, Anne felt they were friendly and had no doubt they could sense she had Irish blood coursing through her veins, and that she loved horses. These ponies were used for farm work such as bringing home turf from the bog, seaweed from the beach, and taking milk to the creamery. They are smaller, thus easier to keep, eat less, take up less space, and are faster and more athletic than donkeys.

Milling through the farmyard and gardens, she happened across a pile of stones tucked away in a small arch. Tiny pale blue wildflowers pushed through any open space they could find, reaching toward the sunshine. Hearing rustling among the flowers, in her wildest dreams she hoped it might be a fairy, but disappointed it was just a light puff of wind that moved the flowers. But maybe? She still had hope.

The sign at The Red Fox Inn, an old traditional pub, read OPEN as they stepped over a lazing wolfhound and in through bright raspberry red open doors. They were taken back in time by old-time atmosphere and décor. "Irish Coffee or Bailey's Coffee?" a server named Kelly Ann offered the house specialties.

Kelly Ann questioned if they knew that Bailey's Irish Cream was truly invented in Ireland, not just a fabricated name.

"In the early 1970s, Gilbeys of Ireland, which is a division of International Distillers and Vintners, wanted to create a product that they could market internationally. A man who worked in the research lab was told that the company would be starting a new brand of drinks for exploration. He wasn't given any details on what type of drink he was to invent, only that it must contain alcohol.

"He and his colleagues invented Bailey's Irish Cream in 45 minutes. He'd come up with the idea of incorporating Ireland's reputation as a dairy producer into the drink. From there, his merry bunch came up with the idea of mixing Irish whiskey and cream. They had purchased a bottle of Jameson's Irish Whiskey and a tub of cream, which they mixed together in their kitchen. It didn't taste all that good but it had promise. They added sugar which helped but it was still missing something. The final ingredient they added was Cadbury's Powdered Drinking Chocolate and were amazed at how good it tasted. It took two years to perfect and in 1974, Bailey's Irish Cream was introduced as the first Irish cream on the market. Over a billion bottles have been sold. Oh, and the guys who invented it, think they are millionaires? They were only paid about 3,000 pounds for their invention. This is my condensed version of the true story." They all clapped and she did a curtsy.

Their souvenir was the recipe for making homemade Irish Coffee and a delightful memory.

Riding in a motorcoach provided them the gift of height

and, therefore sight, as they could see much more than those driving in their cars. They sat above the hedgerows and stone walls and were able to peek into people's second-story windows if they could see through the lace curtains. One particularly nicely painted red home adorned with matching potted plants had curtains with dogs woven into the lace pattern. She wondered what it would be like to spend the night there. Her imagination ran wild, daydreaming of something that might surprise her if she had a chance to explore the home. What did it look like inside? Who might live in a house like this? Surely an artist or veterinarian.

Streams wound like ribbons through farms and yellow-flowered shrubs of gorse. Occasionally they would see clumps of standing stones and ruins of castles, forts, and stone homes.

They stopped for a hearty lunch and one had corned beef with a lemon sauce, with three, yes, *three* mounds of mashed potatoes. Anne ordered the Shepherd's Pie that had a four-inch layer of mashed potatoes on top. Dessert was warm bread pudding with deep rich cream poured over the top, settling in the bottom of the bowl and saturating the pudding. Not one drop of the delicious cream was left.

The Ring of Kerry has a collection of hamlets sprinkled along the coastline. They went through one particular village where the businesses stretched out in a straight line all butting up against each other. The structures are all two stories high with the first being orange, then a cobalt blue store with wording on the front indicating its name, Green Chair, Haberdashery, and Vintage Gifts, followed by an all-white building with chartreuse trim, another white one with Ferrari red trim, ending the row with a bright lime building.

About ten miles from Killarney, they pulled off at Ladies View, a scenic overlook and understandably one of the most photographed places in Ireland. Before them lay rolling emerald hills covered in grasses and low bushes. Beyond is a lake nestled at the base of mountains, and soft and fluffy clouds like pillows, against a robin's egg blue sky. "Maybe a house on the lake? Pretty idyllic." Peter put this arm around his wife. The geography looked particularly vibrant and the clouds with the sun peeking through frequently altered it all. They stood mesmerized gazing up at changing billowy shapes as the clouds passed quickly by. In the distance, dark virga almost reached the ground as they could see a rain shower.

Returning to Killarney by 6 p.m. was important because they had reservations for a Jaunting Car Ride through the national park. Not an actual car but a horse-drawn buggy ride. They wound through the lakes, and saw small deer, a pheasant, squirrels, and lots of bird life. As they rode on, the likable local driver filled them in on what they were seeing, historical facts, and always entertaining Irish folklore.

While walking to dinner, they saw an elegant window display of Katie's Luxury Chocolates and Aunt Nellie's Sweet Shop. Exquisite trays lined with white lace doilies were arranged in a parade of chocolate delicacies, each hand-dipped frippery decorated with a different design on top. Almost drooling, that's all they needed, and in they rushed.

Anne breathed in the fragrance of chocolate, the smell better than any perfume. She made a bee-line for the dark chocolate extravaganza while admiring the artwork depicting what type of soft center, delectable delight she would bite into. It felt like she was in a chocolate gallery or museum. One dark chocolate with a right-hand swirl indicated a buttercream center. Another dark chocolate had a white polka dot top indicating coconut inside. A dollop of ruby frosting divulged this filling was hot from chili pepper. A round dark chocolate patty with a gold embossed twist was filled with white mint cream. A fuchsia twirl indicated berry cream inside. Next to it was a three-inch-long chocolate stick filled with orange jelly. She bought three of these because it is a favorite candy that Peter enjoyed as a child. There were other impressive displays of milk chocolate bars, toffees, caramels, and marzipan. A young woman wearing a name tag that read Kathleen approached them. "Welcome. Did you know an Irishman invented both chocolate milk and milk chocolate?"

"It's like the Irish invented everything yummy," Jeanine said. "Tell us more."

Jeanine, Linda, Nancy, Sue and Anne gathered closer to hear. "During the 1660s, a man named Hans Sloan was a County Down native, that's in Northern Ireland. He was a physician but at one point he was studying in Jamaica. While he was there he came up with the idea of chocolate milk. He noticed the native Jamaicans mixing cocoa with water. He tried it and found it disgusting. But it got him thinking about their mixture and he tried a concoction of his own. He added cocoa to milk and thought it tasted a little better.

"When Doctor Sloan later moved to England, he took the recipe with him and sold it to an apothecary as medicine. It was used to treat digestion and consumption.

"Later he experimented and boiled cocoa with milk and mixed in plenty of sugar. His invention was milk chocolate. Cadbury began to produce his creation which was first sold as 'Sir Hans Sloan's Milk Chocolate.'"

"You're not making this story up, are you?" Anne asked. "Because I am going to repeat this to friends as if I've known this all along. Since I am 12% Irish, I'm taking credit for it."

"All true." She laughed along with Anne. "Then there's Bailey's Irish Cream, but that's another story. Can I help box up what you'd like?"

"We've heard the Bailey's history. Thank God for the Irish," Nancy joked.

Anne selected one each of lavender buttercream, banoffee, and sea salt toffee. Then chose some gifts for her special chocoholic friends and family, carefully hand-selecting sets of four chocolates that were carefully cushioned in boxes, each sealed with flaxen stickers and wrapped with a dainty ribbon tied in a perfect shamrock green bow.

That evening the ten friends ventured out to dinner at a well-known family restaurant called Treyvaud's and substantiated why it received such a high recommendation. Anne had organic Irish salmon with sun-dried tomatoes and herb crust. Fresh green beans were included. Peter had prime Irish beef meatballs (two the size of baseballs) with a sweet and spicy red wine sauce and colcannon. Colcannon is cabbage and potatoes boiled and pounded together. "It's so much better than it sounds." Peter took another large bite. Every single bite of the mammoth meatball tasted scrumptious. For dessert, they tried the restaurant's famous Bailey's Irish Liqueur cheesecake with butterscotch sauce, a perfect way to end a delightful day.

Nancy mentioned, "Remember the Bailey's over ice we had in the bar of our hotel in Reykjavik?"

"Yes! That was the first time I'd ever tasted it. Didn't even have it the first time we were in Ireland. Really didn't know about it until you introduced me to the wonderful world of Bailey's. In hot chocolate, wowza."

"We need to have one or two more before the end of our trip."

Wrenna sat with Bailey, half on her lap and half stretched out on the sofa watching TV. The medium-sized, stocky Manx rolled onto her back so Wrenna could pet her broad chest. Bailey rubbed her face against Wrenna's hand and she recognized the familiar look in the cat's golden-eyes indicated her readiness to play. The cat seemed more like a dog displaying her affection and playfulness. Wrenna stroked her companion's plush double coat that sometimes revealed blue tones mixed in with silver, brown, cream and white. Bailey had been with her since she was a kitten, almost three years. It took her several days to come up her new family member's name. She thought of strong women in politics but Regina, Josepha nor Norma really worked. Then she almost named her after her favorite female singer, Taylor Swift. But her cat definitely wasn't a Swifty and Taylor just didn't fit either. She went with one of her favorite beverages instead.

Wrenna laughed as she remembered folktales about these cats. One myth is when Noah closed the door of the Ark, he accidentally cut off the tail of the Manx cat.

"Give me ten minutes, Bailey, I want to watch the rest of this program." *This Country* was some sibling mockumentary of the rural Cooper family and village idiocy. She really didn't care as long as she avoided the news in case of any updates on Seamus. There was none.

She anxiously awaited a text from Morgan. He had been good about contacting her. Still away doing some undercover work, it made her nervous and she wondered if they married, could she cope with the stress of being married to a guard? He'd texted her a photo of a man she didn't recognize. He admitted it was a selfie and that was exactly what he wanted—to be unrecognizable. Bailey purred as Wrenna told her all about Morgan, again, and how she felt quite sure she loved him. She believed her beloved cat understood every word. *Great, now I've become a crazy cat lady*, she muttered.

CHAPTER TWENTY-EIGHT

They stopped to stretch their legs at the Gap of Dunloe. It is extremely rocky terrain with few trees and more blooming gorse. Anne noticed something hanging from a solitary tree and rushed ahead to explore. Someone had left a chain and lock hanging from a lower branch. She recognized it as a love lock that many couples leave on bridges in favorite cities they wish to return to. She could see why a couple left their lock here. "I could live here," she leaned in close to Peter. He'd heard that comment so many times, that he didn't even need to respond, he just nodded. He did agree that the narrow mountain pass running north to south in County Kerry, which separates the MacGillycuddy's Reeks mountain range in the west from the Purple Mountain Group range in the east, looked stunning and peaceful.

As they crossed a stone bridge, Anne noticed the familiar root beer-colored water flowing over the boulders indicating peat would be close by. Driving through the backcountry, she sighted plenty of bunnies. Some locals purposely run them down as folklore reports that witches unfortunately could disguise themselves as hares. Witch hares supposedly stole milk from cattle.

Occasionally they'd notice an Irish Wolfhound beside their human, or in an outside pen usually the size of a horse corral. As for cats, they learned that black cats were believed to be lucky, and Irish black cats allegedly could understand human speech.

Often Anne would see "Céad Míle Fáilte" or "A Hundred Thousand Welcomes." She did feel welcome and a kinship to the land, nature, and people. She felt this almost as strongly as when she was in Scotland and Iceland. She wished she had in Italy but sadly, she hadn't. Nor did she have a drop of Italian in her.

As they cruised through little villages, she randomly caught a peek through a slightly opened draperies. If the curtains were open wider, she had a fleeting opportunity to peer into someone's life. Anne had overused the words "charming," "cute," and "quaint" as well as "old-world" and "picturesque."

Mickey and Eamon were wrong thinking they were in the clear. Little did they know several of their clients had been burned one too many times. Guards had a file three inches thick and growing daily that included names, locations, websites, transaction details, and photos of a variety of employees and customers. The Revenue Commissioners were supportive of the sting operation soon to be in play.

Graham sat in an old pickup truck, a video camera following the two men's every move at a track miles outside of Derry. Other undercover guards working the case mingled among the crowd. At their nightly meetings, they talked about what they had learned and the next steps in the investigation of Seamus' untimely demise.

On their first visit to Blarney Castle 20 years earlier, all Peter and Anne knew about the infamous limestone block called the Blarney Stone was that kissing the stone endows the kisser with the gift of gab, or nicer, maybe, the gift of eloquence, or skill at flattery. The stone had been set into a tower of the castle in 1446. All Anne could think about were the millions of germs on the rock.

There is much more to see and do than kiss that dirty stone. The process alone was ridiculous: you lay down on a boardwalk, hang upside down, bend backward dropping your head down with some man holding you so you don't slip down several stories. "Nope, not for me." However, Anne did stop and touch it.

Returning to the famous Blarney Castle, they were eager to revisit this historical attraction with friends who were seeing it, and Ireland, for the first time. Anne got great pleasure watching their expressions seeing this special country through their particularly merry eyes, especially some having Irish roots like her. Several were anticipating kissing the stone, which she and Peter had agreed they need not repeat the climb up especially since there were hundreds of people in the line. Before safeguards were installed, the kiss was performed with real risk to life and limb. Participants were grasped by the ankles and dangled from a great height. "Been there, done that for me," Anne told Sue. "Plus, I've got all the luck and blarney I need."

The stone castle reminded Anne of a shoe box standing on end with some cutouts on the top and not much curb appeal. It's a five-story stone tower with windows all around with a wedding cake-like-topper that must have been erected to watch for marauding Vikings. There's an uneven yet walkable stone wall around the castle that's great for gazing down on intruders or tourists, depending on your frame of mind or the century you lived in. A black bird was eyeing Anne and Peter from his perch above. Anne glanced up. "Don't you dare. Skedaddle." She hoped he wouldn't be depositing something white on her only jacket.

They were able to hike all around the medieval fortress and the tower house that was built between the fifteenth and seventeenth centuries. Cheery flowers of all colors and types adorned the well-kept gardens complete with interesting rock formations known as Wishing Steps in the Rock Close. This garden felt as if it might be a mystical place, and reading a sign, it had been the site of an ancient druidic settlement.

Wandering the trail under a vine-covered wooden arbor, they stepped into magnificent gardens of flowers and stood under a leafy canopy of ancient yew and oak trees. Needles and leaves littered the ground. The Bog Garden contains two waterfalls where they strolled on a raised wooden walkway, then through a willow tunnel before passing through large clusters of giant rhubarb plants. The whole scene appeared to be prehistoric, something straight out of the *Jurassic Park* movie.

Anne noticed a crow or maybe a jackdaw hopping from one wooden arch to the next. "He could be a twin to the one from the castle wall," she pointed to Peter.

The oldest trees at Blarney Castle are here. One humongous tree had limbs that could have been individual trees, dozens of them. A group of three yew trees, clumped together on an island, supposedly have been there for up to 600 years. This entire area evoked a sense of calm. Anne couldn't explain it and decided she'd keep her self-awareness hidden.

They came to a 90-foot-long wooden pergola that spans the path through the area called the Herbaceous Border that runs along a south-facing stone wall in the upper arboretum. Extending more than 100 yards, the Border creates an impressive display of color using perennials as well as unusual annuals. The pergola was bare of summertime flowers except for a late-blooming rose here and there. Anne imagined what all those vines would smell like with thousands of colorful roses.

They stood overlooking the appropriately named Fern Garden, in the heart of the castle gardens. A waterfall cascaded dramatically down one side. They followed the path under a jungle-like canopy and came upon over 80 varieties of ferns including one that was more than ten feet higher than Peter and the tallest of its kind in Ireland. He heard rustling and they stood quietly and observed a family of four rambunctious red squirrels.

Hidden behind the castle battlements they located the Poison Garden, which positively wasn't here 20 years earlier. The sign read in bold font "DO NOT TOUCH, SMELL OR EAT ANY PLANT! CHILDREN MUST BE ACCOMPANIED AT ALL TIMES." They entered at their own risk as made abundantly clear by the signage. These plants are so dangerous and toxic that some are kept in large cages. This garden contains a collection of poisonous plants from all over the world and labeled with information about their toxicity and traditional and modern uses. "Notice how quiet it is in here? Creepy. Not even a bird." Peter pulled Anne's arm as they exited quickly.

The Jungle, complete with its own bamboo viewing platform, trails along the back of the Tropical Border. It was designed to surprise visitors with exotic plants that can be grown in the Irish climate. There are banana plants and giant tree ferns. Anne felt like they'd been transported to a completely different country somewhere in the Caribbean.

Her favorite garden within the castle is The Seven Sisters which forms the central feature of a garden of grasses, with velvet-looking flowers which are a contrast to seven large, solid gray rocks that dominate the space. Even the prickly purple thistle appeared softer next to the hot pink Irish Heather. Rows and beds of different colors and types of dahlias, colorful chrysanthemums, plus some surprising hibiscus, all in full bloom created a mixture of shapes, colors, and textures. Children were having a grand time climbing all over the boulders.

A plaque read that legend tells of a famous king who once ruled this area. He had seven daughters and two sons. His rival was a powerful clan chief and the time came when the king had to defend his lands. One terrible day the army rode out to battle with the king, and his two sons led the way. Although victorious, it came at a great price as both sons were killed. The army marched back to the castle, passing the ancient druids' stone circle that had stood for millennia. The king dispatched a contingent of men to the sacred site and in his grief, instructed them to push over two of the nine standing stones commemorating his fallen sons. The Seven Sisters remain standing to this day. Anne made every effort to believe these stories of fantastical Irish history—her history.

Ready for a break, Peter and Anne followed the signs through the stableyard a short walk from the castle, to the charming, appropriately named Stable Yard Café. Lined up in the display cases were decorative cakes, fresh scones, and other tasty treats. Offered were a large range of Bewley's coffees and varieties of teas. All cakes and scones are freshly baked daily by a local baker and the selection of lemon drizzle, chocolate, carrot, coffee, apple tart, and Banoffee pie was overwhelming. They could have had Guinness stew, sausage rolls, pizza slices, or snacks and crisps but agreed on a little lighter fare. She had Banoffee pie in Scotland so knew it was a pastry base or crumbled biscuits, lots of butter, sliced bananas, topped with unsweetened whipped cream, toffee, and a few more thinly sliced bananas. Instead, Anne opted for a cup of tea with cream and sugar along with a lemon scone with a drizzle of honey produced by a local beekeeper and a scoop of their famous ice cream.

"Ice cream, this time of day?" Peter looked at his wife who was almost drooling.

"Who doesn't have homemade loganberry ice cream in the morning?" They were going to sit outside in the sunshine, but Anne noticed a crow eyeing her that creeped her out, so they sat inside and enjoyed the scenic posters scattered around the café walls. Garden flowers brightened each table from the mason jars that served as vases.

Anne caught a bird standing in the doorway staring at them intently. "He's waiting for you to drop something, a speck of leftover scone. This one positively followed us around and he's getting on my nerves. He's spooky and disturbing."

"It's a hungry or very spoiled crow, Anne. Obviously well treated. Or a jackdaw."

"Maybe it's my imagination, but I did take a few photos of him in these different locations, and in each picture the bird is identical."

"There are about a dozen outside. They all look the same to me."

As they left the Stable Yard Café, the winged stalker joined its other inky feathered friends gathered on the rooftop. Uncomfortable due to the bird congregation, they headed directly to the Blarney Castle Shop for some browsing.

Anne felt transported back 20 years stepping into the store where she had intended to find just the right gift for her recently revealed Irish father, and figured Blarney Castle would be appropriate because he sure had the gift of gab and told a story like none other. She had an ah-ha moment—a Kelly green plaid tie with a matching pocket scarf. She knew he'd wear it every March 17 from then on. He dressed professionally each workday as a county official in Oregon. He oversaw the county elections, licenses including marriage, and was the keeper of many records. He had been elected by the citizens for many terms. *He loved that tie*, she said to herself, so glad she'd gotten it for him two decades earlier.

Returning her thoughts to the present, she wandered the aisles and came across a round rack with dozens of bookmarks with family crests and explanations of their origins:

-CAMPBELL for her cousin Patti who is married to Donny. It means "crooked mouth." Anne chuckled when she read this.

-DALY for her friend Sally. Daly means "assembles frequently."

-FINNEGAN for her childhood friend Maleah and her parents who were some of her folks' best friends. Finnegan means "little fair one."

-MARTIN for her longtime friends Mike and Kathy. Mike's parents were best friends with her folks and were like second parents to Anne. It means "devotee of St. Martin." Unfortunately, they also had been on two trips where Anne had come across bodies, all coincidental, of course.

Anne purchased ten laminated Riley bookmarkers for family at home. The crest of two lions standing upright with two front paws holding a human hand appeared rather frightening. The lion's palms faced forward with five dripping droplets of blood that matched the lion's two red tongues in a Kelly green shield surrounded by swirls of gold. Not a happy-go-lucky crest Anne would have preferred.

Dave whispered to Anne and tugged her arm. "I need your help in finding Sue the perfect Christmas gift. Come see my finalists." Anne knew immediately it would be a gold and silver bangle bracelet for her Sisterchick.

"Yes, that's it."

"Now distract her and keep her away from here."

"On it."

She drew Sue's attention to a display case of silver Celtic earrings. Anne and her Sisterchick Sue shared laughter, tears, and many ah-ha moments on this adventure and now an identical pair of earrings.

Anne knew their next stop would be at the Blarney Woolen Mills, established in 1823, known as the home of Irish Knitwear and Belleek Irish china. She didn't *need* any more Belleek after visiting the factory 20 years earlier. Need and want were total opposites like apples and oranges or oil and water.

She'd been *wanting* another Christmas ornament crafted of Belleek china and had saved some of her spending money for this occasion. She bought five, taking one home for each of her precious nieces. One had given her a plaque that read, "Only Aunts can love you like a mother, keep secrets like a sister, behave like a true friend, and kick your butt if you need it!" Anne loved those girls.

All manner of "Woven in Ireland" clothing, blankets, and textiles fashioned of merino wool and cashmere, lined the shelves. Nancy smiled, as she was in her happy place—shopping. Peter purchased a traditional gray herringbone Irish flat cap, while Anne spotted a marble shamrock ornament, the color of Gravenstein green apples for herself.

Walking in the door with a handful of sunflowers, Wrenna was flabbergasted. "My favorites!"

Her smile put the sunflower's brightness to shame, he thought. "I remembered from high school. You wanted a sunflower corsage for your dress but they weren't in season yet."

"You continue to amaze and impress me, Morgan Graham."

"Good. That's exactly what I wanted to hear."

Meeting for a quick lunch whenever possible, Morgan and Wrenna kept their promise not to speak of the ongoing case with Seamus. Sitting side-by-side in a booth, he drank his coffee in a couple of slurps and consumed a ham toastie in three bites. She watched him with eyebrows raised.

"Working in law enforcement makes you impervious to the heat of drinks, along with gulping meals quickly."

"Evidently." She felt so relaxed with him.

He wanted to explain everything but could not tell her a major investigation had begun into Mickey, who had supplied Seamus with the beer and poison, and another man named Eamon, who Seamus owed money. The investigation board in the office had dozens of photos of all the people connected to the case.

Seamus's questionable death wasn't a priority now, the illegal gambling ring was. When Morgan did mention that permissible update, he noticed she took a deep breath and then exhaled slowly.

He closed his unreadable eyes.

"Are you okay?"

"Aye. Sometimes when I look at you, I lose track of what I'm thinking."

"Is that a good thing or a bad thing?" She slid closer to him, feeling content and at ease.

He took her soft hand and gazed into her astonishingly winsome eyes. He wasn't sure about the soulmate thing but he felt as if he was entering a comfortable warm shelter he never wanted to leave. "I'll let you know when I figure it out."

Detouring a few miles west off the main road, they entered the village of Mitchelstown, population 3,000. The River Gradoge runs by the town into River Funshion and it is best known as a center for cheese production. They stopped to give a hearty hello to one of their fellow traveler's grandparents. John's grandparents opened their romaine lettuce-green door and gave them an enthusiastic wave. Anne would have loved to have gone into their home but didn't dare ask. John would be having dinner with them that evening in Cork. Their squared-off door was bordered by a white stone-carved arch and surrounded by ivy. Anne took a picture of their emerald front door.

"You know, some of Dad's relatives came from Cork. It seems half of Ireland was named Riley." Peter nodded and chuckled at his wife's comment.

After dropping off their luggage in a cozy hotel room, Peter suggested they go for fish and chips. They meandered past row houses, one Kelly green with windows and roofline painted tangerine, and a two-story orange sherbet building. On the waterfront, they stopped at a small chipper. Anne overheard a man say, 'wan an' wan.' "I think that's one-and-one," she whispered, "like a standard order."

"I would just like a few chips and one piece of fish. Do you have tartar sauce?"

"We make our own." Obviously, he was proud.

"Could you please add that too?"

"Let's just split one order and then we can get a dessert somewhere." Steam rose from fresh-out-of-fryer fish and chips. Peter sprinkled malt vinegar all over his half of the meal.

In a small paper cup, Anne dipped her piece of hot crispy coated hake into a mix of mayonnaise, finely chopped dill pickle, green onion, and capers.

"Oh, my goodness, this is the best tartar I've ever had. Peter, try a bite, not much though, I'm not sharing. It's perfect with the dill pickles, not sweet pickles which should never be in any tartar sauce as far as I'm concerned."

"Yes, dear. I know how you love tartar sauce and are a dill pickle snob. And gelato. Oh, and crème brûlée. Yum, that is tasty but I know you enjoy it much more than I do. I think we need a second order."

"Agreed. Forget dessert."

Sunrise and sunset were possibly Anne's favorite time of the day. Mainly because of the colors. "Peter, doesn't the evening sky remind you of a stained glass window, all ablaze with the setting sun's brilliance?"

"Quite eloquent my dear, and you are right." They watched amber, pink, coral, and crimson reflect off the River Lee with several Canada geese and a Bewick's swan family making the only ripples in the water before stepping into their hotel.

Knowing they promised to never ever ever discuss the fateful Seamus episode, Fay read Wrenna's text in all caps.

GUARDS CONCLUDE THAT S DEATH IS FROM DRUGS AND POISON CONTRIBUTING TO HIS FALL. CASE CLOSED!!!!

What a relief. Let's have a drink!

NOW!

Fay saw a thumbs-up emoji, very unlike her cousin.

CHAPTER TWENTY-NINE

Back in their spacious motorcoach, the Americans headed to Waterford where Anne anticipated stopping since it would be their first time here. Enjoying the drive through the agriculture of multiple shades of mint, pear, lime, fern, and moss farms separated by short stone walls, she didn't want to miss a thing. Dozens of navy-colored magpies were hanging around the sheep. The birds supposedly foretold the future.

April noted that there's a superstition relating to the sighting of these birds. The saying goes "One for sorrow, two for joy, three for a girl, four for a boy, five for silver, six for gold, and seven for a secret never to be told."

Why not? In Ireland anything can happen, Anne was finding out.

Anne had some Waterford collectibles at home and would be searching for a Christmas ornament. She'd lost track of how many special mementos she'd purchased thus far. Peter had given her a few starter pieces, and after several years she finally had a complete set of a Waterford nativity scene that they brought out for the entire month of December. She already had a Celtic Cross and a thatched cottage.

They were staying in Waterford, home of the House of Waterford Crystal, with their hotel conveniently located just down the street. But before being released to support the local economy, they toured Christ Church Cathedral Square complete with several all-white houses lined up in a row. One had a bright crimson door with a cute ceramic birdhouse nailed to the upper right-hand side of the door casing. The next home had a bright azure door with an ebony #7.

The Georgian-style cathedral with pillared portico, internal columns of varied styles, and a spectacular fancy stucco plasterwork ceiling is stunning. Sparkling at Anne were two jaw-dropping, shimmering Waterford crystal chandeliers. "They look like maybe an upside-down ice cream cone with the cone quite long," Sue decided. Prisms of light ricocheted off everything, bouncing colors all over. The white scrollwork on white columns and arches with the soft yellow ceiling radiated a cheery peaceful ambiance. The internal walls are adorned with many elaborate memorials, monuments, and reliefs. April drew their attention to the elegantly carved pulpit, baptismal font, and magnificent organ.

Additionally, in the square, is a life-size Viking boat outside of Reginald's Tower, a Waterford landmark monument and Ireland's oldest civic building. The tower occupies the site of the fort and was built by the Vikings, led by Reginald when they first settled in Waterford and established the city in 914 AD. The fort was built to guard the entrance to their harbor, the tidal marsh where St. John's River flowed into the River Suir in the area of the present-day city hall.

Anne took several photos of Dave, being of Norwegian heritage, who sometimes acted like a Viking.

The ground and first floor date to King John's time. John visited Waterford twice, in 1185 AD as a young prince then again as king in 1210. The walls on the ground floor are over 13 feet thick, impressive yet typical of towers of the period. The ground floor is tiled, and the upper floors are wood. Built into the wall of the tower is a staircase with steps that were deliberately designed to be of different heights and widths, making it difficult for attackers (and visitors) to climb. Steps like this are known as stumble steps. The spiral staircase was oriented to the right making it impossible for right-handed attackers to swing their swords properly as they climbed up. "Those Vikings were a skillful and shrewd lot. We're going there next." Dave was obviously proud of his ancestry as both of his parents emigrated from Norway.

"Never mind the pillaging and plundering," Sue added.

Rebuilt by the Anglo-Normans in the twelfth century, the top two floors were added in the fifteenth century to house a cannon. Until about 1700, the tower was the strongpoint of the medieval defensive walls that enclosed the city.

In the archways are many displays presenting a view of how the town would have been around the year 1050, almost 150 years after it was established. The modern streets of Waterford still follow the lines of the original streets set out over a thousand years ago.

In a display case is a Viking lead weight decorated with an enamel bearded human face. This weight, dating from about 850, is one of over 200 dug out during archaeological excavations at the Viking site near Waterford. Before coins were used by the Vikings, for currency they traded pieces of silver which were weighed using lead weights like this one.

There is a brooch called the Waterford Kite Brooch crafted about 1100 AD and is Ireland's finest example of personal jewelry from this period. These kite-shaped brooches were basically cloak fasteners with elaborate heads worn by high-status women and men. This brooch would have been used to tie a cloak or a shawl. It is made of silver and decorated with extravagant gold foil and amethyst studs. This piece shows the wealth of Waterford's residents during this time, as well as the exceptional talent and ability of its craftsmen.

There is a cannonball on the top floor of the tower and April showed them one embedded in the outside tower wall. The cannonballs date from the siege of Waterford by the army of Oliver Cromwell in the 1600s, when ships on the River Suir bombarded the city with cannon fire. Even though a small tower, it is packed with impressive history and treasures and a fine education for all of them.

After the tour the visitors had the afternoon open to explore, so Anne headed right for the Waterford Crystal store hoping to find the perfect souvenir. She had to find just the right Christmas ornament. A terrific marketing piece propped up in the corner of the store window was a full-size harp adorned with thousands of shimmering crystals.

Anne stuck her hands in her coat pockets for fear of bumping or breaking something. To the right stood a door, and not just any door, but a door with an oval-shaped mirror. Surrounding the mirror was a myriad of distinctive crystals, row after row around the entire mirror. Impressive and extraordinary are understatements and only 32,000 euros, not including delivery. A display case held the Reginald Tower engraved on an exquisite crystal vase. She glanced to the left and spotted several types of ornaments. It was hard to select just one, but she did, a wreath of ivy complete with a bow at the bottom with 2018 engraved on it.

While walking back to the hotel to drop off her Waterford find for safekeeping, she noticed a colorful poster promoting *Kyle Riley & The Temper Tantrums*, a folk and rock music show for toddlers under eight. They would be performing the following week at the Theatre Royal. Rileys were everywhere. A black cat crossed in front of her and she remembered that the Irish believed that meant good luck was heading her way. Unless you're the first person that the black cat sees in the morning. If that happens you might as well go back to bed because nothing good's going to happen all day.

She didn't want to question the folklore too thoroughly, like how would one know if they were the first to see that particular black cat that morning? *Just go with it* she told herself. Another ism she heard was about death. If a wild bird enters your home or a picture falls off the wall, you can expect a death in the family. Crossed knives on the tabletop or counter? Better uncross them immediately or there will be an argument in the household. She did chuckle at the itchy palms. If the palm of your right hand is itchy, it means you'll soon be shaking hands with a stranger. If it's the left hand, you're about to come into some money. She actually enjoyed these cultural quirks.

Gazing out their hotel window that evening, reflecting on the day, she watched as the iridescent sunset transformed the colors of the river. Light clouds turned apricot and then pink against the amber dusky sky. Lights were twinkling on each home lining the roadway across from the river. The homes and lights disappeared from view as they wound around the corner.

Now twilight with the window slightly ajar, somewhere in the distance Anne could hear a familiar sound that she loved. And sometimes she was the only one who heard it. Anne knew there were bagpipers somewhere, but Peter didn't hear them. He reminded her they were in Ireland, not Scotland and he noted she tended to hear bagpipes when no one else did. But once the music got closer thus louder, he agreed that somewhere there were indeed pipers.

Anne gave him her squinty-eyed, well-deserved "I told you so" glare. Down in the dark parking lot below huddled a group starting to warm up for a performance. "I needed to find out where they're performing. See you later..." as she ran out of their room, down the corridor to the lobby to inquire about her favorite Scottish musical sounds. At the same time, the band marched into the lobby and it turned out they were playing at a fundraising event in their hotel. Anne sat outside the dining room for some time listening to their distinctive and sometimes haunting melodies. What a perfect way to end a lovely day.

CHAPTER THIRTY

Someone started singing "On the Road Again" as they stepped onto their bus the next day and soon came upon the Rock of Cashel. Also known as the Cashel of the Kings and St. Patrick's Rock, it is a historic site located in County Tipperary. Legend says the Rock of Cashel originated in the Devil's Bit, a mountain 20 miles north of Cashel, when St. Patrick banished Satan from a cave, resulting in the Rock's landing in Cashel. The limestone outcrops rise 200 feet above the surrounding plain. In 1001, the King of Munster donated his fortress on the Rock to the church. Outside, Anne viewed the twelfth century Irish High Cross at the Rock, a perfect Celtic cross constructed of sandstone.

Cormac's Chapel, the chapel of King Cormac on the hill of Cashel, is magnificent Irish Romanesque architecture constructed in 1127. It has opposing doors on the north and south sides, twin square towers, a steeply pitched stone roof, an altar bay, and arched windows all done in white, beige, yellow, and chestnut bricked-shaped stones. Peering through the bars in the castle windows, Ireland was aglow in goldenrod gorse. Farther out were acres of multiple shades of green divided by uneven rows of bushes and rocks. The oldest and tallest of the buildings is a well-preserved round tower about 90 feet high, dating from 1100. They used the dry-stone method when building the tower. Anne had seen this in Scotland and recalled being told that it was a method by which structures were constructed from stones without any mortar to hold them together. This technique was used frequently in building stone walls, traditionally for boundaries separating property or as retaining walls for terracing.

When entering the chapel's south door, under vaulted ceilings and wide arches Anne felt a warmth from the sunbeams pouring through windows. Frescoes were magnificently restored in the 1980s after somebody exposed they had been whitewashed. At the north door are five arches supported by five columns, and above the doorway is a centaur shooting at a lion.

But it's all about the views from this vantage point. There are extraordinary views inside and out. Wandering outside Anne explored old grave sites and saw the abbey below.

Stopping for a snack this day wasn't that outstanding. Some days were like that because of where they were driving. Some gas stations in the UK and Europe have a restaurant and full grocery store. They had an hour in one such locale. In the market Anne read their version of ABCs: A-Apple juice, B-Beef, C-Cheese, D-Duckling, E-Eggs, F-Fresh salmon, G-Green beans, H-Handmade chocolates, I-Ice cream, J-Jams, K-Kippers, L-Lagers, M-Mushrooms, N-Nibbles, O-Ostrich, P-Prepared meals, Q-Quality, P-Pork, R-Rashers, S-Stout, T-Truffles, U-Unsalted butter, V-Venison, W-Whiskey, X-Xtra Large Pizza, Y-Yoghurt and finally Z-Zucchini. Anne couldn't resist grabbing four handmade chocolates for the road, dark ones, of course.

Wrenna and Morgan met for an hour, as he'd come home for a brief break. He missed her and his dog, Flynn. They had kept their vow not to discuss Seamus but he did inform her about the drugs and gambling case he was involved in. However, he didn't share the extent he was involved. She kept their conversations light and entertaining and told him about Fay's new love, the Greek shipping magnet.

"Do I need to do a background check on this guy?" he chortled. "I can let you know his details next time I get a break. The case might be over in a month or so."

"Let's wait for a check on him for now," she laughed. "Do you want me to help more with Flynn?"

"No, that's okay. My brother can stay as long as necessary. But visit Flynn when you can. He's quite taken with you, as am I. But I've got to go." He took her in his arms for a long kiss that sent tingles to her toes.

Just before the busload of tourists arrived at Kilkenny, Anne noticed dozens of sooty black birds about the size of crows, on fences, rooftops, and lampposts. April told them that according to Kerry tradition, jackdaws of Kilgarvan could once talk. To escape the unwelcome attention of the crows, they requested to move into the towns. At first, due to the opposition of the chief druid, the king refused, but later, when a jackdaw unearthed the king's missing ring, he relented.

"So, are crows and jackdaws the same?"

"Jackdaws are a type of hooded crow that have very pale blue eyes."

"Okay, those were jackdaws that were stalking us. I glared at one, right in his creepy bluish-white eyes."

Stopping at Kilkenny on the River Nore was yet another

of the many "step back in time" sensations Anne had had on the trip. She and Peter did a city tour on a miniature train, more like a trolley pulling two cars, that held around ten tourists.

Around the first corner, one charming house had brightly painted yellow trimmed windows upstairs and down, and double doors in the same cheery yellow. Window boxes overflowed with cadmium red geraniums and tiny delicate creamy flowers. The train followed closely by the original rock wall, about ten feet tall with ivy trailing down from the top. She touched the roughness of the rocks. Around another corner stood a sunshine yellow house next to a pink house which stood right next to a teal house. They rode by St. Canice's Cathedral, looking bleak because of the drizzly weather. Two side-by-side houses attached by a brick wall showed off a bright cardinal red door and the other a soft lemon yellow one.

As the train putted along, they received an education on banshee, fairies, and leprechauns. As she was Irish, Anne thought it was important to keep them straight. Apparently, she'd forgotten the differences over 20 years.

—A Leprechaun is a solitary fairy, a shoemaker, or tailor, resembling a small man of grumpy temperament. The leprechaun is said to have a pot of gold, which he must surrender to whoever catches him.

—A Banshee is a female fairy attached to a family. It warns of impending death by giving an eerie wail. She recalled hearing about the banshee in Scotland as it is also prominent in Scottish lore.

—Fairies are either pint-size beings or a little bigger like a leprechaun or someone of normal human stature and can be either female or male. They roam around in troops and have the gift of healing, which they can pass on to humans if they wish. Sometimes a mortal may be sought by a fairy lover. If he refuses her advances, he is her master; if he surrenders, she dominates him. Fairies live in mounds.

Anne just wanted to see one, or any one of them.

After the 30-minute tour, they popped in for ice cream at Murphy's. It wasn't a surprise to find Dave and Sue already sampling the goods. A picture of a content brick red-tan cow read, "Creamy, creamy milk from the rare, indigenous Kerry cow breed." When Anne read "One of the best ice cream shops in the world," they were goners. Not only did all the publicity on the walls create high expectations, so did the handsome Irish guy serving up the delectable delights as he told them about certain favorites like Dingle Gin, Irish Brown Bread, Irish Coffee, Elderflower, Dingle Sea Salt—stop right there—she had to have sea salt. But wait, Sticky Toffee Pudding? Yep, another must try. He told them that the worst flavor they created turned out to be smoked salmon ice cream. "It tasted awful." He faked a gag. The best unusual flavor, blue cheese and caramelized shallot. The oddest customer request that they actually concocted into ice cream was green pea and mint, reportedly not great.

Drizzle and gray clouds matched the same color of Kilkenny castle and church. Kilkenny means "Church of Cainneach" and sits on both sides of the River Nore. They explored this small medieval town and its castle. Like other towns, the castle was built, and walls were added to protect the residents from the invaders.

Standing behind a plot of prickly-stemmed ruby roses, a portion of Kilkenny Castle loomed across the grassy acreage. This part of the castle seemed like it was being held up by gray stones, seamlessly constructed into a gigantic round container of Quaker Oats, perfectly round and tall. The middle section with four chimneys poking out the side reminded Anne of a soda cracker box tipped on end. It stands grand and stately but not all that handsome. However, few buildings in Ireland can boast a longer history of nonstop occupation than this castle. Founded soon after the Norman conquest of Ireland, the castle has been rebuilt and modified to fit changing situations over 800 years.

The town's coat of arms is the castle flanked by two columns, beside which are two soldiers with a bow and arrow, slanted outward. Below in the grass is a bright tomato-red lion, smiling; not a growl but a smile, with a cobalt tongue that matches his claws. Everything has meaning but this one wasn't clear to Anne.

Kilkenny is a historic old city and celebrated its 400th year in 2008. Its incorporation began in the early sixth century with a church built in honor of St. Canice, now St. Canice's Cathedral, also known as Kilkenny Cathedral. The tower and the church are about the same height.

Touring the inside they appreciated the hand-carved wood, highlighting the details and workmanship. Anne noticed dogs at the feet of some of the tombs. Dogs represent loyalty. Anne felt the hairs on her arms prickle not because it was scary, but because of its history within the walls of this architectural marvel. Worship has taken place at this site for over 800 years. Sue pointed out the remarkable stained glass windows, and The See Chair of the Bishop of Ossory dating back to 1120.

The Round Tower is the oldest standing structure in Kilkenny City, and only two people at a time can climb it. "Well?" Anne eyeballed Peter.

"No way! I'm not climbing that steep wooden ladder with 121 steps." No one did.

CHAPTER THIRTY-ONE

The next day their bus load of jolly tourists departed for the Wicklow Mountain range south of Dublin. Thick deciduous trees cover over 50,000 acres. It is littered with bogs and heather blanketing the hillside, slopes, and peaks. They saw fast-flowing streams and sometimes short waterfalls emptied into deep lakes of sapphire. These mountains weren't like the Cascade Range in Oregon, but lower and more meandering with a myriad of green hues depending on which type of vegetation grows there. The colors reminded her of green grapes, green pears, honeydew melon, asparagus, broccoli, cucumbers, green peppers, lettuce, peas, and zucchini, a smorgasbord of colors.

The cheery sky was dotted with cotton-ball clouds that moved quickly overhead. White ones to thicker gray were common in short periods of time. Anne concluded that the Irish weather would be difficult to predict. Clouds moved quickly creating distinctive profiles and silhouettes with their shadows making unique figures on the ground. One cottony cloud had a dark center that resembled an angel blowing a horn. The shadow it created on the ground gave the appearance of a miniature horse.

Acres of bright yellow moved with the breeze like rolling wheat fields. Vibrant yellow petals gave the appearance of millions of miniature suns. A farmer's stand had buckets of platter-size sunflowers for sale.

Miles of purple heather had peaked two weeks earlier, April said. Now the entire setting looked like it had been covered by a dusky burgundy carpet rolled out for expected royalty. April mentioned that the mountain range is the largest continuous upland area in the Republic of Ireland and the mountains stretch into County Dublin and are sometimes called the Dublin Mountains.

She pointed out the highest peak, Lugnaquilla, about 3,000 feet. The mountains are composed of granite but there are much older rocks of quartzite. Copper and lead have been the main metals mined, with a brief gold rush in the eighteenth century. Several rivers have their source in the mountains including the Liffey in Dublin. Powerscourt Waterfall is the tallest in Ireland at 397 feet.

On a hilltop, Anne stood observing a mountain that dropped off sharply into a pasture with hundreds of fluffy sheep, like large slow-moving golf balls. The land disappeared into a light sandy beach. Peter observed a light bluish-gray-backed bird with white underparts and a dark head, about the size of a large crow, flying rapidly. Later when checking their *Birds of Ireland* book, he identified it to be a peregrine falcon.

Glendalough is littered with ponds and lakes, probably because it is a glacial valley. It is well-known for an early medieval monastic settlement established in the sixth century. The clouds created shadows on a calm lake. Gray ones hovering over rolling hills in the distance matched the stone arch color.

The low stone arch led to the site of an early monastery built between the tenth and twelfth centuries complete with round towers over 100 feet high. Anne shivered while meandering through stone ruins once sturdy and sacred.

Across a creek, they ambled through St. Kevin's Cemetery, just a short distance from the village of Laragh. The cemetery is part of the monastic site they had just explored. Celtic crosses in all shapes and sizes adorned family plots where headstones were crafted in many different styles, some standing straight but most tilting one way or another due to centuries of erosion. Many were in surprisingly good condition. It is an old graveyard still in use. A quail and her family scampered away, obscured behind a headstone. Momma bird had an interesting white-streaked pattern on her hazel face. Anne sauntered for a while hoping to scribble names and dates in her journal. She didn't discover even one O'Reilly in the bunch.

The size of this cemetery was modest yet quietly haunting, and she found it hard not to be moved by the dozens of headstones. A few people, not part of their group, were milling about, clutching bunches of flowers and Anne assumed searching for some familiar family name. At one end of the grounds sat an elderly woman resting her hand on the corner of a stone. Anne felt a powerful pull toward her. She couldn't see what was written on the gray, weathered headstone. Anne whispered "Hello" not to startle the lady. When she glanced up, Anne saw the lady had tears in her mournful hazel aging eyes. Then Anne did, too.

Stepping into the old church, she peered out a long window. It provided a view of a portion of the cemetery with the tallest Celtic cross tipping to the right. It is set in the foreground of shrubby trees, a stream, and harvested crops creating different shades of tan and green rolling hills. She could see the appeal that St. Kevin saw.

Going outside, there were several handsome horses in a nearby field. Their coats were shiny and tails swung freely. A small, red hand-painted sign read, "DANGER" in capital letters and "Keep Away From Horses, Please." One horse came trotting up, clearly expecting a carrot or treat of which Anne had none. He acted friendly enough and not at all dangerous as the sign would imply. He lowered his chestnut head over the flimsy wire fence and Anne rubbed his neck and then simultaneously scratched both sides of his handsome face. She spoke to him in an even voice explaining her Irish roots, convincing herself he could be a descendent of her kin. She was a horse lover and this steed could tell. He tipped his head down and she scratched the bridge of his nose moving up to what had the appearance of a poorly painted abstract white diamond on his forehead.

Weekday afternoons were usually slow at the tracks. Mickey had a pocket full of cash from business acquaintances to bet on the afternoon races. His associates knew the chance they took dealing with Mickey, but the risk was worth it as several had come out farther ahead than using regulated channels.

It was pretty simple. The gamblers placed bets with bookie Mickey in private places like a bar, social club, a barber shop, even the corner market, or his own illegal betting parlors. They relied on his inside information and never asked when he'd gotten lucky for them. He'd never disclose his connections with the jockeys or betray them.

Eamon's gang never worried about violating the law. Mickey consistently fixed the odds in his boss's favor and more than a few times Mickey refused to pay out winnings because Eamon told him so. He didn't care that there were no guarantees of fairness and that profits often were channeled into Eamon's other illicit activities, drug trafficking and money laundering. He just did what Eamon told him to do and now his debt had dropped to $14,500.

Driving on a long driveway, past a golf course, and up a hill they arrived at Cabra Castle in Kingscourt. They respectfully veered around a wedding party who were in the picture-taking phase. The wedding couple stood by their parents, mothers dressed in floral attire each with a feathered hat.

April selected the room keys hanging on a railing in an arched doorway. The keys were large and heavy, and attached to a silver oval fob that would never fit in a pocket. They were sent out much like on a scavenger hunt to find their rooms. The numbering system had nothing to do with the location of the room and after helping everyone get to their rooms, Anne and Peter ferreted out theirs at the back of the property in the Carpenter's Workshop.

Up the narrow stairs to the second floor, they entered a spacious room with a king-size bed, a large bathroom, snacks, and water in Cabra Castle bottles, similar to a wine bottle. Anne did a complete circle seeing a large portrait of an Irish setter, an antique floor lamp in the corner, a desk cluttered with brochures, and a crock that held umbrellas. A mishmash of pictures in non-matching frames filled the walls like a jam-packed museum. Throw rugs hid most of the cold tile floor.

They only unpacked what they would wear the following morning for the flight home. Anything delicate had already been wrapped in the bubble wrap that she always took on any trip. And by now, she didn't have room for much more in her carry-on.

Several meandered around the inside and outside of this marvelous castle, but since it was nippy and misty outside, Sue, Nancy, Jeanine, and Anne retreated to a cozy alcove inside to order a warm drink and split an order of Sticky Toffee Pudding which all had been introduced to on this trip. Each bite was like a party in Anne's mouth. A glass of Bailey's was placed before each woman as a treat from Nancy and she was dubbed their Bailey's Queen.

Wandering around inside, the women met up with their spouses. Jeanine mentioned that allegedly this is an extremely haunted castle, apparently by the ghost of a woman who was killed here, and disclosed, "I'm sensing some bad juju here."

While the eight stood in the lobby underneath a large chandelier listening to the story about the ghost, the chandelier swayed and the ceiling creaked. They scattered like songbirds when a hawk is overhead. No one had an explanation for this coincidental occurrence.

"Did you see that? That about scared the bejeebers out of me," Sue whispered.

"Haven't heard that one used in a long time," Peter said to Dave.

"Maybe too much Bailey's?" Jeanine whispered to Nancy.

When Anne suspected someone could have been directed to walk above them at the exact time they heard the ghost story, a clerk overheard as he ventured by and politely objected, "Oh no, Madam, that area is cordoned off due to some repairs." Hmm, not a leprechaun, fairy, or spirit but maybe a ghost finally, Anne hoped.

Greg and Linda, Chris and Jeanine, Dave and Sue, Bruce and Nancy, and Peter and Anne had dinner together, feasting on lamb shank, chicken, and sea bass. The dining room exuded opulence, with light fixtures dripping with crystal fobs. For dessert, they were served a layered anniversary cake celebrating 100 years. This cake was more like strawberry pie with five inches of whipped cream on top. After dinner drinks would be served next.

Anne was still fuming over her discovery while reading the back of the menu, finding out that the castle and the surrounding land belonged to the O'Reilly family until it was confiscated in the mid-seventeenth century by Cromwell's orders and given to Colonel Thomas Cooch.

She had read in *The Irish Times* newspaper that this castle was the second scariest in the world. Anne hoped her O'Reilly clan was floating around haunting it, preferably starting with the nasty Englishman Oliver Cromwell and the Cooch family. Malarkey? Maybe not.

Settle down, she told herself. Anne knew her great-great grandparents on her father's side had come from somewhere around the Dublin area. *What if?* She couldn't wait to tell her dad this cool news. *Oh wait, I can't*, she remembered.

Excusing herself, she explained she needed some time alone. They understood. Wandering out to the gardens of the grand castle, now turned into a splendid modern-day hotel, gray clouds hung low and a gentle drizzle misted the air. The light mist affected the end-of-the-summer flowers and bushes to create a silver shimmery glaze.

What if? What if, what? Anne spoke aloud, then did a 360 to make sure no one stood too close to hear her talking to herself. As she ambled around the grounds it felt like she wasn't there but instead outside of her body, more like a shadow—slightly off-kilter. She had a similar sensation when taking too much cold and flu medicine.

Looking toward the ruins of the original castle, she saw movement in the distance. In the field, a person she assumed a woman because of her medium-length hair and her flowing skirt or dress, but she couldn't tell her age.

Anne closed her curious eyes and tipped her face upward

enjoying the soft vapor on her pale skin. Her eyes still closed, she peeked once to make sure she hadn't journeyed somewhere back in time like in the book *Outlander*. No way did she want that to happen.

She imagined a young woman with cinnamon long locks standing overlooking the sea, or had Anne suddenly been teleported back to the mid-1800s? She watched and felt the breeze blow inland off the water as the waves rose and fell with their snowy white peaks reaching to heaven. The waves crashed against the rocks leaving a foam that bubbled as the water rolled out. Several seagulls on the beach were squawking noisily. Their bright yellow beaks were accentuated in color due to their head, neck, and undercarriage pure white, blending into a soft gray body. Two had obsidian backs. Each one's tail feathers gave the impression they had been dipped in the same design and color painted on zebras.

Could this woman actually be my great-great-grandmother Maggie? Two gray wolfhounds romped around the woman. How did Maggie get there, some 20 miles from what was possibly her husband's family home? She wondered if Mauve and Moyrah knew the castle history.

The mist turned to heavier raindrops, maybe trying to wake Anne up. Shaking her head attempting to snap out of the trance-like state, she retreated back to the castle wearing no headgear or coat to save her from getting drenched. Anne became concerned about her mental state, wondering where all this hallucinating about her great-great-grandmother and Irish Wolfhounds had come from.

Protected from the rain under an original stately arch in the hotel garden, she glanced around the exterior of the current castle and visualized her O'Reilly ancestors. While hopeful, she knew it was unlikely that this could be her ancestors' home, the family castle. She wondered how it might have been—regal, noble, majestic, stately? Or did it resemble the bones of a relic gradually crumbling and deteriorating? Did ivy and weeds tug on the remaining walkway and creep in through the broken empty windows and up staircases stretching to claim every last pillar and rock? Visions of her Mother's family castle, now ruins, in Sanquhar, Scotland, came to mind.

Ten minutes later she sat again at the table with her friends. Anne shared some history explaining that the O'Reillys and Reillys are the descendants of the Gaelic Irish sect, the O'Raghailligh of Breffny whose influence extended to many counties. The O'Reillys were such a powerful influence that at one stage in their reign of power, they issued their own coinage. The O'Reillys throughout the centuries have produced churchmen.

At the time of the Old Gaelic Order in the seventeenth and eighteenth centuries, the name was established on the continent of Europe, where the O'Reillys joined the armed services of France, Spain, Italy, Russia, Prussia, and Austria. The name was also established in America, where many with the name became prominent. There was Henry O'Reilly (1806-1886) of Carrickmacross in County Monaghan who was a pioneer in telecommunications; John Boyle O'Reilly (1844-1890) was a poet and newspaperman. There was Dr. A.J.F. O'Reilly or, as his friends called him, Tony, born in Dublin in 1936, who was an international rugby player for Ireland, solicitor, and industrialist. He became president of the Heinz Corporation in 1979 and was an initiator of the Irish-American Association.

"What about a souvenir from here?" Bruce picked up a Cabra Castle glass water bottle on the table.

"I mean really, who wouldn't want a bottle from their family's castle?" Sue added. Anne thought to check first with April and their driver, Bill, about purchasing a bottle. After rambling on and on telling them her family story, and that this could be her family castle (and the gift store sign read CLOSED), it was insinuated she take one from the table. Bill winked, emphasizing the wink several times. "It's your family castle, just take it." April agreed.

Anne told her tablemates what had been suggested. After dinner, she discovered several at her disposal from accomplices who had hidden them in their jackets. They drank a lot of water during that meal.

Back in their room, Anne wrote an elaborate note to the cleaning staff explaining her plight and she left a donation with instructions for them to kindly pass it along to the proper authorities in the gift shop. She packed two for home in her carry-on, one for her youngest brother and one for herself. She assumed they would be the only residents in the state of Oregon with a Cabra Castle glass water bottle. Stuffed in her carry-on was also the menu from dinner with the castle history printed on the back.

CHAPTER THIRTY-TWO

Returning to Dublin, Anne, Peter and friends wandered the city not like wide-eyed tourists but more like returning guests who knew much more than when they started.

At the waterfront, Peter said, "Remember when we were here 20 years ago and what a surprise it was to see those incredible sailboats, or I guess tall ships, that were ending the Cutty Sark Tall Ships Race? That was so cool watching as the crews sprinted up poles and proudly unveiled their country's flag coming into the harbor. I recall that the crews had been racing for six weeks and we learned that the races were among the world's most prestigious maritime events."

"And Dublin basically turned into one vast street carnival from morning to night with parades, street theater, and music of all types. That evening those extravagant fireworks and water displays lit up the night sky. Nearly 5,000 crew members, from over 30 countries throughout the world were visiting this city. Do they still have the races?"

"Yes, but I think it's called something different now. We'll have to google it and find out."

After strolling all morning with hunger pains becoming sharper, Anne and Peter shared a Beef and Guinness, a thick, dark brown savory stew with two generous scoops of mashed potatoes on the top. That afternoon they moseyed along the river seeing boats, memorials, and people.

Situated right next to Christ Church, and linked by an elegant bridge, is DVBLINIA, a trust to recreate a journey of everyday life in medieval Dublin. They saw a scale model of the city showing the original location of public buildings and street layouts. They climbed St. Michael's Tower for a unique panoramic view of Dublin's city and surrounding area. Then they stopped at the gift shop, buying lace handkerchiefs and anything with a shamrock.

"Remember going to the service here two decades ago for the bombing victims?"

"Yes, and I remember Mauve telling us that the bombing caused outrage both locally and internationally. The Real IRA denied that the bomb was intended to kill civilians and apologized. Shortly after, the group declared a ceasefire. The casualties included people of different backgrounds and ages: Protestants, Catholics, teenagers, young children, a mother pregnant with twins, Spanish tourists, and others on a day trip from the Republic of Ireland. Both unionists and Irish nationalists were killed and injured. As a result of the bombing, new anti-terrorism laws were swiftly instituted by both the UK and the Republic of Ireland. Mauve thought this was a turning point. Women stood strong and did the right thing by reporting the murderers, many within their own families. Relatives reported relatives, friends reported friends, and vowed it would not happen again."

"And that minister shared and we sang the old hymn, 'Be Thou My Vision.' That was a sad time for sure." Peter ended that trip down memory lane.

At their final dinner together, Peter lifted his glass to

toast to their friends. "Here's to grand friends, Irish or not—never above you, never below you, always beside you. Sláinte."

Sue inched near Anne. "Great. I was already emotional," as immense tears rolled down her cheeks.

At the end of their adventure, Anne's traveling friends gave her a splendid one hundred percent merino wool Blarney Woolen Hills scarf in various shades of pink with a light celery herringbone pattern and muted blue vertical stripes. Anne truly had the kindest friends in the world.

CHAPTER THIRTY-THREE

Flying out of Dublin, from her window seat Anne gazed down at the giant jigsaw puzzle of plentiful greens and browns, with sections of red and orange. Poppies, she knew, in various shapes and sizes, were getting smaller and smaller until they flew through a cloud bank, and only white remained.

She thought about what lay ahead of her, a memorial service for her darlin' Dad. She heard a familiar voice whisper, "Darlin' daughter, you must return one day." *I will, Dad.*

While napping, she dreamed she was on a cruise ship, sitting in a lounge chair gazing at tropical Mediterranean islands. A Viking dressed from the middle ages barreled through the crowd, yelling her name. In a Norwegian accent, she heard, "Anne, Anne, Anne! It's me. Your great-great-great grandfather from Norway." She felt troubled and tried to run away or maybe running toward him.

Peter woke her. "Hon, are you okay?"

She shook her head, clearing cobwebs. "Way too much family drama, I'd say."

CHAPTER THIRTY-FOUR

Three months later, just before Christmas, Anne opened an email from Mauve, assuming it would be about an upcoming family wedding. She'd just read one from Moyrah with updates on Fay's Greek God, as they all called him. Interesting that their parents would be meeting Stephan's in January when Patrick and Keira went for the winter to Malaga. Instead, she opened a newspaper article.

Man's untimely death leads to dismantling large-scale illegal gaming ring

Gardaí have concluded an investigation of Seamus Jamie Kennedy, age 26 of Derry, who died in Malin Head on September 10. Found were high amounts of marijuana, alcohol, and traces of foxglove in his system contributing to a fall down a hillside.

After much investigation from CCTV footage, and through mobile calls and texts, guards discovered Kennedy was heavily in debt to Eamon McCallum, who ran illegal gambling rings and distribution of drugs.

Following months of investigation, gardaí arrested McCallum after finding evidence on the victim's mobile and emails of middle man, Mickey Tucker. Mr. Tucker provided the poison in Kennedy's beverages on the day of his death. Tucker provided state's evidence and was sentenced to ten years for criminally negligent homicide.

McCallum has been charged with murder and is awaiting trial. Texts between Tucker and McCallum indicate the intention of Kennedy's murder due to unpaid debts.

The article continued with details and other nefarious endeavors of the accused.

Peter heard, "You've got to come read this email from Mauve."

Peter moseyed in from the mailbox with a handful of holiday cards. Anne noticed one from Ireland but didn't recognize the handwriting and opened it first. In swirling calligraphy lettering she read,

> You are Invited
> to celebrate the wedding of
> Wrenna Mauve O'Riley and
> Morgan Callum Graham

Her thoughts floated back to September with the colossal disclosure of her cousin's secret and the happenings at Malin Head. She handed the invitation to Peter.

"Looks like we're going back to Ireland soon." His faux Irish accent had improved significantly. "Did you notice there's writing at the bottom?"

Anne reached for the invitation. Scanning down she read in elegant cursive lettering, "Family First."

The End.

ANNE'S FAVORITE RECIPES

Irish Blonde Cocktail - A very popular drink for anyone who doesn't care for beer.

- 2 oz Michael Collins blended Irish whiskey
- ¾ oz orange curaçao
- ¼ oz La Ina fino sherry
- 1 dash Regan's Orange Bitters
- Garnish: flamed orange peel
- Add the blended Irish whiskey, orange curaçao, fino sherry and orange bitters into a mixing glass with ice and stir until well chilled.
- Strain in a chilled martini glass.
- Garnish with a flamed orange peel.
- Sip!

Irish Coffee

- 4 T Irish whiskey
- 2 tsp brown sugar
- 4 oz hot coffee
- 1 oz heavy cream

- Steam a glass.
- Pour in four tablespoons of Irish whiskey.
- Add 2 teaspoons brown sugar and boiling coffee to within ¾th of the top of the glass.
- Stir briskly until sugar is completed dissolved.
- Add cream, lightly whipped, and pour into the glass over the back of a teaspoon so that the cream will not sink.
- Do not stir!
- Sip!

Try using French press or high end coffee beans, medium- to dark-roasted coffee works best.

Preheat your glass.

Use freshly whipped cream. Avoid the stuff in cans, it will ruin the coffee. Instead begin with a little heavy whipping cream and vigorously whip with a whisk or fork until it is light and fluffy. It's worth the extra effort.

From John and Olive Mulvihill of the Red Fox Inn in Glenbeigh along the Ring of Kerry.

Shepherd's Pie

Shepherd's Pie is made with lamb, Cottage Pie with ground beef. Both are comfort food casseroles that originated in England. This recipe calls for both meats but you can do all of one or the other.

- 3 pounds pealed potatoes
- 1 T kosher salt
- 1/4 c milk
- 3 T salted butter, divided
- 1 c shredded white cheddar cheese
- 1/4 c sour cream
- 1 large egg yolk
- 2 tsp ground black pepper, divided
- 1 T olive oil
- 1 c diced onion
- 1 c diced carrot
- 1 pound ground lamb
- 1 pound ground beef sirloin
- 3 T flour
- 1 tsp finely chopped fresh rosemary
- 1 tsp finely chopped fresh thyme
- 1 c beef stock
- 1 T tomato paste
- 1 T Worcestershire sauce
- 1 c frozen peas (A big NO for Anne, substitute corn if you wish)
- 1 T chopped fresh parsley

Cut and place potatoes in large saucepan and add enough water to cover by 2 inches. Stir in 1 T salt and place pot over medium-high heat; bring to a boil. Cook until potatoes are fork tender, about 20 minutes. Turn off the heat and drain.

Return potatoes to the hot pan and set over the same burner. Add milk and 2 T butter, allow butter to melt from the residual heat. Mash potatoes with a masher until smooth. Stir in Cheddar cheese, sour cream, egg yolk, ½ tsp salt and ¼ tsp pepper. Set aside while you prepare the filling.

Preheat oven to 375 degrees. Grease 9x13-inch dish.

Heat olive oil and remaining 1 T butter in large skillet over medium-high heat. Add onion and carrot and cook, stirring constantly, until onion begins to turn translucent, about 5 minutes.

Add lamb and beef and cook, crumbling with a spoon and stirring often until browned, about 5 minutes. Sprinkle meat mixture with flour, remaining salt and pepper, rosemary and thyme. Cook for 2 minutes stirring constantly.

Add beef stock, tomato paste and Worcestershire; cook, scraping any flavorful bits from the bottom of the skillet. Bring mixture to a simmer. Cook until thickened and vegetables are tender, about 8 minutes. Stir in peas (or corn). Transfer mixture to the prepared casserole dish and top with the mashed potatoes.

Bake in the preheated oven until golden and bubbly around the edges, 25 to 30 minutes. Sprinkle with parsley. Let rest 10 minutes and serve.

After making this once, Anne decided to purchase it at Costco and pick out the peas on her piece.

Cousin Mauve's Sticky Toffee Pudding

- 8 oz medjool dates, pitted
- 1 c boiling water
- 1/3 c butter, room temp
- 2/3 c light brown sugar, firmly packed
- 2 tsp vanilla extract, real vanilla
- 2 large eggs, room temp
- 2 T molasses
- 1 2/3 c flour
- 1 1/2 tsp baking powder
- 1 tsp baking soda
- 1/3 tsp salt

Toffee sauce:

- 1/2 cup heavy whipping cream

- 1/2 c butter
- 3/4 c light brown sugar, packed
- 1 pinch of salt
- 2 tsp vanilla
- Chopped walnuts, optional

Preheat oven to 350 degrees. Lightly grease a 12-cup muffin tin, ramekins or an 8" baking dish.

Add the dates to the bowl of a food processor or blender and pour boiling water on top. Set aside for 5 minutes.

Meanwhile, prepare the batter: cream together butter and brown sugar. Add eggs, one at a time, beating after each addition. Add the molasses and mix well.

In a separate bowl, sift together the flour, baking powder and salt, and then stir into the batter.

Pulse the date mixture in a food processor, then stir in baking soda. Pour the date mixture into batter and fold gently to combine, but don't over mix.

Pour batter into prepared pan. Bake 18-20 minutes or until toothpick inserted in the center comes out clean or with a few crumbs. Don't over bake or cake will be dry. For a square baking dish, bake for 22-25 minutes.

Serve muffin cakes flat-side up with warm toffee sauce on top.

Toffee sauce:

Add cream, butter, brown sugar, and salt to a saucepan. Cook over low heat, stirring until sugar dissolves and sauce is smooth, and slightly thickened about 7-10 minutes. Remove from heat and stir in vanilla.

Spoon toffee sauce over cake and garnish with chopped walnuts, if desired.

Store cakes and sauce in an airtight container separately for up to five days in fridge.

If you don't like dates or don't have any on hand, prunes make a good substitute.

If toffee isn't your taste, try a warm caramel sauce or a butterscotch sauce.

You can make this dessert up to five days in advance. Warm the cake in the microwave or oven and reheat the sauce on the stove or microwave until warm and pourable.

BON APPETIT!

TRIP TIPS

Remember to study up on the country you are visiting. There are many inventors and artists who got their start in Ireland and these are great conversation starters.

Actors-
Pierce Brosnan, Liam Neeson, Saoirse Ronan, Enya, Bono, Oscar Wilde, Mary Robinson (first female president of Ireland from 1990-1997)

Inventions-
Color photography, in 1894 by John Joly
Guided torpedo, in 1877 by Louis Brennan
Hypodermic Syringe, in 1844 by Francis Rynd
Ejector seat, 1949 by Sir James Martin.

The Irish have proof and take credit for inventing modern chemistry, chocolate milk, croquet, tattoo machines, portable defibrillators, design of modern submarines, boycotts, and seismology.

Some Pronunciation help...well maybe.

Letters have the same phonetic values as in English except for the following:

A is pronounced like o in hot or aw in thaw.
    Bh is pronounced like v or w.

Ch is like k, never like s.
Dh is like y or is unpronounced.
Fh is unpronounced.
Gh is like y or is unpronounced.
Mh is pronounced like v or w.
S is pronounced like sh when it precedes I or E.
Sh is pronounced like h.
Th is pronounced like h.

Some words that might help:

Fáilte	Welcome
Cheers	Thanks
An Lár	City center
Bonnet	Car hood
Boot	Car trunk
Deadly, Brilliant	Great, Excellent
Jumper	Sweater
Lift	Elevator
Quay (Key)	Waterfront
Ring	To telephone

Bangers	Sausages
Champ	Mashed potatoes with onions
Chips	French fries
Fry or Fry Up	Traditional Irish breakfast
Salad	Salad and garnish on sandwich
Shandy	Sprite/Lemonade and Lager

Don't forget most British words are the same in England, Ireland, Northern Ireland, Scotland and Wales. And what Americans call the second floor of a building is the first floor in the U.K.

Don't forget the metric system is used almost everywhere in the world so weight and volume are calculated in metric. A kilogram is 2.2 pounds and one liter is about a quart. Temperatures are generally given in Celsius. Twenty-eight Celsius is a perfect 82 degrees to us. Twenty is 68 and zero is our 32 degrees.

Before visiting Ireland, please purchase a vocabulary guide; it's educational and humorous. Spend some time on YouTube for pronunciations and a laugh or two. And be sure to purchase a well-respected travel authority's book on Ireland like *Rick Steves' Ireland* and read each word.

Traditional Gaelic Blessing

May the road rise to meet you.
May the wind be always at your back.
May the sun shine warm upon your face;
the rain fall soft upon your field
And until we meet again,
May God hold you in the palm of His hand.

ANNE'S READING LIST

Rick Steves Ireland
By Rick Steves
Avalon Travel Publications
ISBN 978-1-63121-671-8

Lonely Planet Irish Language & Culture
Published by Lonely Planet Publications
2nd Edition
ISBN 978-1-74104-815-5

The Great Book of Ireland History & Fun Facts Vol. 1
by Bill O'Neill
Self Published
ISBN 978-1-79864-959-6

Irish Myths and Legends
Appletree Pocket Guide
Ronan Coghlan
ISBN 978-1-84758-003-0

71050899R00174